CHAPTER ONE

October 193-

He was the cleverest man John had ever known, but sometimes it seemed as if Henry Cleavis didn't live in the real world at all. Like many brilliant fellows he was caught up in the life of the mind and everything that he had going on up there. John knew that, in their partnership, he would always be the one who must attend to more practical affairs. Times such as now - when they were settling into a new town, a new college, a new everything – were precisely when a bit of pragmatism was required. But John saw that Henry was walking around in a daze.

Just today, at lunchtime, Henry came back to their disordered rooms and said he'd been to pick up a huge pile of post that had been waiting for him at the porter's lodge. It had been building up during the summer months, awaiting their arrival at Darkholmes and the porter was keen to get all this stuff off his hands. John knew the kinds of thing Henry received in the post on a daily basis and didn't blame Mr Mack the Hexford college porter for wanting it out of his tidy lodge.

When he came back though, Henry was holding not a single parcel or letter. He looked befuddled and distracted.

John was carrying a tea tray and saw at once there was something the matter with him.

'Oh, sorry, John,' he smiled. 'I don't mean to alarm you. It's simply... I was down in the porter's lodge just now and I could have sworn... I saw a... *faun*. Curly hair, little horns and a goatee beard. Devilish-looking creature on goaty legs. Picking up his own post. He nodded good morning and trip-trapped out of the place and no one else seemed to notice but me. The fellow was half nude, for goodness' sake! I was too flabbergasted to say anything...'

John put down the tea tray and frowned at him. They'd had this kind of thing before. It was often down to overwork and stress. 'Come and sit down. Look, hot buttered muffins. I found a nice little bakery on Cathedral Wynd...'

For once, High Tea didn't mollify Henry. He sat down heavily in his favourite armchair, which was one of the few pieces of furniture in their rooms that didn't have boxes or heaps of gubbins piled upon it, looking for a home. His dear face seemed so confused to John. 'I know what I saw. It was a faun. Straight out of the *other place*. Here, John. Right here in Darkholmes.'

His friend nodded. All right, he thought. Give him the benefit of the doubt. Say he's not just seeing things. 'What would a faun be wanting here? Is it on the faculty, do you think?'

Henry glared at him, and John saw that levity wasn't the way to get him out of this funk. 'He bade me good morning, John. I was too startled to say anything at all in reply.'

John nodded and they stared at each other.

'Is there something uncanny here, do you think?' John asked him.

'I think it rather looks like that, yes,' said Professor Cleavis with a folorn expression. He sighed and leaned forward to take up his china cup. The steam curled and misted up his tiny, round glasses. 'We were fools to think we could simply move away and find somewhere free of enchantment.'

2

'It was worth a try,' John said grimly. 'A new start. Somewhere you can settle and get your strength back. I fear that the rigors of the past few years have worn you out, Henry.'

'There's nothing wrong with me,' he snapped. 'I have a job to do. And I'll do it to the best of my abilities.'

'It might even have been a *good* faun that you saw, and not an evil one at all...'

'I'll be the judge of that,' Henry said darkly, and slurped his tea.

*

John knew that Henry was dismayed. More dismayed than he would ever let on to anyone, even to John, his loyalest friend and companion. John knew that, for all his shows of bluster and intent, Henry would have relished a more sedate life in that beautiful, leafy, ancient northern town. It would have done him so much good to relax into its lofty, gothic splendour and to be for a while simply the fussy old academic that he was meant to be. He could finish that book he had been trying to get done for years. He could have students who would follow him around and flock to listen to his every utterance. All these things would be good for this exhausted, ageing man.

He had worn himself ragged, these past few years, living among enchantments and mystical beings.

When Henry went off to his room for an afternoon doze, John found himself hoping fervently that maybe the faun had been a hallucination. John even hoped Henry might be going bananas. That way at least there wouldn't be any magic involved.

John set about unpacking a few more boxes. Books, books and more books. Some of them were very musty, stodgy things relating to Henry's expertise in mythology. Gilt-covered, leather-bound things from all over the world in a hundred different languages. Also, lurid paperbacks – murder mysteries and curious scientific romances. Some of these he had enjoyed, as much as Henry. When they took their frequent walking holidays around England and Wales and Scotland, and when they travelled abroad, they would carry heaps of these things with them, and read aloud to each other in their tent or their shared pension rooms at night.

Stories, Henry Cleavis always said, were meant to be read aloud. Like the old, old tales and myths. They were passed on by word of mouth. And so we ought – he always said - whenever we can, sit around the campfire and liberate them once more by speaking them aloud.

It was hard for John to see his mentor and beloved friend become so doddery and unsure. For the past six months, John mused, he'd been in quite a state. As the date for their removal to the north and Darkholmes approached John had rather hoped that Henry would rally and that the challenge of a new position and new surroundings and interesting new people would put the colour into his complexion again. John was waiting for the spring to come back into his step.

Henry was looking a little lost. He looked daunted by the new place with its soot-encrusted buildings and its winding streets and the green sluggish river that looped the whole town, almost making it an island.

He looked like he felt he had been brought here to face something terrible.

Ah, John thought, but I'm letting his mood get to me. Come on, John. Buck up. Don't get gloomy. Henry Cleavis needs your help and your strength. He needs to be shown that you are both going to be happy in this university town of Darkholmes. John

4

told himself that he needed to forget about his own shivers of foreboding and just get on with it.

With that, he decided to take himself off to the porter's lodge, down in the quad below. He'd fetch up the post and the parcels that Henry had left behind down there. Maybe there was something amongst all that lot that might cheer him up?

*

By evening Henry had rallied somewhat. When he emerged at suppertime he was bright and breezy. John could see the way he wanted them to play it. Nothing at all had happened down at the porter's lodge earlier that day. He had never seen anything untoward. All right, John thought. If that's the way he wants it.

Briskly, Henry was rubbing his hands and looking spick and span, with his face scrubbed till it was gleaming and his fluffy white hair and beard washed and combed. He was wearing a red velvet jacket and checkered trousers. He could be quite the dandy, in his own way.

'What's it to be, John? Shall we brave the refectory for supper?'

It was the first time dining there for both of them, and it was a big moment. Henry was the new appointment to Hexford college. A star in the world of obscure mythology. When he took his place at one of the long wooden tables and John slid in next to him, they were both aware of the eyes of dozens of scholars upon them. A few of them muttered to each other. Henry beamed broadly with goodwill at all of them, nodding affably and John's heart twinged slightly. Henry was always so friendly towards the world at large. He behaved as if everyone was going to be his friend.

John was wearing a striped rugby top and some decent trousers. Henry had suggested he wore his best – i.e, not torn or dirty – black blazer. Just to show some respect. They hadn't known in advance how formal the meal was going to be. Not very, turned out to be the case. Many of the dons were slouching about in everyday attire. John even noticed one chap tottering by in an ancient pair of slippers. Only a handful were wearing the full regulation black dress and mortar board. In the guttering candlelight they looked like hideous crows flapping about, pecking here and there before they settled to roost.

All in all, it was pretty shambolic. Much less grand than the last place Henry had worked, and where John had studied. John had expected more from Hexford College and the University of Darkholmes.

Women with thick arms and smudged aprons brought round vast tureens of soup. Henry peered at the contents, nodded and smiled, but there was no charming the dinner lady looking after their table. All around them rumbled quiet, cultivated conversation.

'I don't think I can stick eating here every evening,' John said.

'We won't,' Cleavis told him out of the corner of his mouth. 'Once we're fixed up in the rooms I'll get the old camp kitchen assembled again…'

John grimaced at the thought of this. He lived in fear whenever Henry had that portable gas ring burning. His culinary achievements might have been astonishing with such basic equipment, but it was still entirely possible that one day he would burn the whole place down. Henry was very easily distracted.

'Do you think you'll like it here?' John asked him bluntly.

'Oh, I'm sure I will,' he said, dunking a hunk of rustic bread into his bright green soup. 'Why, I like just about anywhere, don't I? There's always something to love about a new place. You just have to go looking for it a bit harder sometimes...'

'The river's rather beautiful,' John told him. 'And all the woods and things around it, all about the outskirts of the Medieval town. Very stately, the river, very slow and ancient. Unspoiled.'

'There you go, then,' Henry smiled. 'You've found something good straight away! Well done, John! I can always rely on you.'

John had been for a run in the late afternoon, as the sun was going down over the Cathedral and the lofty battlements of the castle. And it was, he thought, truly spectacular down in those dells where the river wound its graceful way. He did think Henry would enjoy it. Whenever he went out on his evening constitutionals, wherever they were living or staying, he would look for places and things he knew Henry would enjoy.

'Professor Sneagle,' said a high, rasping voice all of a sudden. It came from a stooped figure in Professorial robes. He was glaring at the two men across the refectory table.

'I beg your pardon?' asked Henry. And then, 'Oh! Professor Sneagle, of course! How are you?' He jumped up and grasped the old man's hand, shaking it with such force it seemed like he was in danger of breaking him apart. 'John, John, this is Professor Sneagle!'

The old man gave John a wintry glance and he could feel a shiver go through him. Sneagle's face had a look of a crab apple, rotten and withered and still on the tree.

'You're very welcome here, Professor Cleavis,' said Sneagle. 'However, some of the faculty have expressed…'

'Aha!' cried Henry. 'I remember what you're famous for! *Rare and Fabulous Beasts*! That's what the world knows of you, Professor Sneagle!'

This put the dessicated old chap off his stroke. 'What?'

'Your marvelous book,' nodded Henry enthusiastically. 'About all the Rarest and Most Fabulous Beasts in the world. Astonishing work, I must say. Essential reading. I keep my copy on my bedside table for regular consultation. World-class, Professor Sneagle!'

'Oh!' gasped the old cove, looking like he had never received any kind of compliment in his life. He looked, John thought, almost like a young girl who'd just had her first ever kiss.

'Oh, wonderful, wonderful,' said Henry, sitting back down to his soup and tucking in with relish. John knew that Henry's copy of Sneagle's book of monsters wasn't by his bedside, in the new place or in the old. It was kept in the lavatory. Henry always said he'd never read such claptrap in all his life. Now John remembered where he knew the name Sneagle from. It was at the top of every sheet of their toilet paper.

Henry asked: 'Now, what is it I can do for you, old fellow?'

'Erm,' said Sneagle, wrong-footed by the new boy's kindness. 'It's just some of the others, you know. Well, you know what academics can be like. Bitchy and so on. Well, they're just agitating a bit because word has got out about your new position…'

'Oh yes?' asked Henry, with that gleam in his eye. The one that John hadn't seen in a while. Henry had rediscovered his sense of mischief, and when he realised this, John felt like giving a loud cheer.

'Some of them are saying it's a disgrace, how few duties you have been given,' Sneagle said, very snidely. 'No teaching, no tutorials. No pastoral care. Nothing.'

'Ahh,' said Henry. 'I see what you mean.'

'They're all up in arms,' muttered Sneagle, glancing at the other tables. John could tell by his tone that he himself was chief among the whingers. Henry was enjoying watching him squirm. 'They want to know why you've been given such an easy position.'

'I must say,' Henry said mildly, mopping the ends of his moustache with a piece of bread. 'I was surprised when I received the letter offering me the job. You're quite right. It's shocking! It's completely unheard of! I'm here and they've got me doing almost nothing in return for my bed and board and salary. Most curious, eh?'

'Most,' frowned Sneagle.

'But, you see, I didn't care to probe too far into the mystery,' Henry added, lowering his tone. 'In case it's all some dreadful mistake and suddenly they land me with ten times the workload.'

'Ten times nothing is still nothing.'

'Quite, old fellow! Quite! But I figured that the Brains Trust who run this university of Darkholmes must have their own reasons for this strange state of affairs. And do you know what? I'm loath to pry into other people's mysteries. They will have their own reasons for doing things the way they do. And *I* know better than to shove my sticky beak where it isn't wanted.'

Henry smiled very pointedly at the wrinkled expert in impossible creatures.

'Ah,' said Sneagle. 'I see. Well, I shall leave you. It seems that our main courses are being... erm, dished out.'

'Lovely!' cried Henry, as the heavyset server approached them with a gigantic dish of what looked like a golden crust of dumplings surmounting a delicious, steaming meat stew. Professor Sneagle went scuttling off to his colleagues. 'Huh,' was all Henry had to say about their encounter.

They're like a bunch of schoolboys, John marvelled, and then forgot all about them as supper was served and it turned out to be the most heavenly meal they had eaten for months. They had been in the process of relocating their lives for simply ages, it seemed, and hadn't really felt settled and comfortable since the spring. Chicken stew and dumplings made for a proper homecoming, John decided. Even if they were forced to enjoy it in the company of jealous old crows.

*

A few days in residence saw them settling into their new rooms.

Henry thundered about the place looking like he was permanently confused, coat tails flapping and hefting great piles of manuscript about, but that was quite normal. He would be like that anywhere.

John suspected that his friend was starting to like it in Darkholmes. Just as John himself was.

Their rooms looked onto the walled security of the college on one side, where tall holly bushes and myrtle had been growing for what must have been centuries. And on the other there was a precipitous view of the town's rooftops and the swaying canopies of conifers that were thickly planted all the way down to the river. It was quite a drop and, the first time John looked, the view made him feel quite dizzy.

They had a mantelpiece filled with invitation cards, to this and that. Henry stared at them blankly, and John had found him dropping them surreptitiously into the wastepaper basket. This was no good. John decided that he would not have him burying himself away in his work and living separately to the other dons. He dug out all those drinks and dinner invites and ordered them and sorted them and told Henry that he was going to keep the diary for him and simply tell him where he ought to be and who with.

Henry's face darkened at this. 'I am *your* mentor. I should be telling *you* what to do.'

'Mentor!' John laughed.

Then Henry looked quite serious. 'Yes. Yes, I am. And you need to remember that. When they go asking who you are and what your role is. You're my younger brother. I have looked after you since you were sixteen, when our parents were killed on holiday in Switzerland.'

'I know the story,' John glowered at him.

'Keep the story straight,' Henry said gruffly. 'Keep it straight in your head. Make it trip off your tongue when anybody asks. Be plausible. Don't stand out too much. Cloak the past in tragedy and people get too embarrassed to ask further questions. It's a very English way of carrying on.'

John nodded. He knew he was right. They didn't want any untoward questions, did they?

'This is the first date we've got,' John told him, shoving a rather fancy embossed card under his nose. 'Before any of the official college stuff, even. It's drinks with a Professor Tyler and his wife, at their home... Can you make out this writing?'

Henry seized the card from John and he blinked at it. 'Ahh, the famous Professor Tyler.'

'Is he? What's he famous for?'

Henry made a flabbergasted noise. 'Nothing in the outside world. His fame is bounded within the rather esoteric, closed circles that I move in. But he's quite a figure. Quite an interesting man. Oh, you'll enjoy meeting him, John. We both will, I imagine!'

'Both?' John was surprised by this. 'You want me to come along, too?'

'Of course,' Henry said. 'I don't want you hanging around at all of these tepid college jamborees, of course. You'd hate it anyway. But Professor Tyler's will be a different kettle of fish, I imagine. Quite different. Oh, you must come with me tomorrow night to… where is it?' He squinted through his smudgy glasses. '199 Steps Lane…'

*

That evening it was getting dark as John pulled on his running outfit and hurtled out into the college and beyond the antique gates. He was using his nightly exercise sessions to explore their new environs, running elaborate loops through the cobbled streets and the myriad tangled alleyways. Henry warned that, sooner or later, he was bound to come a cropper on those slimy cobbles and the frosty paths, but as usual John didn't heed him. He found that he was hungry for new sights and smells. He loved poking his nose into the old market place, with its covered section that reeked of dead poultry and fresh fish.

The students were coming back, and they had doubled the town's population inside a week. They stood out quite sharply against the drab, local folk by virtue of their fancy clothes and their braying accents. John felt a bit embarrassed by them, because they were southern, like him, coming into this town, flaunting the bright colours of their college scarves and honking the horns of their cars, some of them, as they toiled up the narrow, steep lanes. The locals scuttled out of their way, muttering to themselves...

John kept on running, down to the river, where a brown mist was emerging from beneath the tall stone bridges. It curled and curdled and obscured what was left of the daylight. John kept on pounding, out of breath now. He wasn't as fit as he'd been a year ago. The stresses of the last while had sent his system out of kilter. He would have to take better care of himself.

On the towpath beside the river was where he had his first encounter with the uncanny in Darkholmes. It happened that very night.

At first he thought it was another solitary figure, out for a stroll in the inclement autumn weather. He was slipping about on the fallen leaves as they approached each other and he felt compelled to make some asinine comment about the dreadful mist. But all at once the words froze and died in his throat.

The figure coming towards him seemed to be hooded. Like a monk, he thought, at first. He wore the flowing robes, too, of something liturgical, perhaps. John knew there were still monks at the Cathedral. Perhaps he had wandered down from the cloisters for a breath of foggy air? But then something clutched at his abdomen. A horrible feeling of dread.

The man appeared to be wearing a cloth sack over his face. Lumpy, dirty canvas masking all his features. Two lumpish, awkward corners made grotesque ears or horns... he looked as if he was wearing a pillowcase over his face. This made it sound comic, as John tried to describe it to himself in terms that made sense to him, but there was something very horrible about this spectre.

John stopped in his tracks. He stood there, winded, as the robed stranger approached. There was a vile smell. Something burning. Something rotten was being put to the torch. A whiff of corruption and woodsmoke.

He drew level and John found himself powerless as he whispered in his ear. 'You should have never have brought him here.'

John gagged at the feel of the breath on his cheek. Twiggy fingers stroked his arm. 'I-I didn't bring him here. He came here of his own volition...'

The being snorted nastily. Mockingly. 'He should never have come to Darkholmes. This will end badly.'

John was paralysed. Why should he fear a figure in a cloak and a hood? There was something insubstantial about him. The fingers that brushed his bare flesh were sticklike and thin. He could have fettled him easily, he was sure. But he was frozen solid.

And then the cowled figure swept away, into the mist, leaving John alone by the slow brown river that circled the heart of Darkholmes.

*

'*And so it begins again,*' Evelyn Tyler wrote to her mother. '*Another academic year in this hellish place...*'

Given how many years she and Reginald had lived in Darkholmes together, she thought it all might have become less bothersome by now. But it hadn't. Hordes of new, scrubbed young men came seething through the town each autumn and

14

her husband was called upon to be away from home at all hours. There was always such a lot for him to do at the start of the Michaelmas term, and did he ever complain? Did he ever kick up a stink? Did he even mind that, in all this kerfuffle, he was neglecting his beautiful wife? No, and he never had.

Secretly Evelyn believed he was glad when his college duties meant that he had to be away from home even more than usual.

The only thing he missed was having quite so many solitary hours in his smoky office upstairs at home writing his stinking masterpiece.

Either way, Evelyn would see neither hide nor hair of him.

Writing about all of this to her mother, she did regret sounding so shrill and vexed first thing in the morning. She was writing at the breakfast table in all the debris, while Brenda fussed around her. She could already imagine what her mother's weary expression would be like as she read her daughter's latest, at her own breakfast table the next morning.

'I'm just ever so tired, Mother,' Evelyn wrote. 'I want things round here to change...'

She didn't suppose her mother could empathise really, or even understand. Her mother had had Father. He had worshipped her as a husband ought. He put her on a pedestal and wouldn't let her down for a moment. And when he was taken from her she still didn't get down from there. He made Evelyn's mother feel like the most important woman in the world.

Reg made Evelyn feel like someone he hardly even knew.

He would come flying down Steps Lane on that deathtrap bicycle of his and enter the house in a hurry, shedding scarf, overcoat, papers, boots, all his paraphernalia in the hallway.

Brenda would fuss round him, helping him with things, and he would be wriggling to be free to shoot straight up to his study and his precious opus. Evelyn would stand by the staircase at the end of the hall, feeling a fool, trying to catch his attention. All dolled up after a day of doing not very much. And he barely ever spared her a glance as he thundered by. She hardly got a nod and a 'good evening.'

Most evenings he didn't even join her for supper. She was at the dining table alone as the housemaid lumbered round dishing out. Then Brenda went to take Reg's tray up to his study and he nibbled as he worked at his massive desk. Then Brenda went off to eat in the kitchen. What kind of life was that? They were all sitting in different rooms in that great draughty house, eating Brenda's indifferent food.

Oh, when she thought about the house she was brought up in. Her parents' parties, their marvelous celebrations. The festive dinners with music and champagne and cigar smoke and ladies in evening frocks and how, even when Evelyn was tiny, the adults would let her come down to see all the glamorous ladies and gentlemen.

When she first came as a young bride to the august town of Darkholmes, she imagined being a social success in the way her mother always was. She always seemed to be such a hit, effortlessly. But when Evelyn started up in her own home and she would try to throw parties and soirees for the people there – for the other dons and the academic wives – her efforts always fell rather flat. They didn't like her. They still didn't like her. Now she realized that they thought the parties she threw were rather vulgar and silly. They stood about awkwardly. Reg was mortified. At first she thought he was embarrassed on her account, and sorry for the efforts she had gone to, for such an ungrateful crowd. But then, as the snooty beggars filed out into the night at the end of another damp soiree, she realized that he was actually ashamed of *her*, of Evelyn. Her food wasn't sophisticated. Her chatter wasn't bright and brilliant. When her guests wanted to talk about learned things in their usual way, she tried to get them to play silly party games, or to dance to rubbishy music on the phonogram. She looked back and shuddered at herself. But she was only trying to have fun, wasn't she? She was only trying to liven them all up.

Some people, she thought, were simply happy being half-dead.

*

She was sorry almost immediately after posting that letter. She popped it into the post box at the end of Steps Lane and thought, well now, Evelyn. Does your mother really need four more sheets of Basildon Bond containing nothing more than complaints from you that she must have already heard a hundred times?

But, she thought, her mother must understand that she was all she had to talk to. Pathetic, wasn't it? She was forty-three and had no one – no one at all – with whom she might unburden her soul. Reg was a dead loss. Brenda was a brutish lump of a woman. Naturally Evelyn was not above speaking to serving staff but Brenda really was the end. A mouth-breathing monster of a woman, fit only for mashing potatoes, scrubbing smalls and hefting the hostess trolley about.

Anyhow, today Evelyn was in a better mood because she was actually looking forward, for once, to hostessing a little gathering to celebrate the beginning of term. In recent years she had taken to fulfilling her social obligations in the manner that Reg approved of, and didn't even try to make it fun for anyone. Sausages on a stick, schooners of sherry. All these tweedy duffers and their ugly wives standing around chortling and guffawing over their snobby in-jokes.

This year, though... this year she had a feeling that it might be a bit different. She couldn't say why or how exactly. There was just... a tingle in the air. Early frost, one might say. Or perhaps she was not untouched by the excitement felt by many at the start of the academic year.

There were new members of faculty to meet. And one or two of them intrigued her. And, just that afternoon, in a tearoom in town, she had met one of the gentlemen that she had invited to her drinks do. A younger man than she was expecting. A mutual acquaintance introduced them to one another and it was the young gentleman who made the connection. He said, 'Oh! You are the lady who invited us for sherry! The beautiful handwriting!' And he smiled at Evelyn.

He was the brother of the new professor in Reg's college. And what a handsome young man, she thought. So gallant! He seemed to be looking forward to her party a great deal, to judge by his reaction. He wore a rugby top and his sandy hair was all ruffled. He looked hardly older than a student himself. Somebody young and vital, she thought. Coming round to her home. Someone not too sophisticated to laugh and smile and be friendly...

He had put her into a good mood, she recorded in her next letter to her mother. It didn't take much, did it, she reflected. Just a little kindness and attention flung her way.

Perhaps she would even buy something new to wear for the do.

All of a sudden the beginning of term seemed to be looking up.

*

Steps Lane was in the north of the city, where the streets were wide and all the horse chestnut trees were dropping their gingery leaves. John could only just restrain himself from collecting up conkers and stuffing them into his jacket pockets. This evening he was all togged out in his finest. He was even wearing a dress shirt borrowed from Henry. The collar was too tight and they couldn't find cufflinks amongst all their still-scattered possessions.

John hadn't ventured this far north into the city on any of the runs he took, and it was a little further than they were expecting. Henry was grumbling about the time and how they should have caught a cab. He was a dashing sight in his velvet jacket and a rakish scarf. John was glad he'd dressed up. For their first two weeks in the new town they had both been too secluded.

'It's quite grand, out this way, isn't it?' John observed, nodding at all the fancy houses, set back behind high walls and trees, hidden at the end of driveways.

Henry made a vague noise of agreement, but he was miles away.

They hadn't talked about any of the uncanny things they had witnessed since arriving in Darkholmes. John tried to relate his strange encounter by the riverside to Henry the very night of its occurrence, but he put up a trembling hand like a barrier between them. It was as if he knew what was coming and was trying deliberately to shield himself from it. Not very like him at all, John thought. He seemed almost fearful. That night he was feverish and withdrawn. Every night since he had slept rather badly, and went to sit by the empty grate with a rug flung over himself, reading and writing.

Yes, writing. He had immersed himself in the world of his book again. With, as it turns out, so few duties for his new college or the university, he was taking advantage of his ample time. John realized he should be glad about this. He had been the one urging him to return to his Chronicles. But there was something that John wasn't sure about. Something unsettling about his mood.

At least tonight there was a gathering to take their minds off their somewhat stifled days in the college rooms.

Evelyn Tyler greeted them in the doorway of her home. Number 199 wasn't, perhaps, as grand as the other homes along that street, but it was still pretty impressive. And so was she, in a beaded black cocktail gown. She cried out effusively – acting as if she was glad to see them. She treated John as if he was an old friend, on the basis of their brief meeting in that café the other day. He thought then that she was a strange bird. He detected something slightly desperate about her. Lonely. The way she was seizing upon them now did nothing to dissuade him from that point of view.

'We have heard so much about the famous Professor Cleavis,' she said, turning her charm on Henry full force. John loved the way Henry stammered and flummoxed and cleared his throat, unused to such attentions. If he wasn't mistaken, Evelyn Tyler was three sheets to the wind, rather early in the evening.

They were drawn into the house, which was noisy with jazz playing on a gramophone in one of the downstairs rooms, and from everywhere there came chatter and laughter. It was all a bit more animated than John would have expected. He had been to plenty of academic shindigs in his time, and this one seemed to be at the jollier end of the spectrum.

'My Reg can't wait to meet you both,' Evelyn winked at them, and made savage gestures at a large woman dressed up as a Victorian housemaid. 'The great Professor and his... his handsome protege.'

Protege, am I? John thought. He couldn't help smiling at this and Henry caught his eye, frowning. The large woman in the mob cap and pinny tried to take their jackets, but they demurred. It was best to keep them on at affairs like this, just in case one needed to make a quick getaway. Besides, John's shirt was slightly too small and he had just had his jacket cleaned. He felt like showing it off. The large maid grunted and shrugged and moved off again. Poor dear, thought John. Fancy having to dress up like that and dance attendance on the likes of us.

'These are the last of our guests to arrive, Brenda,' her mistress called after her. 'Perhaps you'd like to start taking the canapés round, hm?'

She shouted this at the broad retreating back of the woman and she seemed piqued by Brenda's surly manners. Evelyn turned to her new guests with a silly laugh and said, 'Staff!' As if this was going to impress them.

Then John and Henry were urged to mingle. Evelyn virtually dragged them through several downstairs reception rooms, which were clean but dowdy and crowded with half-familiar looking academic types. The air was thick with pipe smoke and genial guffawing. There was a flurry of names and explanations and they both did a lot of shaking of hands and murmuring of platitudes. John knew that his presence attracted a few comments and a few interested stares. Not hostile, not intrusive. Mostly interested. A few were appraising him in a hungry way. A furtively sexy way. He could sense that. He must be the only person there under forty-five, he realised. Most of the folk present had known each other for donkey's years. Henry and John were new blood in Darkholmes. The old-timers' interest was perking up.

Henry flattered and charmed them effortlessly, leaving a little ripple of laughter and pleasure in his wake as he moved from group to group.

The lumbering housemaid came round pushing a golden hostess trolley. It seemed to be quite hard-going, wheeling it over the rucked-up and faded carpets. What's more, the trolley was rather low for her and even moving around these rooms looked like back-breaking work. She brought egg and tomato finger buns and sausages on sticks to where Henry and John had retreated, between the French windows and the upright piano in the dining room. John juggled a paper plateful of nibbles for them both.

He decided to be extra nice to the maid. She squinched her lumpish features to listen to him. 'Did you prepare this delicious feast yourself, Brenda?'

A light dawned in her eyes. 'Ooh, er, yes. Ha haha. Yes, my own fair hands. Um, yes.' She grinned at him, revealing a mouthful of broken teeth. Then she lumbered away, yanking the trolley on its obstinate castors.

'Poor woman,' said Henry softly.

'How long do we have to stay?'

'Not long,' he grinned. 'I just want to say hello to our host. And I promise we won't be here all evening.'

Usually Henry was as good as his word. But that evening and that soiree were different. He vanished off by himself and was missing for at least an hour or so. And John was left at the mercy of a gaggle of faculty wives, who surrounded him and plucked at him and quizzed him mercilessly. For a while, with his back up against the French Windows, he felt as if he was being pecked to death.

Meanwhile, Henry was away with their host, Professor Reginald Tyler, who couldn't abide parties and had retreated to his upstairs study, where he asked Henry to join him for brandy and a cigar.

*

'Sounds a lot more fun than the interrogations I had to put up with from those harpies,' John complained, as they trudged home, much later than was promised. 'What did you talk about in the great man's study? Why did he want to see you?'

Henry glanced sideways, and John noticed that he looked a little pleased with himself. 'I rather think I've been asked to join a gang!' he said, twinkling.

'You what?'

He chuckled at himself as they wandered down the hill, back into the north of the city centre, via a warren of somewhat slummish streets. The evening mist was rising from the river and there was a curious quiet about the place. But it was a soothing quiet. Nothing sinister.

'I've always been a rotten mixer,' Henry sighed. 'Back when I was a boy, at school. I never really played with the other boys. They never wanted me to join in with their rough-and-tumble games. But I think that might have changed, this evening.'

John snorted with laughter. 'Goodness! Whatever has Tyler asked you to join?' For himself, he felt miffed that he never got even a glimpse of their host.

'I have been invited to join a select band of scribblers, John. Tyler's inner circle of writers. They meet once a fortnight in his sitting room and discuss their works-in-progress.'

John pulled a face. Now they were walking amongst the dark-shuttered shops and the streets were narrowing: their ancient, tumbledown roofs almost meeting above their heads. 'You've never been interested in joining a Writers' Circle before…!' he scoffed.

'Ah, but this is a pretty special one, old chum. This group is called the Smudgelings.'

'So?'

He raised his eyebrows. 'Oh, Tyler's group is well-known. It gets talked about. Hushed whispers. Rumours. Tittle-tattle.'

'Oh yes?' It was altogether possible that Henry had mentioned this rarefied club of Tyler's before, but John had completely blanked it from his mind.

'It's said that Tyler reads from his own work and that the other members are like acolytes. Gathering to hear his chapters as they emerge, hot from his study…'

John shook his head, tutting. 'Hot from his study!' He was glad to hear that Henry could at least gently mock Professor Tyler's pretensions. But he also knew that Henry was truly flattered and excited by the invite. He really wanted to belong to this Smudgelings' gang.

'Tyler seemed to know all about my own works,' Henry said modestly.

'Did he indeed?'

'Oh yes. Yes, he seems a most well-informed and civilized sort of person,' Henry said musingly, as they crossed the old stone bridge into the very middle of the city. 'I think we might get along rather well…'

And so they made their way home.

*

There was a hideous surprise awaiting them in their cloistered rooms.

They toiled up the staircases to the sixth landing, and at the very top they were both instantly on the alert. There were noises coming from behind the heavy wooden door that bore both their nameplates.

Henry's eyes went wide. 'Some beggar is burglarizing us!'

John eased him aside gently, interposing himself between the door and his friend.

And they listened.

And listened.

And there came a rustling. And then a thump. Rustle-thump. Rustle-thump.

There was something in there. Had they left a window open? Had a bird or a cat got in somehow? John shook his head. Too heavy. A burglar. A person. Or… maybe…

He reached out to touch the door and found that it was open. It was slightly ajar.

'Henry, stand back..!'

When John flung himself into the passageway he grabbed for the first weapon that came to hand. Admittedly one of the African spears, or the Carpathian axes that they had hanging on display might have been better. But instead he reached for the odd assemblage of items that were cluttering the coat-and-hat stand and produced his very oldest, and favourite, cricket bat.

John didn't even pause. Brandishing said bat, he hurtled into their living room-cum-study in order to confront the intruder.

Henry was right at his back and it was he who burst out: 'Goodness me!' at the sight of the hideous creature.

It was Mr Mack the college porter, rifling through their belongings. He had made quite a mess. Everything they had unpacked and for which they had carefully found homes, had been flung about the place with wild abandon.

Wanton chaos-making, or was he looking for something deliberately? John was in no mood to argue the finer points. He went at him with his cricket bat not because he'd made a mess, but because he was in a semi-transformed state somewhere between college porter and fiendish bat-thing.

'Mr Mack!' cried Henry, appalled at the sight of the porter in the nude, sporting grey, leathery wings and flapping them with deadly intent. 'What are you doing here? Did you bring my post?'

The heinous being just hissed and flapped the most outrageous forked tongue in their general direction.

'Hmm,' said Henry. 'A Gyregoyle. I should have known.'

Then, with almighty force, the being once known as Mr Mack lunged towards the pair.

John gave him a good battering with his willow, but those limbs and those claws were too strong. He snapped the bat easily in half and – imperiled as they were – John would not have been ashamed to admit that he felt a pang of loss. But, as Henry later pointed out, Mr Mack sealed his own fate with that blow, for the cricket bat splintered nastily into two jagged halves and John was left holding what was, to all intents and purposes, a very serious-looking stake.

The porter hissed and frothed his boiling spittle and slashed the air with his wings.

'Where is the manuscript?' he gurgled and, even as they watched, appalled, it seemed that his human features were distorting even further. They were turning even more monstrous as he tried to spit English sentences at them. 'It must be here… Your manuscript, Professor Cleavis…'

Henry looked dumbfounded. 'Look, here, Mr Mack,' he started remonstrating with the thing. 'You can't just go breaking into a chap's private rooms and demanding…'

'The book!' roared the porter, and they were assailed by the infernal reek of his breath. A gout of flame popped out of his now beak-like maw, which surprised everyone present, including Mack himself. 'Give me your book!'

'There are lots of books here,' John pointed out equably. 'And you've made rather a mess of them.'

'YOUR BOOK, HENRY CLEAVIS!' he shrieked. 'YOU MUST HAND YOUR BOOK OVER TO ME.'

'My book, old fellow?' Henry asked in a mild tone, shuffling forward and looking bemused. Now he was standing well within range of those fearsome claws and teeth and John wasn't happy about that at all.

'The book you are *writing*,' snarled Mr Mack, the porter.

'Aha,' nodded Henry, as if this cleared up some small matter that had been puzzling him of late. 'I see. Well, I think that's all I need to know for now, Mr Mack, thank you. Would you leave my rooms, please?'

The winged fiend flung back his now almost unrecognizable head and laughed. 'You think I'll just leave? Empty-handed?'

Henry shrugged. 'I think you ought to. You've made quite a nuisance of yourself up here. Poor John will have to spend quite some time clearing up this dreadful…'

The creature lurched forward again, murder clearly on his mind.

'Oh dear,' sighed Henry. 'Stake him through the heart, would you, John?'

*

Which was, more or less, what John did. The shattered willow proved deadly, and he was on his mettle, but it still took several hefty thrusts to pierce the brute's armoured chest.

The porter squealed and went into a frenzy. Bright purple blood, semi-coagulated, sprayed about the sitting room. John hung on for dear life as the creature thrashed and howled in protest and made for the window.

John had staked the porter of Hexford College in the chest with a broken cricket bat! Even in those hectic moments he still had a calm place in his mind in which to consider this absurd fact. That genial, witty, rather slow-moving old chap. They had seen him every day since they had moved to this town, going about his business and helping them settle in. Evidently he had been this abomination in secret all along...

John was gripped between the creature's desperate limbs and the cricket bat had become lodged inside its ruined chest cavity. Even in all the hullaballoo John was gripping onto the gore-spattered handle of said bat with all of his might. This, it turned out, was quite a mistake for, just then, Mr Mack utilized all his remaining bodily strength to smash through the sitting room window. He even managed to mangle the ancient metalwork of the window frame, and with a terrific crash, he flung himself out into the dark air high above the college – with John still squashed between his brawny arms.

'John!' Henry cried from the window as they rose and rose higher into the sky. Way below in the college quad, tipsy scholars and other burners of midnight oil came to see what the matter was. None of them could quite believe what was going on and John wished that he couldn't, too.

'John!' Henry called again, equal parts concern and testy impatience. His friend knew what he meant. Why couldn't John have staked the brute accurately to death and had done with it? Without getting carried away and playing the hero and ending up making a show of himself?

He had learned something interesting that night. Henry had called the monster a 'Gyregoyle', not a gargoyle. And that was because, when it flew, it went round in tight little spirals through the darkness, flapping its wings like crazy. They went round and round high above the towers of the college and the spire of the cathedral and the battlements of the castle. And then, eventually, the creature bled out of the last of its infernal strength and plummeted to the ground, taking John with it.

They landed in the trees at the back of the castle, on that sheer drop down towards the river. It could have been worse. John broke two ribs but, as Henry kept pointing out, when he went to visit him in hospital, it could have been very much worse. John had to learn to stop trying to be quite so showily heroic.

Of Mr Mack the Gyregoyle – and John's favourite willow – there was no sign.

*

'You said he was a Gyregoyle,' John frowned at Henry, sitting up in white cotton sheets the next day. He was wearing crisp borrowed pyjamas and keeping a wary eye on Matron, who wasn't happy with Henry visiting outside of the official hours. Henry never did care much about official hours though.

'Hmm?' said Henry, flipping through the story magazine he'd brought ostensibly for John, and sucking a Satsuma. 'What's that?'

'You said the monster Mr Mack had transformed into was a Gyregoyle. I've never heard of those before. How did you know what he was?'

Henry stared over his glasses and sighed. 'That's quite simple, my dear chap. You see, it was I who made them up!'

*

When Evelyn Tyler next wrote to her mother in Scotland, she was glad to report that her soiree hadn't been an utter washout after all.

For once she had held a drinks party and it hadn't been a complete failure. She even imagined that people might have had a good time...

Not that Reginald cared, particularly. He barely emerged from his study to honour the guests with his presence. He passed through the downstairs rooms briefly, only once, nodding stiffly at the people he had known for years. Then he scurried back to his rotten study where, apparently, he was deep in conference with Professor Cleavis – someone he had known for all of five minutes. A genial, bumbling, eccentric chap – but those lesser mortals downstairs hardly saw him.

Luckily they had his protégé John instead – who was a great boon to the party. As Evelyn had already reported to her mother, John was a handsome, strapping fellow and all the ladies were pleased to see him and bask a little in his attention. Splendid manners he had.

Soon, however, this party Evelyn had spent so long in preparing was over and done with and all the guests were gone. The house was in a dreadful state and, next morning, she had that sinking feeling. That awful faded feeling she always got when the fun was over and done with and ordinary life took over again. She went back to bed, she was that browned off. She listened to the bleak noise of Brenda lumbering about with her dustpan and shovel, and then the vacuum.

Reg never said anything. He never passed comment on the party's success or otherwise. Nor did any of their ungrateful guests thank them for a wonderful time. Except for one – John (she never got his surname.) He sent them a little note, both of them, thanking them for the wonderful time he and Professor Cleavis had experienced in the Tylers' beautiful home. Now, that was good old-fashioned manners, wasn't it?

Plus, it was a surprise, too, because university gossip had it that those two new gentlemen encountered something of a nasty surprise that evening of the shindig on Steps Lane. Upon returning to their Hexford College rooms (which they apparently *shared*) they encountered a burglar or somesuch. A very violent person who, when disturbed by their return, caused a dreadful scene. John flew to his friend's rescue and there ensued a fearful fight, with windows being smashed and – if the gossip was to be believed – there were scenes of bloody violence and gore.

Details were being hushed up, of course, as ever. The University of Darkholmes wouldn't want scandal. They didn't like to involve the local constabulary, though Evelyn didn't see why. If there were vicious attackers lurking around colleges then surely the matter needed looking into via the official channels?

When she asked Reg about this, later in the week, as they tackled one of Brenda's suppers together, he pursed his lips and shook his head. 'The University authorities know what is for the best,' he told his wife, and returned his attention to the charred kippers.

'I heard it was some kind of...' Here she lowered her voice, because Brenda was dragging that infernal hostess trolley into the room.

Reg frowned. 'You heard it was what?'

Evelyn dabbed her lips with a napkin. 'Something not quite human.'

'Nonsense,' he said gruffly. 'Not human? Eh? What? What's that supposed to mean?'

'It's just what I heard. On the grapevine.'

He sighed heavily. 'If it wasn't human, this intruder who so rudely surprised our new friends, then what do you suppose it was, Evelyn?'

She was brought up short by the fact that he actually used her name. I must be so very starved of affection, she thought.

Brenda was standing right behind her and Evelyn could hear the change in her breathing as she readied herself to break into their whispers. 'I heard it was a demon,' the servant announced darkly. 'I heard it was like a demon out of hell.'

The Tylers were both surprised that she had the nerve to burst out like that, so abruptly. It wasn't something she was given to.

Reg flew into a fury. He jumped up, scattering dishes and cutlery. He berated her in the strongest terms. How dare she bring her silly superstitious speculations into their home? How could she sully his supper table with her idle peasant gossip?

He gave her such an acid tongue-lashing that Evelyn felt quite sorry for the poor fool. She hung her head and took hold of her trolley and backed clumsily out of the room.

'Reg, that was uncalled for.' Evelyn told him. She tried to sound frosty, but was shaken by his outburst.

'I want her out of here,' he snapped. 'I'm not having talk of demons from hell. You tell her, Evelyn! Tell her tomorrow that she can collect her cards! I'm not having her in my house a day longer!'

And so that was where they were up to. It seemed to Evelyn that she was to lose her only company about the place, and her only help with the mountains of work that need doing at 199 Steps Lane. She was sure they would never get a replacement who would tolerate the pittance they doled out to Brenda.

Evelyn was starting to wonder whether Reg wasn't going doo-lally.

*

It felt rather like Henry had gone into an almighty sulk with his best friend. John tried talking to him, but he didn't want to go into it. All he would say regarding the unfortunate scuffle with Mr Mack the college porter was that he wished there could have been another way. Why had John had to make it quite so violent?

As if I had a choice! Thought John, crossly.

But he didn't argue the point with Henry because exerting himself in the smallest way – even raising his voice – resulted in crippling pain. His ribs were all bandaged up and he was wheezing and hobbling about like someone twice his age. As it happened, he wished his encounter with the porter hadn't been quite so violent, too.

They had hushed the whole thing up of course, the college. Interesting, how quickly the authorities had moved on that. Mr Mack had been called away to his extended family in

Australia, apparently, and his replacement was Mr Briar, who donned the man's spare uniform and cap and calmly set about doing his job in the exact same way.

And nothing more was said about the business of the savage Gyregoyle.

Henry didn't mention the name again. He wouldn't discuss the business at all, beyond enquiring after John's sore ribs. He sat in his chair by the fireplace with his trayful of papers upon his lap and all his writing materials scattered about him, and he pushed further into his book.

His sequel. His second children's book. The follow-up to 'The Other Place.'

John backed away. Who'd have thought the composition of anything as benign and cheery-sounding as a children's book could render him so glum and introspective? But that's what it did. He sat and stewed over his fantastical adventure story and looked like hell.

It was the same last time, the previous year, when he was coming close to the end of his first book. John had tried to tell him – you take it all much too seriously. You will damage your health, getting so obsessed and abstracted…

And Henry just about snarled at him in response. 'This is how it has to be!' he yelled. 'This is the way it works!'

Evidently John didn't understand these things. He realized that he didn't have Henry's genius. He would never understand what it was he was going through.

All he knew was that Henry hadn't been entirely happy since starting to write about that fantasy world of his. When he first invented the 'Other Place' – as he called it – he had changed. John was best placed to observe this, and he knew it for the truth.

Since then he had been like a man possessed of a dark secret, the workings of which he could never share.

Even with John.

*

In a matter of mere days Henry Cleavis and Reginald Tyler became close as anything. They sought each other's company like revolutionaries or would-be assassins. They were meeting up in town for special pow-wows.

Henry wasn't exactly furtive about it, but he didn't seem to want to discuss it with John.

Mornings were frosty as October wore on, and Henry was dressing up warmly and winding a scarf around his head until he was almost unrecognizable. He shoved his leather satchel full with his messy papers and hurried out.

John was left to his own devices.

Still, he had his own things to do. Shopping to get in. Repairs to the window and doors to oversee. The rooms to tidy. A new town to get used to. He had plenty to be getting on with.

Henry and Tyler seemed to be having get-togethers at the pub. John had seen them with his own eyes. Not that he was following them, of course. He was just out for a (very cautious) walk. He was down that part of town, walking past the front of LeFanu College and happened to notice, across the street, Henry hurrying happily into a pub. *The Phoenix and the Carpet.* A quaint old place. And there was Henry, popping in for a tipple in the late morning.

John would not be ashamed to say he followed him in. The place was almost empty. Quiet, too. His feet were too noisy on the bare boards as he went from room to room, peering in alcoves. He hung back as he heard Henry's voice at the bar.

He hid beside the cloak room and Henry didn't have a clue he was being watched as he carried a tray bearing two foaming tankards of ale.

Henry went to settle in the front room, by the crackling fire and the bow window overlooking the street. A hawk-faced, angular man in tweeds was waiting for him. Their table was scattered with books and papers and they were intent on their hushed conversation. John knew at once this must be Tyler. He was the complete physical opposite of Henry and radiated a kind of… John didn't know what he would call it. Haughtiness, he supposed. Plus a general air of malaise. Quite different to Henry's ebullience and charm. Tyler hardly seemed a natural candidate for the post of Henry's new best friend.

John knew he couldn't stand about there all day, hovering and trying to eavesdrop. Soon enough the landlord might discover him, lurking there in his scruffy running clothes. He would feel a fool if he was turfed out in front of Henry.

So he left. Very carefully, leaving them to it.

Secret meetings. Hushed conversations. All their books and papers.

They were talking about their writing. That's what it was.

Silly of me to feel so wounded and left out, John thought. But really, he almost felt betrayed.

It was he who Henry used to turn to. It was he who used to hear all about his work. But he supposed, on that front, Henry had more in common with the esteemed Professor Tyler.

John buried all the unworthy thoughts he was having and hurried into town, to continue with his chores.

*

One of the things he had to do was set up an account with a local bookshop. Just like the one they'd had in their old town. It was something as vital as having an electricity supply. Or running water.

John had his eye on just the place. It was somewhere he had discovered when he was out on his exploratory trips through the city.

Chimera, it was called. The kind of place that looked as if no one had set foot in it for years. In fact, one had to look quite hard to see that it was even open at all. The windows were dark and grey with matted cobwebs and several small panes were cracked and boarded up. But he knew at once, as soon as he saw it, that it was bound to become his and Henry's bookshop of choice in this new town.

Not for them the shiny, everyday, respectable establishments where everything was new. Not for them the shops catering to the humdrum tourists and the student brigade. And they wouldn't even patronize the run-of-the-mill antiquarian bookshops that filled the winding streets of the old town almost to bursting point. No, all the bookshops they had ever used had been just like this – and he knew that *Chimera* was the place for them as soon as he saw it.

There was a splendidly bewhiskered old lady in charge of the place. She sat at a desk underneath the staircase at the far end of the room. The whole place smelled deliciously of the very strongest Turkish coffee and, on his very first visit last week, she had given John several cups of this crunchy brew, which made him swoon. And then she regaled him with the history of this filthy, crumbling shop, where she had worked for an unbelievable sixty years.

Today she blinked at him over her knitting – a dirty, lime-green muffler – and stared like she had never clapped eyes on him before.

'I've come back to open my account,' John mumbled, feeling curiously self-conscious as he stood before her. 'A joint account, for Professor Cleavis and myself.'

She frowned. Really hard. Her flesh had the texture – and the smell – of fruit gone rancid in the bowl. 'Cleavis?' she whispered. 'Professor Cleavis?'

He didn't like the urgency in her tone. Why was she being so odd? Last week she had been delightful company. 'Y-yes,' said John. 'Professor Cleavis… my mentor.'

'Mentor – pah!' she spat. And she really did spit. A wad of chewed tobacco flew out of her mouth onto the filthy carpet.

'You know Professor Cleavis?' he asked.

'Never heard of him,' she snorted phlegmily. 'Unless you mean Henry Cleavis the author. The children's author. 'The Other Place'. That man.'

'Why, yes!' John burst out. 'I do! That's exactly who I mean!'

She narrowed her eyes at him. 'Yes. I'd heard he had come to Darkholmes.' She bit into her bottom lip, chewed at it thoughtfully and seemed to come to a decision. 'You may open your account here, young man. On the condition that you bring Henry Cleavis here. To my shop, so that I can see him in the flesh.'

John nodded readily, knowing that there was every chance in the world that Cleavis would want to come here. Once he heard about the existence of this dirty and labyrinthine place there would be no holding him back.

And was it foolish to suppose that he would be grateful to John for finding it for him? Perhaps for a moment he would forget about his new friend and the excitement of pints and prolonged meetings in the pub with Reginald Tyler. Perhaps he would remember his one-time best pal?

*

John buried his morose thoughts and went hunting through the upper rooms of *Chimera*. He was looking for books for himself. Something to indulge himself in. To fill up his idle hours. With his ribs as they were, he couldn't run and explore Darkholmes as he really wished to. He had been instructed to stay at home and recuperate.

The shop became narrower and grimier, the higher one climbed its rickety staircases. The going was perilous, too. Several times he almost came a cropper in avalanches of old tomes. Soon he was out of breath and stooping painfully under the low, sloping roof of the attic, where he had found stashed hundreds of old Penny Dreadfuls. His very favourite kind of reading matter. The pulpier and more violent, the better. Henry always made fun of his tastes. Though he loved adventure stories too, his favoured tales were always a bit more cerebral than John's.

There was a heady scent up at the top of *Chimera*. Wood smoke and old paper, tobacco and spiders. Then there was an almost spicy scent, too. Exotic. Otherworldly, as if the pages of these lurid books had blown open in the breeze.

Yes, there was a breeze. But the skylight was shut. It was painted shut with coats of gloss and pale, sticky cobweb. There hadn't been a breath of air through that cramped room in years. And yet… there was one coming now. And it wasn't chilly like it ought to be. This wasn't a riffle of breeze from the river and it had nothing Octoberish about it. It was warm. Warmer than John's own breath. It was like someone breathing down his neck, or on his cheek. It was like standing close to a loved one and waiting for a kiss…

What was he thinking about? What was he doing? Standing there and going off into a dream like that?

But there was definitely something altered in the atmosphere. There was a swirl of dust in the air. The breeze was blowing more strongly and the air was even more laden with strangely evocative scents.

He thought the room where he was currently standing was the last room in *Chimera*.

But no. There was a doorway between the final two bookcases. Behind the aspidistra, the greying leaves of which were stirring in the breeze.

The door was painted an indefinable colour and it was sticky as toffee lodged in the corner of a pocket. John touched it briefly and it sprang open. He crouched – gingerly, wincing with pain – and stepped through into another room.

There was noise. Impossible chatter. The clattering and chattering of hundreds of people. It was baking hot and the room he was in seemed to have fabric instead of walls. Billowing fabric with wonderful sunlight glimmering through. Here there were more books, heaped on tables and in piles upon the sandy floor. He was standing in a tent.

He found a door and poked his head out.

He was in a market place. A loud, brash, busy marketplace. An Arabian souk, by the looks of it.

This cannot be, he thought.

He was very calm. Though sweat stood out on his forehead, along his arms and all down his back. Suddenly he was roasting hot in his duffel coat and the sun, peering over the canvas rooftops, was searing his eyes.

This just couldn't be.

'Have you found anything you like the look of?' asked a voice at his elbow.

It was the woman who had been sitting at the desk of *Chimera*. Downstairs. He had just seen her down there. With a fuzz of old lady beard. She was still clutching her knitting. She must have followed him all the way upstairs... and into the attic... and out into this impossible place.

'I...' He stared at her and then at the other people crowding by. They were dressed in brilliant colours. They gave him only the most cursory glances. Some were scornful. They must think I'm mad, he realized, togged up like I am against the autumn cold. 'I haven't found anything,' he told the old woman. 'No.'

'Are you sure?' she twinkled at him. She was even being flirtatious. 'You haven't spent much time looking. I've got some amazing books here.'

'I imagine you have,' said John, very stiffly.

Then he turned away and hurried back inside her tent. He blocked out all the sounds and smells and impossible stuff he had just witnessed. He crammed himself back through the small door and breathed a massive sigh of relief that he was back in the prosaic attic at *Chimera*.

He didn't want the impossible stuff. He didn't want the magic things. They could just take them all away. They could stop presenting themselves to him. He'd had enough already.

John hurried down the stairs, dislodging precarious stacks of books as he went.

He was thinking: *it's never been like that. I've never been transported before. I've never been to Another Place.*

Why now? Why here? And where the devil was that?

He descended the levels of *Chimera* and he was near to panicking. The sweat had turned chilly on his face and all over his body. The hair prickled on his scalp. Now he was disappointed in himself. He'd never thought he'd react like this.

He had seen magic things before. He had seen sorcery close to.

But he had never been to Another Place.

He was scared. When it had happened, he was scared. He hadn't been excited or amazed. He didn't relish a second of it. He was just scared and he turned tail and ran.

She was still sitting at her desk, clacking her needles and clucking her tongue. He had no idea how the whiskered hag could be in two places at once and, just then, he didn't care.

He left the bookshop, hardly sparing her a glance. He thundered out like he was furious.

'Come again soon,' she called after him. 'I know you will. You are bound to return. And why not bring your friend, next time? I'm sure he'll be astonished...'

By then John was standing on the cobbles outside in the freezing wind. The door slammed shut behind him, with a rushed carillon of bells.

He wouldn't go back there in a hurry. Perhaps he would find somewhere else to buy their books.

CHAPTER TWO

Sunday was one of Reg's evenings.

Evelyn was quite used to the routine. Every fortnight she was banished to her boudoir. She took a light supper on a tray and read herself to sleep as, downstairs, goodness knew what was going on in her parlour. All those men, trooping into her house. Fifteen, maybe twenty of them. She didn't know exactly. She wasn't really sure who came visiting on the nights when the Smudgelings had their meetings at 199 Steps Lane.

And what did they even talk about? They were stuck in there for hours on end, slurping sherry and pots of tea and smoking themselves blue in the face. Reg always said it was to do with the books they were writing. Their Works in Progress, he called them. But really, how long could they talk about boring things like that? Men getting together and drinking and smoking. It had to be women they were talking about, hadn't it? Evelyn dreaded to think.

Upstairs she was supine on her candlewick bedspread with a whole heap of magazines and a box of choccies and a racy novel from the library and she would pass the time all on her own.

In many ways Smudgelings nights weren't all that different to any other night.

She tuned the radio to play some jazz. Lots of tinkly piano music. Tea for two and two for tea. That song brought a little tear every time. One of their courting songs, though she doubted Reg would remember that.

Her mother would never put up with it, would she? A bunch of strangers traipsing into her home and getting up to drunken shenanigans. Evelyn was far too forbearing and patient. Just as her mother had always told her.

Bored, earlier this evening Evelyn called Brenda upstairs and asked what was going on down there. Well, as per usual, the housemaid didn't have much to say. Oh God, Evelyn cringed. She's so guttural. I can't bear it. Why did we ever hire the terrible lummox?

But hire her they did, ten years ago, useless as she was and Reg said that they couldn't ever get rid of her. Complete turnabout the other day, when all he wanted was to see her gone. Now he was back to saying they couldn't sack her at all, ever. Who would look after her if they turfed her out? That was the kind of thing Evelyn's tender-hearted husband said.

The meeting had begun, was all Brenda could tell her mistress, and she'd served them tea in the best china, along with Battenberg cake. All the usual faces were there. Evelyn asked if there was anyone new. A queer light came into Brenda's deep-set eyes. 'Oh, oh, yes,' she went. 'Yes, indeed, madam. Prof – Prof – Prof Cleavis. He has come. He is at the Smudgelings' meeting for the very f-first time.'

Aha! She knew Reg would bring Henry Cleavis into his little gang. It seemed inevitable. Surely Reg was cooking something up. He was making furtive, secretive plans of some kind.

Evelyn asked Brenda: 'Is Professor Cleavis's young friend here as well, then? That nice John?'

Brenda shook her head brusquely. 'No young man. There's no young man. Not here.'

Which was a shame. Evelyn could have done with another look at that burly, bright, dependable-looking young man.

Then she was thinking – there was all that recent business, wasn't there? There was a terrible story about some kind of intruder in their college rooms. Yes – and the young man was injured. Broken ribs, wasn't it? Everyone was very shocked when they heard, but the details were sparse. Evelyn wondered if his injuries were the reason he wasn't at her house that evening. Perhaps he was incapacitated. What a terrible thing, for such an active-seeming young person. She could pay him a visit, perhaps. Just to see that he was all right. The next time that she was in town, when she was close to Hexford College, she could pop in, couldn't she? There would be nothing wrong with that. With her showing a little concern for a young man's health and well-being.

She could even drop by tomorrow, couldn't she? She was having lunch in town. She had just remembered.

With her mother's old friend. Catriona Mackay.

*

She fell asleep fully dressed on top of the bedspread. All her glossy magazines strewn around her. She woke feeling drab and disheveled. Reg had been to bed and not even disturbed her. He hadn't thought to wake her, or encourage her to undress and sleep under the covers like any normal husband would.

By the time she was up and about it was 9 am. Reg was out at work already. Brenda was dusting the parlour and, even though she had the French windows open to air the place, Evelyn fancied she could still see that fug of blue smoke hanging about. And, though the room was quiet, she felt she could still hear the endless chatter of Reg's cronies in there. The echoes of all their boring twaddle, never knowing when to stop.

She made Brenda brew up a strong pot of tea and then got her to run a hot bath.

And then Evelyn dressed herself up so she looked her most tip-top. Really, by rights, that oughtn't to be possible, not after all the gin and soft-centres she had put away the previous night. But she did look rather marvelous. Her complexion was wonderful, as if stifling bedrooms and chocolate liqueurs were all she needed to make her bloom. She had her mother's bones and skin. She knew she had no one but mother to thank.

It was chillier today. She donned her new winter cape, trimmed with fox fur. Her birthday present. She tried her matching hat at a jaunty angle and off she went to catch the bus at the end of Steps Lane. Trundling into town, she was feeling rather excited by the prospect of company and a lunchtime spent at *Aphrodite's Salon*.

She was in her mother's debt for everything that was worthwhile in her life. This new friend was only the latest thing. Evelyn would never forget that she was mother's friend first. She was glad that her mother had lent her out. Mother knew that Evelyn had been starved of witty, elegant, sympathetic company and Catriona Mackay was a godsend.

Evelyn could still recall how her heart lifted that morning back in spring when she opened her mother's letter and learned all about how Catriona Mackay was a very special person. How she was starting a new job at the University of Darkholmes and knew no one at all in the town and how Evelyn must go out of her way to introduce herself and befriend the new girl and look out for her. It was almost absurd to think of that now, since she felt Catriona had been the saving of her and not the other way round at all.

Evelyn knew at once, upon first sighting this slim, elegant figure with her inquisitive smile and those amused green eyes, that they were destined to become famous friends. The silvery, frosty scent of her cologne and her dainty clutch bag. Everything about her was just so chi-chi and perfectly sophisticated. She seemed almost other-wordly in the context of the pokey, wood-panelled room in Hexford College where she was beginning her job as secretary to the Dean.

Evelyn had imagined a much plainer person. Someone she might perhaps need to bring out of herself. Not so with Ms Mackay, who was a much more naturally vivacious person than Evelyn herself. Evelyn happily conceded that when they lunched together in public places Catriona was the one who typically draw the admiring stares of strangers. Evelyn was not envious. She hardly cared one whit. She was deeply under Catriona's spell as anyone.

There was one thing which Evelyn still didn't understand. And that was how Catriona could possibly be, as her mother had first claimed, a school contemporary of hers? Surely Catriona was no older than Evelyn herself? Mother must have made some mistake. Even after Evelyn asked, several times, in her letters, mother had never given an adequate reason for this queer-seeming discrepancy of age.

*

Last time Evelyn's mother came to visit they had made a special trip to *Aphrodite's Salon*. Even Reg had come along. Mother had pronounced that the place was *drenched* in the ambience of 'a more refined era'.

Evelyn believed that it was the only place in town fancy enough for her mother – and for Catriona, too – all plaster angels and candlelight. A breath of *fin-de-siecle* glamour, is what her mother said. Evelyn had been thrilled by her mother's reaction. At last she had done something to impress her. And now she loved the place herself. She could almost imagine lolling about in Paris, say, smoking Gauloises and nibbling caviar off a tiny spoon, rather than being here in this town, feeling herself getting smothered in the mist and the ivy of a Northern University.

Catriona Mackay was waiting in what had become their regular corner banquette. She had ordered gin slings, the naughty girl. She rose from the red velvet plush and kissed Evelyn on both cheeks.

Whenever Evelyn was with her it felt like breathing a different atmosphere. Catriona was full of news of everywhere. She was like a cyclone who had been hither and yon, using up every single day she could get free of her job to tootle away to London or even to the Continent. She got to go to all the best places and, rather gauchely, Evelyn had once wondered aloud how she could afford to gallivant on the pittance Hexford College was undoubtedly paying her.

'My dear Evelyn, I don't need the money..!' That day she chortled low in that perfect white throat. She laughed at the very idea of working because she had to. A lovely guffaw of real amusement at Evelyn's confusion. Oh, everything Evelyn ever said seemed to tickle her so. 'I work because it amuses me. And – my dear – what a privilege it is to be in the proximity of so many stellar geniuses – your husband paramount among them.'

Now it was Evelyn's turn to laugh. She didn't know for sure, but she suspected that Catriona was making fun of her hubby. But Evelyn didn't care either way. She knew a thing or two about basking in the proximity of geniuses and it felt in no way as thrilling as sitting right there on a banquette in *Aphrodite's Salon* with Catriona. Evelyn was enthralled at the way Catriona dealt with her mussels. She twisted open their little black shells and toyed with the lucky occupants, one by one. Evelyn had foolishly ordered Welsh Rarebit and was stuck with prodding at a plateful of stodge.

'In all seriousness, Evelyn, dear,' Catriona told her. 'The reason I am here in this dingy town is to glory in the presence of the many brilliant, inventive minds of these men. Oh, yes.'

Evelyn could hardly believe what she was hearing. Surely Catriona was worth ten of any Professor one cared to pick out?

'Your husband's little society, for instance,' Catriona smiled, sipping her gin sling and finding it almost all gone. 'Its members really fascinate me. I would love to know more about them and what they get up to.' She clicked her fingers at a superior-looking waiter, who brightened when he saw who was doing the clicking.

'I can't tell you very much about the Smudgelings, I'm afraid.' Evelyn sighed. 'On those nights I'm a stranger in my own home.'

'Banished to your lonely tower like Rapunzel, yes,' Catriona smiled at her. Those jade eyes reflected the chandeliers. Yes, *Rapunzel*. She was quite correct. And Reg was the horrid dwarf keeping Evelyn prisoner. Rumplestiltskin. Yes – that cast her everyday plight in a much more flattering, fairy-tale light. 'You know, I'd love to know what they discuss in these little gatherings of theirs,' Catriona mused. 'All sorts of amazing things, I'm sure.'

'It's just stories!' Evelyn blurted out. 'That's all it is. I've listened at the door and Brenda has told me things that she's heard, too. And it's just silly old stories that they talk about. Stories about… magic and all that mystical stuff that Reg is so bothered about.'

Catriona looked delighted by this. 'Have you ever read any of his chapters? Have you seen any of this long, ongoing, everlasting novel of his? Have you ever heard him read from it?'

Evelyn shrugged and suddenly the elegant room seemed to be tilting around. The waiter arrived with more greenish gin for them both. That was better. 'I've lived with him all these years – seventeen bloody years! – and all that time he's been scribbling away at that same book. I've picked up a thing or two. Had a look in his study, had a poke in his briefcase. And really, it's just kid's stuff, you know.'

'Kids' stuff?' frowned Catriona.

'Yes. I mean… it's all goblins and ogres and witches and… pixies! It's ridiculous! Bloody pixies! A grown man like him scratching away in his books and working all those hours into the night, for all those years, and getting together in a huddle with all those other men and then it turns out that what he's writing about is fairies and pixies and magical spells...!'

Evelyn was off on something of a rant at this point. She was giving herself free reign because it felt good to raise her voice in a public place and snigger with derision at that man of hers. Plus, she was making Catriona hoot with laughter and that felt good too. Evelyn was actually enjoying herself.

Then Catriona said, 'But you see my dear, to me it all sounds wonderful. You make it sound just like heaven to me.'

'Do I?'

Catriona drew her closer. 'I dabble, you see. I write a little, too. I write just the kinds of things that you're describing so hilariously…'

Now this brought Evelyn up short. At first she didn't know what Catriona meant. She *wrote*? She wrote things like Reg did? She noticed Evelyn's reaction as the notion settled in. Surely I have insulted her? Evelyn thought. By making it sound silly it's possible that I have cut her to the quick. But Catriona was so well-mannered she would never give away her hurt feelings. She just smiled sadly and suddenly Evelyn remembered something her mother had once told her.

'Oh!' she burst out. 'Yes! I recall now... Mother said that once you had *aspirations*...'

'Hardly aspirations,' she demurred. 'A fantasy. A childlike whim. A mere caprice.'

'I'm sure it was more than that,' Evelyn interrupted. The memory gained force. 'Yes... mother told me about the days when you were at school together. In the big house in the Highlands. Those draughty dormitories in the attics. She told how you wrote and wrote everyday in your private notebooks, and each night you would gather your favourite girls into your bed and you'd make a little tent out of sheets and lighted candles. And you would read to them all.' All at once Evelyn could picture the shadow-play of yellowish candlelight and she even got a whiff of the starchy smells of sheets and clean nightgowns. 'Mother said that you told them all the most wonderful tales. Ones that you made up inside your own head...'

Catriona was nodding and smiling. Almost shyly. This was so rare for her. In their short friendship Evelyn had never seen her look abashed. She lowered her face modestly towards the pale candlelight and the effect was most becoming. 'A girlish hobby.'

'But you are still writing these stories?'

'Why yes,' she said in deadly earnest. 'Oh, I never gave them up.'

Evelyn remembered how her mother looked, when she talked about the tales told by her best friend at school. When Evelyn was small her mother even tried her hardest to bring those midnight tales back into her mind. She thought she could pass them onto her daughter. But she could never quite recall them in their entirety. All she could conjure up were nonsensical fragments. Shards of stories only. Evelyn remembered mention of *The Time Gentlemen* and *The Goodnight Ladies* and *The Moss Queen* and *The Staircase that Fell out of the Door*. Yes! Those tiny bits… they came back to her even now. Catfox and The Regurgitator and Devilish Hugh.

Across the gulf of years from Evelyn's own childhood… it was like hearing footsteps in the next room. And she sat there on the velvet banquette with the very woman who supposedly originated these half-remembered things. This impossibly young woman who was their creator. And she looked no older than Evelyn herself.

All at once Evelyn realised something that, when she gave it any thought at all, was quite obvious.

There was something magical about Catriona Mackay. Something delicious and dark and quite out of the ordinary.

'I would love to hear your stories.' Evelyn told her and it came out in a croak. Her cold lunch lay untouched between them like a sticky wasteland. Catriona had finished all her mussels and the shells rattled like dark little skulls when she pushed the bowl aside.

'Perhaps you will, Evelyn,' she said wistfully. 'You might be ready.'

Their jolly get-together had shifted into a different key. Evelyn wasn't sure when or why it had happened. A certain mood crept over them. It gathered them up and delivered them back to the windy street, where leaves went shivering by on the pavement. Students and housewives scuttled past, bicycles and motorcars were whizzing along.

They were back in the humdrum again.

Evelyn was pulling her fur-lined cape over her shoulders again and the now rather somber Catriona helped and fussed over her, praising the priciest, most stylish item of apparel Evelyn had ever owned. All at once, in comparison with the indigo coat that went right down to Catriona's tiny feet, Evelyn felt shabby. Her cape felt like a horrible scrap of affectation: a nasty, cheap rag hanging round her neck. And then she thought – my goodness, who paid for our lunch? And she understood that Catriona must have seen to the bill, so quickly and blithely that she never even noticed, never gave it a moment's consideration.

Catriona linked arms with her as they walked to the crumbling courtyards and towers of Hexford College. She had to return to what remained of her afternoon with the Dean and Evelyn was going to pay a visit.

'My dear,' Catriona suddenly murmured, ever so softly. 'If you could obtain for me an invite to join your husband's little society, I would be eternally grateful.'

All Evelyn did was nod at this.

It was impossible. Reg would never have it.

Women weren't allowed. Of course they weren't.

But Evelyn nodded, because she knew that, for the sake of the captivating Catriona Mackay, she would see to it that Reg agreed and welcomed her with open arms into the fellowship of the Smudgelings.

*

Evelyn took directions from the new porter, who seemed all of a-dither, poor man. Evidently he was still getting used to everything in Hexford College and learning where everyone belonged. Even for those long-used to being there Evelyn imagined it being a perplexing place. Pale stone corridors and staircases, galleries criss-crossing bright courts and darkened halls. She felt as if she had walked several miles before she reached the rooms of Professor Cleavis and John. At the porter's lodge she found to her slight embarrassment that she still didn't know John's surname. She had to refer to him as Cleavis's young friend and companion, which didn't sound quite nice or respectful, somehow. Even the porter – though knowing who she meant – couldn't supply the correct name. It was as if the poor young man wasn't quite a person in his own right.

At last she knocked at the dark door and, after several moments, John answered. Tousled, sheepish, wearing a tartan dressing gown and clearly not expecting company today. There was a fusty aroma in their sitting room. Evelyn glanced about at the newspapers, opened books, used plates and cups and heaped ashtrays. It was all unmistakable evidence of men left to their own devices. A wife such as Evelyn recognized the signs at once. It felt rather like wandering into a messy lair.

'Mrs Tyler,' he smiled, wincing as he steered her in. She realised that he was in pain.

'Sit down, you poor man. I heard you had damaged yourself...'

He looked rueful. 'Yes, ribs. They should be mended by now. I'd be all right had I not gone out and tried to run about the town before I was quite healed.'

'But you didn't want to be cooped up in here,' she said, indicating the room's close confines and hoping that she wasn't coming across as too judgmental.

'I'm not used to days of inactivity,' he sighed, dropping heavily into a well-upholstered armchair. The Oxblood leather had worn to pale pink in places. Yes, his body was big, robust. It was just as attractive injured and stiff like this. Even more so, actually, to Evelyn. All her training as a nurse and all her most natural impulses made her want to take care of him.

'You should be very careful,' she admonished. 'And do everything your doctor tells you.' She smiled. 'I was a nurse in the war. I know whereof of I speak.' Why am I putting on this fake, fancy voice when I talk to him? she wondered. He wasn't snobbish and clever like the rest of them. Why did she feel the need to put on an act...?

'A nurse?' he said. 'Oh, I think I knew that. Henry might have told me that about you.'

It pleased her to think that they had been discussing her. Even if the conversation had been wholly banal, the idea of being invoked between them made her glad. John offered her refreshment, but she told him no. She didn't want him going to any effort for her sake. He must just sit there and tell her how he was. That was what she was there for. (Though in truth she could have murdered a hot, sweet cup of tea. Those lunchtime cocktails with Catriona had given her a pounding head and a raging thirst.)

'So, I understand Henry was at your house last night,' John asked suddenly. The question seemed to jump out of him unbidden. 'Did he enjoy himself?' There was something queer in his tone. It took Evelyn a moment to recognize it. Peevishness. A feeling of being left out.

'You'd know more about that than I would,' she frowned. 'Reg tells me nothing about his meetings. The Smudgelings are a closed book to me, I'm afraid.' Her weak joke made him chuckle, and she went on to describe how she hid herself upstairs, gorging herself on chocolates all night and perusing Movie magazines. She was making herself sound foolish in order to amuse him, and she was pleased to get him laughing. It was a rich, raucous, *unguarded* sound.

All at once Evelyn felt very strongly that John was a good man. She wanted to spend more time around him. She gave him a few more tidbits, making light of how Reg treated her. She painted a verbal picture of his tetchiness, his casual snobbery and frosty neglect. She was making fun of her whole life in order to make it all seem less hurtful.

As John laughed she studied the new window. She could smell putty. Tools were lying about in that part of the room. Curls of wood shavings were scattered on the floor. There were smudgy fingerprints on the new panes. Already it was getting darker out there. The afternoon light was retreating across the ancient rooftops. She said to him, 'I was sorry to hear about your... attack. This... this intruder you had. I must admit, I felt almost responsible for your trouble that night. Given that you were attending my drinks do...'

He pulled a face. 'It was hardly any of your fault, Evelyn. But it was most curious. The... erm, former porter of Hexford College, you know. Mr Mack...'

'I know him! I have known him for years. I wouldn't have believed it of him. He was such an old man. Well past retirement age. How could he ever have been a physical threat to one as wonderfully strong and... and... fit as yourself?'

John stared at her and he was frozen for a second. She could sense that he was considering whether or not to confide in her. There was something he needed to tell her. And it was something he wasn't meant to talk about. Evelyn sensed that an embargo was about to be smashed through. He was about to break a promise. She just knew it.

'Can I tell you something?'

She leaned forward. 'Yes.'

He looked fretful and nervous.

'Please,' she said. 'Tell me what has you so worried.'

And then he told her.

It took about five minutes for him to give her a matter-of-fact account of the terrible events of that night after the soiree at her home. He described what he and Henry had discovered upon their return to their rooms. The shocking sight of the intruder. The violence. The impossible things that went on.

Evelyn kept her mouth shut and her expression as neutral as she could make it. Her pulse was racing, though. She drank up every word he was saying with such rapt attention it was as if she was trying to memorize it all.

'There's more to it,' he said, and burbled on, in a rush. He described every bizarre thing that had befallen him and Henry since their arrival in Darkholmes. It was a month-long catalogue of uncanny encounters. To hear him talk like this was exhilarating to Evelyn. She found it thrilling. She began to perspire. Her arms, the very backs of her knees.

It was rather like someone had unstoppered an old, colourful glass bottle and let the genie out.

John was a very talkative genie. He babbled about goat men in the porter's lodge, picking up their parcels. Hooded men loitering by the riverbank and university employees who grew vampire wings and circled and swooped around the sleeping towers.

'You'll think I am mad,' he said, interrupting his own flow.

'No, no. Not at all.' She tried her best to sound sincere. She *was* sincere. But why couldn't she ever drop this polite party hostess act? Why couldn't she sound more genuine? He was a good man. A safe man to speak to. And he was scared. Why couldn't she just say to him – I know that you aren't mad. And I know that everything you are talking about is real.

I know this because I have experienced such things too.

But she didn't say this. She didn't say anything. Nothing useful.

She made noises. Consoling, platitudinous noises. She told him to rest and recuperate. She told him to get plenty of early nights and more fresh air.

She hated herself for being a liar. She knew that everything he was trying to tell her was true.

There were monsters in Darkholmes and she had seen them too.

*

Evelyn went home.

She said nothing of any use, and gave him no real comfort.

She made him feel as if he was going crackers and then she left.

She hiked all the way home. The freezing rain started and she felt leaf mulch and muck from the pavements splattering up her tights. Her face was frozen like a mask by the oncoming wind. Halfway home she had tears streaming down her cheeks. If anyone noticed and stopped to ask her why, she wondered if she would be able to explain.

Both significant encounters of her afternoon – with Catriona and with John – had been quite overwhelming. She felt as if she had been laid bare by both. Her nerves were twitching and overwrought.

She was not used to so much attention. That was what it was. And, heading home, past crowds of school children in uniform and other folk going about their business in the lowering gloom, she was starting to feel like no one all over again.

She was being rained upon and preparing herself for home, where she would be once more confined, and ignored and back in her domestic box. She walked home and readied herself for the everyday again.

Except…

When she got indoors she found a scene of unholy disruption.

There was something wrong with Brenda.

*

Their maid was having a funny turn in the scullery. Evelyn could hear all the carry-on as she stepped into the hall. She had never heard Brenda screaming before and the noise was alarming. It was a high-pitched wail like a siren going off, or a cat that had been trodden on.

In the kitchen Brenda was backed up against the Belfast sink and the back door was wide open, with the dark wind and sodden leaves blowing in. Glass panes were cracked as if someone had flung it open with all their might.

Evelyn had a go at slapping her. Her fingers stung from contact with her coarse flesh and Brenda barely flinched. My God, Evelyn thought, what's she *made* out of? Naturally she had never touched her before. She was *cold*. But perhaps that was shock and the effect of the door standing open?

'What the devil's got into you?' Evelyn shouted.

Brenda gibbered. Her mouth made the shape of words.

'Oh, do pull yourself together, Brenda,' her mistress snapped and dashed over to slam the door. Crash, tinkle, smash as shards of glass toppled onto the tiles. 'What's wrong?'

'Hurrrr, hurr, hrrrr...' Brenda said. 'Horrrrid goblin men...'

'*What..?*'

'There were four of them,' she said. 'They come bursting into the kitchen. Little horrible goblin men. Babbling and squealing. They took me by surprise. While I was making the steak and kidney...' She gestured vaguely at the scattered utensils, the ruined pastry. 'They ate the kidney and steak,' she mumbled throatily. Evelyn noticed that gravy was slopped all over the work surface. It was a strangely gory sight.

'Who were they, Brenda? Burglars?' But what kind of burglars would break in to steal the contents of a pie? How desperate could they have been?

'Not normal men,' Brenda gasped, and her face contorted as her panic rose again. 'Goblin men. Like toads or newts, their faces. All naked. Horrible grinning mouths...' She certainly seemed to believe what she was relating to Evelyn.

On the floor there were footprints in splatters of rainwater and gravy, garden mud and greenish slime.

'Do you truly expect me to believe in goblin men?' Evelyn asked sharply and Brenda nodded firmly. 'They came with a message.'

'A message? For whom?' Evelyn had gone quite frosty with her. That was because she herself was becoming nervous. She didn't like the way this conversation was going one bit.

'They said that… whoever is making all the… the *holes*… needs to stop it! Stop the *holes* forming! Stop, stop! They kept shouting in my face. Stop making the *holes* or you'll find much worse than just goblins coming through. And then they laughed this horrible laugh all together. Like frogs in the mating season. Oh, madam, it was terrible.'

Quite an extensive speech for Brenda, this was. Evelyn was impressed by her conviction, too. She was gibbering like a mad thing, but she clearly believed what she was saying. 'But what does it mean, Brenda?'

Brenda fixed her gaze upon Evelyn. Grey eyes with stern, crinkled lines radiating all around them. They were wise eyes, Evelyn suddenly realised, for the very first time. She had never noticed that hard-won wisdom in her servant's eyes before.

'But madam, you know. You already know. Making *holes* in this world. You know what it means. Same as I do.'

She hesitated. 'Do I?'

'We both know. And we both know who and what is causing it. When the goblin men say stop it, stop it happening, we both know who they mean.'

A vast gap lay between Brenda and Evelyn. It yawned between them, but suddenly Evelyn knew what Brenda was going to say.

'It's your husband, Madam. Every word he writes and every word he reads aloud. They're making *holes*. He's creating dangerous *holes*. Great big gaping *holes* in the world. *Holes* that go from this world to the other one. *Holes* like in floorboards or like cheese or old lace. And we both know that he's doing it. It's been happening for years. Too many *holes* to patch up. There's too many by now to keep it quiet any more. The *holes* are making everything fall apart, Madam. Your husband has gone too far...'

*

Evelyn set Brenda tasks that she knew she would find consoling. Turning the evening's pie into cheese and onion, and pulling out all the stops to make sure they would still have food on the table when Reg came home.

He was like a tattered scarecrow when he arrived back, sodden with rain, cold and stiff. He pulled his bicycle into the hall, where it stood dripping and shedding slimy leaves on the clean parquet. He took a bath and soon thereafter joined his wife in the dining room. When Brenda unveiled her replacement pie he took a long, thoughtful, quizzical sniff.

'There was a terrible incident with the steak and the kidney, sir,' she said, and beat a hasty retreat to the scullery.

'Whatever's the matter with her?' Reg snapped. He fiddled with the steaming greens and poked at the molten orange contents of the pie. Actually, it looked rather appetizing to Evelyn.

'Brenda had a fright today,' she told him. 'We had visitors. Not very nice ones.'

His bristly eyebrows went up. 'Indeed? Did you meet them? Who were they?'

Evelyn found herself blushing. Ridiculously. Why should she blush because she wasn't at home all day? She wasn't doing anything wrong. She believed she was blushing because that day she had come perilously close to enjoying herself. She had abandoned her post in the house, and Reg could sense it at once. Now she felt guilty. But she explained crisply to her husband that she was out all day, about business of her own. Important business. But she'd had an account of the unwelcome visit firsthand from Brenda, who was still in quite a state of shock.

'Who were they? Ruffians?' Reg frowned darkly. It was obvious that he resented his supper being disturbed by this irrelevant chatter.

'She said...' Evelyn took a deep breath. 'Reg... Brenda said they were... goblins.'

He was fiddling with his plate.

'Reg, I said...'

'I heard what you said.'

'Goblins, Reg. Four of them. Men. With nothing on. No clothes. Like great slimy toad men in our kitchen.'

'Is she injured?' he asked, meeting Evelyn's eye. He was calmly questioning her as if she was one of his students in a lecture hall. 'Did they in any way harm or molest our housemaid?'

'Well, no,' she said. 'I don't think so. They scared her and pushed her around a bit. They brought a message. For you, it seems.'

He dabbed his lips with his napkin. 'A message from the goblins?'

'It's no use being horrid and sardonic,' Evelyn snapped, and felt her colour rising. 'I know what you do. Anything you don't want to listen to. Any single thing that you don't want to give credence to – you contrive to make it seem petty and silly and small. And now you are doing it with this. But let me tell you, Reg Tyler. I believe her. I believe every word she says.'

Reg shook his head slowly. 'Four naked men came into our kitchen and shouted at her? Surely you can see why I'd balk at such a thing. Brenda is clearly hallucinating, my dear. Obviously she is repressed and sex-starved. Or perhaps she is undergoing some particularly female kind of problem. Possibly she is suffering from all of the above...'

'Goblins, Reg. She said that goblins came into our home in order to warn you about the *holes*.'

'*Holes*?' he chuckled. 'Oh, dear.'

'*Holes* in the world.' She was sounding desperate even to herself. 'They told her that it's your writing. You are making *holes* open up between this world... and the next.'

'Arrant nonsense. Have you checked the drinks cabinet? The cooking sherry? It sounds to me as if Brenda is losing her faculties. Perhaps it's time I looked again at our domestic arrangements.'

'She isn't drinking. She isn't going doo-lally.'

'But Evelyn – dearest. Goblins? Really?'

She stared at the picked-over remains of her dinner. Neither of them had eaten very much. She was glowing with anger but also, on account of the fact he had called her 'dearest,' she glowing with pleasure too. How *stupid* of me, she thought. How needy and ridiculous.

That evening they made love for the first time in weeks. One might have expected awkwardness. The two of them were so clumsy and stiff with each other in everyday life. But it wasn't so. The love-making that went on between them was generally satisfactory. Sometimes it was more brisk and businesslike than others, and sometimes it could be quite vigorous. Evelyn never felt cherished exactly, during or afterwards, but it did the trick, anyhow.

She lit the lamp afterwards so that she could smoke a cigarette and see where the ashtray was. He was sitting up with his pipe.

They shared a companionable, smoky silence for a few minutes. It was while he was at his most vulnerable, like this, that she went for the jugular.

'Reg..?'

'Yes, dearest?'

'My mother's friend. Catriona Mackay.'

'Oh, yes. The secretary. How is she?'

'She's a very remarkable woman.'

'No doubt.'

'She writes, you know. She told me today that she writes stories. Just like you.'

'I doubt that.' He sighed and pulled hard on his pipe.

'Would you...' she began.

'Hm?' He tapped out his pipe.

'Would you perhaps let her join your gang?'

'My *gang*?' He smiled, turning to look at her and reaching out to touch her again. Oh, much more tenderly this time. So much more carefully. He looked at her. Really looked at her. She was so surprised by this that she almost forgot what she was trying to ask.

'Yes... Would you let... Catriona... become a member...of the Smudgelings?'

He kissed her throat, nibbled around her earlobe and whispered into her ear: 'Absolutely not.'

*

Catriona was very disappointed of course.

It was a few days later when Evelyn saw her. The weather was so wonderful that they took a walk along the river front, circling the island. Evelyn was so accustomed to the place that she hardly saw the beauty anymore, but Catriona's noises of appreciation brought it all to life again. It was a *golden* day. The leaves underfoot were frosty and crunchy. It was like bliss, really, just ambling along beside the bronze depths of the water, both in their long coats and puffing out white plumes of breath.

'Only men can write the kinds of stories your husband is interested in,' Catriona said. Her voice buzzed with venom.

'He doesn't think women can write at all. He doesn't think they can read with any taste or discernment. You should hear his opinions on the books I borrow from the town library.'

'I'll make him see,' Catriona muttered. 'I'll make sure he understands.'

Evelyn wasn't sure how she imagined she could do that. Evelyn knew her Reg and how much he was stuck in his ways. 'The point is,' she sighed. 'These meetings of his. They aren't just about what they are writing. It's all about their fellowship. Being men together. It's comradeship, I suppose. Being in a boys' club, apart from all women. I suppose that's the point of it.'

Catriona's whole face looked pointed and determined. She almost looked ugly, the way she was today. 'I deserve to be among them. I deserve their respect, regardless of my sex.'

'But why, Catriona?' Evelyn was becoming exasperated. Shrill, even. 'If they don't want you – who really cares? You don't need them. Start your own society!'

She snorted. 'My own society of one?'

'There's me as well,' Evelyn pointed out, sounding shy.

'You?' Catriona laughed. 'You don't write.'

'No, but I can listen. I love stories. I could listen to you reading yours. I'd be glad to. I'd be more than glad...'

Catriona slowed right down and turned to her friend. She smiled with the sun on her face and all at once she was beautiful again. Her jet black hair shone so brilliantly it was almost blinding. 'Oh, I'm being such a monster. I'm truly sorry, Evelyn. Thank you for your words. You are very kind and I don't deserve you as a friend. And what's more, I believe that you are right. We shall have our own Fellowship, you and I. We must have a... a Sisterhood of our very own. And I will indeed read my work to you.'

Evelyn thrilled a little at the thought of this.

A Sisterhood!

Evelyn pictured herself listening to Catriona tell her wondrous stories. Just as she had once told them to Evelyn's mother. Back when mother was just a girl. Evelyn was wondering whether Catriona's tales were still concerned with The Good Night Ladies? With The Golden Colossus or Mr Tweet? She hoped that soon she would find out for herself.

How would they start? Where would they do it? Evelyn hadn't been to Catriona's place yet. She often described it as a very spinsterish bedsit. She lived at the top of a crumbling house covered with Virginia Creeper. Catriona claimed to sleep under eaves blanketed by scarlet leaves so thick that no natural light penetrated her solitary room. Evelyn was longing to see inside. She was longing to sit at Catriona's feet as she regaled her with stories. She imagined they would be surprising in all sorts of ways.

As they approached the stone steps that would take them up to Oaken Bridge and back to the heart of town Catriona suddenly announced: 'Now I wish to buy a present for you, Evelyn dear. Please will you indulge me?'

*

Catriona had managed to find a shop Evelyn knew nothing about. How was that possible? In just a few months Catriona had uncovered a place Evelyn had never been to, nor even suspected existed.

It was in a part of town where Evelyn rarely ventured. These were the leafy inclines of the south side. She believed that it was round here Catriona lived, in this student-filled part of town, where the old houses were pressed tightly together like grimy books on crooked shelves.

And the shop when they found it was sepulchral and dark. It was like clambering inside an old wardrobe, or into a trunk left in a hidden corner of an attic. Except, among the bric-a-brac and musty swagged curtains and towering heaps of China, there were living things on display, too. There were birds in gilded cages. Dowdy, ordinary birds. Who would go to the trouble of keeping pigeons and sparrows captive? A single magpie glared at Evelyn from his silver prison. Those bright button eyes stayed on both women as they penetrated deeper into the shop's gloom. It turned out that the shop was called *Chimera*, which seemed a most peculiar name to Evelyn.

Catriona was saying: 'I saw something in here the other day… Something I want you to have…'

Evelyn plunged both her hands into a wooden casket of junk jewellery. Every bauble and crystal was coated with black dust. A host of clocks were ticking, roosting on shelves and every bit of wall space around her. Catriona pointed out a devil-faced monkey watching them from behind a curtain. He was chained to the frame of a miniature doorway and bared his teeth as they passed by. Goodness, Evelyn thought: I hope she doesn't intend to buy me a monkey. What would Reg say about that? And what kind of a pet would a primate make, anyhow?

Strange music was playing. Heavy, swirling, thumping, dirgelike. Evelyn could hardly even recognize it as music at first. It was getting incredibly noisy all of a sudden. 'What *is* that?'

Her companion frowned. 'Jimi Hendrix.' Now she looked rather piqued. 'There's no way on Earth she should be playing that.'

'Who?' Evelyn sounded squeaky and scared.

'The owner, of course.' Catriona pursed her lips.

The burning incense was giving Evelyn a headache. Its exotic scent was tainting the freshness of the chilly air they had taken during their walk. The place felt decadent and ghastly. Evelyn wasn't sure she was glad they had come here at all.

Somewhere in the shop's darkest recesses there was a china cabinet and when she peered into it everything had the dull, oily sheen of old gold. Her heart gave a jolt. Was Catriona going to buy her something expensive after all? What a strange thing. This friendship couldn't possibly mean so much to her, could it?

Catriona opened the cabinet carefully and groped inside with one hand, knowing exactly what she wanted to find in there. Ooh, what was coming? Evelyn wondered. A necklace? A brooch? A ring? There was all kinds of treasure in there.

Goblets, bracelets… could that even be a crown she could see? Catriona saw how pale her friend had become, how quiet she was and she laughed low in her throat.

'A token of my great esteem,' Catriona whispered.

'Nothing too expensive… I hope…'

'Mrs White – the owner and proprietress of *Chimera* – is bound to give me a very good deal. We go way back.' Catriona smirked and suddenly she was holding in front of Evelyn's nose a golden object. A small, dark golden thing.

Evelyn wasn't sure what it was. Nothing to wear. Nothing decorative. She was disappointed.

It looked like a model of an animal of some sort. About as big as her hand. She took hold of it and examined it. She decided that it was the most hideous thing she had ever seen. It was an abomination on four tiny legs. Sitting in the hollow of her palm.

'It's a golden basilisk,' Catriona said, and her voice sounded like she was giving Evelyn the world. 'And it will bring you startling fortunes.'

*

She tried to be pleased with Catriona's gift but, really – what was she supposed to do with it?

For such a stylish person Catriona didn't seem to have a clue about the giving of presents. Evelyn thanked her effusively, of course. It was gold. It must have been expensive (though she heard none of the transaction with elderly, whiskery Mrs White.) She put the basilisk (too big for a charm bracelet, too ugly to put on show) in a small wooden box. Catriona smiled graciously.

Then she bade Evelyn goodbye moments later in the cold street. 'I must return to my work. But may I come for tea? To your home? Tomorrow at four, say?'

Evelyn agreed readily. She would be more than welcome. 'We've got so much to catch up on,' Evelyn gabbled. 'I've told you nothing about the past week. I haven't even told you about Brenda and her goblin men...'

Catriona raised an eyebrow. 'Her what..?'

'Our silly maid. Seeing things. Reg says she's gone doo-lally. But I believe her. I think there's something in it. Also, I believe John, too, and all the things he claims to have seen. I believe there are strange things going on in Darkholmes.'

Catriona shivered deliciously inside her white jacket. Exquisite white fur. 'Oh, I agree.'

'The goblin men told Brenda that it's all Reg's fault. Reg and his friends. They are making *holes*, is what the goblins said.'

Here they were, standing on the windy corner by St Frances' churchyard. Evelyn was clutching her wicker basket, weighed down by fruit, cheese and meat from the indoor market, plus that heavy trinket bought for her by her friend. And she was standing there discussing what the goblins had said to her housemaid.

Evelyn felt that, at last, things were actually starting to happen in her life.

'Holes..?'

'*Holes* in the world.'

'Ah, the *world*,' Catriona nodded, giving a twisted little smile. 'This makes complete sense, then.'

'Between their world and this one,' Evelyn supplied, and she nodded again. Evelyn didn't know if she was humouring

71

her or making fun, or whether she actually knew what she was talking about.

'You must take care, Evelyn my dear,' she said, leaning closer. The breeze almost whipped her words away before Evelyn could hear them. 'Your beloved husband doesn't understand what he is doing. That seems very clear to me.'

'He wouldn't believe Brenda…'

'No, he wouldn't. He doesn't understand the damage he's doing to the Very Fabric, the silly man.'

Evelyn's heart quickened at the way Catriona casually dismissed Reg. The most brilliant man in all of Darkholmes and she called him silly. She really was breathtaking.

And… the *Very Fabric*…? What was on Earth *that*..?!

'I might have helped him,' Catriona mused. 'If he had allowed me to join his *fellowship*. Perhaps I could have done something useful. I could have saved all our souls from the impending disaster…' She trailed off, biting her lower lip. Bright, berry red, her lips. Her skin so pale and smooth. Her very complexion made Evelyn feel Christmassy.

Catriona marched away smartly. Her boots rang out loudly on the frozen path.

Evelyn mistakenly thought she knew this part of town better than she did. She took a short cut through the churchyard. The grass between graves was overgrown and boggy and she felt that if she stopped she'd be sucked into the ground. She dodged past yews and massed banks of mistletoe.

There were bristling thorns everywhere as the afternoon leaked out of the sky. Darkness was welling out from the church. Evelyn believed there was a gate on the far side, just a few steps away, and a path that led down to the river walk. She could avoid walking back over the island and the teatime crowds.

But on her way to the riverside the hedgerows were wild and noisy. There was the chattering of blackbirds and rustling of things unseen. Bats wheeled shrieking overhead. And all of a sudden there was a man, striding towards her. He was clad in rough, sack-like garments, some kind of dark gown, and a helmet with two twisted corners sticking out like horns. There was a face painted on the cloth covering his face. Snarling, terrifying, smeary features.

Either he or Evelyn had to give way so that the other may pass. She shrank back instinctively against the bushes and he walked straight up to her. His breath was harsh and snorting, like a horse's, she thought, absurdly. His smell was indescribable. He smelled like something dug out of the soil.

She wanted to flee. But she could not move.

'Let me pass,' she said, rather high-pitched.

He grunted and a cloud of white steam hung between them. But he relented. Her basket felt heavier than ever. It was as if her golden present from Catriona was weighing more by the second. Or as if it was somehow magnetized, and drawing her ineluctably closer to this horrible person.

'You'll come with us,' he said. At first she was shocked that he was speaking actual words in English. It seemed to her that he should talk in some unheard of tongue. Something brutish from the past or another realm, perhaps.

'I'm not about to go anywhere with you,' she snapped.

'Not now. Not today. But we have marked you out, Evelyn Tyler. And you will come to the Other Place. It won't be long now.'

She felt sick with the way her heart was banging inside her chest. It wasn't just fear. It was excitement, too. This is *me*, she thought – Evelyn Tyler – plain old Evelyn Tyler and I'm having one of these strange encounters. For once it wasn't just her hearing about someone else's weird adventures. This was actually happening to her.

'Let me pass,' she said determinedly.

'You are free to return home,' he said.

There was a magpie watching them from the hedgerow. It cackled loudly just then. Its mate appeared with a crash. Then it was like they were earwigging.

The cloth-faced man didn't say anything else. He just made another guttural noise at Evelyn. It was a sort of growl. Like the sound a predator might make, right before it snapped its teeth upon one's neck.

Evelyn had never experienced anything like this encounter on that obscure pathway down to the river. It was frightening... but also, it was *proof*. It was first-hand experience. It was – Lord help her – real life!

She scurried away and soon found herself by the rank grasses and reeds of the riverbank. They were matted with outrageous cobwebs. The waters were heaped with mist. But she wasn't scared now. She was excited and furious and desperate to share her adventure.

Which was why, when she bumped into Professor Henry Cleavis, she leapt on him and blurted out everything that had just gone on.

'My dear girl!' he cried as she flew at him, brandishing her shopping basket. He must think I'm a mad thing, she thought, manifesting out of the foggy gloom like this.

'Professor Cleavis!' she shouted.

'Catch your breath! Breathe properly, young lady. You'll do yourself a mischief. Evelyn, isn't it? Reg's wife?'

She was surprised he even recognized her. She looked rather wild. She had brambles, berries and thorns stuck in her jacket and skirt and leaves in her hair. 'Yes, yes… I've been… I've been attacked!'

'What?' He was alarmed.

'I'm not hurt. I don't mean attacked, not really… but a person – a *thing* – met me on the pathway from St Frances' just now and he said such… such strange things!'

'I'd better get you indoors,' said the Professor kindly. 'I can't have you running about like this. You're miles from home. Look, come up to the college with me. It's only back up the hill. You can sit by our fire and have a mug of tea. You can talk to John and I and tell us what's been going on. And you can even pick the leaves and vines off your outfit.'

The idea of being in the sanctuary of their messy rooms within the old stone walls of Hexford College suddenly sounded glorious. 'Oh, please…'

'Come along then. We'll have muffins and lavender honey and actually, now I remember, I was already wanting to get in touch with you, anyhow…'

He was leading now, up a steep path, even narrower than the one where she had met the hooded man. They were threading between ash trees and oaks and ascending into the heart of the island and its watchful spires. 'Why did you want me?'

'I need to ask you something, my dear,' said Professor Cleavis, suddenly grim. 'What do you know about Catriona Mackay?'

*

Well. She simply wasn't having it.

She did like the Professor and she enjoyed the company of his young companion a great deal. She was sure she respected his intellect. And John's too, come to that.

But she was afraid she would not harken to his wild talk about Catriona.

'I *beg* your pardon?'

She was sitting in their living room with a tea plate upon her knee. She had already eaten a muffin with honey and now she was having a slice of the most deliciously molten Bakewell pudding – made by John (who, it turned out, was not just a pretty face.) She felt rather as if the pair of them were trying to fatten her up for the cooking pot. Tart raspberry jam and that golden almondy paste. She was in heaven even as she listened, astonished, to the good Professor vilifying the woman who had recently become her closest friend and confidante.

'This must come as a shock to you, my dear,' frowned Henry Cleavis, looking very woebegone. 'But I don't believe in beating about the bush. This woman Mackay is devilishly dangerous and I have reason to believe that your friendship with her will put your very life in peril.'

Evelyn still couldn't quite catch her breath. She took a calming sip of the rather hot tea John had brought her.

'Come now, Henry,' the robust young man laughed. 'Don't scare the poor girl. Explain yourself, won't you? And don't be so melodramatic about it.'

'Melodramatic!' said Cleavis hotly. 'You know as well as I do, John, the stories about Cat Mackay. You know the legends about her.'

'Do I?' asked John innocently, settling into the oxblood chair where he had sat during Evelyn's previous visit to these rooms. He took a healthy bite out of his golden tart. 'I get so forgetful with all the legends and tales...'

Professor Cleavis looked annoyed at his protégé. 'She is a very great and noxious witch-woman. A very ancient one. We've heard many whispers and rumours of her whereabouts and activities over the years. We've even felt her malign and wintry presence in the background, sometimes, in affairs and misadventures with which we've had involvement. I myself have only ever felt the slightest touch of her shadow...'

John glanced at Evelyn and his eyes had a humorous look about them. Cleavis was being so incredibly earnest. It was as if John was goading her into laughing. But she would not.

'Imagine my horror,' said Henry Cleavis. 'When I went to talk to the Dean of Hexford College. We were to discuss my duties in my new post at last. And there, sitting at the tidy desk outside the Dean's office I find his secretary. And she is the quintessence of all evil. The most reviled and renowned supernatural being on the face of the Earth at this moment in history.'

Evelyn just stared at him.

Of course, it was all piffle. Catriona could never bring herself to hurt a single soul. Why, surely Evelyn's mother would have known if there was anything iffy about her, after all. And she would never have asked her own daughter to befriend such a person? Also, even if she was this quintessence person that Professor Cleavis was ranting about, Evelyn was certain that she and Catriona were close enough as friends by now that she would have confided in her about such a thing.

Yet at the same time Evelyn was thinking – *this man is quite correct.* Catriona was older than the ages. She was powerful. She was magic personified. Right down to her painted nails.

Evelyn knew that Cleavis was right. She felt the truth of this. Catriona was terrible, deep down in her soul. She was a witch.

And yet Evelyn was not scared of her.

'I believe she has made you her special friend,' said Cleavis softly.

Evelyn snapped without meaning to: 'How do you know that?'

'This is a small town,' he shrugged. 'It isn't hard to get a hang on everything that's happening. If one keeps an ear to the ground.'

'Henry!' John burst out laughing. 'Don't tell me this is what you have been doing with your time. Surely you haven't been following Mrs Tyler about? What will her husband say about this?'

The Professor scowled. 'I imagine Professor Tyler will be most troubled to hear about his wife's friendship with this person. He will recognize the danger, when I tell him. He will believe me what I say that this foul succubus must be dealt with. We must send the Mackay person hence, out of Hexford College and the city of Darkholmes forever.'

He pronounced this very impressively. John and Evelyn gazed at him in astonishment.

'I can't see the Dean being very pleased about that,' said John. 'He told me that he's never had such an efficient secretary. He's most pleased with her work.'

Very carefully Evelyn placed her cup, saucer and plate on their crumb-speckled carpet and stood up. 'Thank you both ever so much for your hospitality, gentlemen. I believe I'm over the effects of my queer encounter by the river. I am most obliged to you, Professor Cleavis, but I will not stay to hear my friend's good name dragged through the dirt...'

Cleavis advanced on her. She received a sudden impression of how powerful this squat, tree trunk body actually was. 'Mrs Tyler, I insist that you listen...'

Was he really going to physically prevent her from leaving these rooms?

'Henry, you have startled her,' said John reproachfully.

'I really must return home,' she said, sounding less sure of purpose now. Her shopping basket felt weightier than ever.

'Honestly, Henry, you're being too ridiculous,' John told him, standing and ushering Evelyn to the door. There was none of that earlier stiffness to his movements now, she thought. He must be feeling fully healed.

'All right,' Henry grumbled. 'But John – I insist you walk with her to the bus stop and see her safely installed...'

'There really is no need,' she began, but privately she liked the idea of a few minutes alone with John. She found his presence rather comforting.

They left the disgruntled academic on his own then, and walked quietly through the calm, dimly-lit labyrinth that was Hexford College. They were passing out of the main gates into the misty street before one of them spoke. It was John. Apologising.

'You needn't,' she told him.

'But I must,' he sighed. 'Henry isn't usually like this, you know. It's since we've been here in this town, this university. For some reason all of his obsessions to do with the supernatural have leapt to the fore... He's acting most bizarrely.'

'He's a clever man,' she shrugged.

They came to stand by the bus stop. 'But the Dean's *secretary*! Your best friend! He's saying she's a witch-woman, for goodness' sake..!' John chuckled and then he suddenly took note of Evelyn's expression.

She looked through the gloom straight into his eyes. Frozen droplets – tiny, infinite – hung suspended as icy mist between their faces. 'I think he's right,' she said.

CHAPTER THREE

John was surprised to be included in the invitation.

'Are you sure he means me as well?'

Henry frowned, winding his scarf around his neck several times, and looking piqued. 'Reg never says anything he doesn't mean. In our relatively short period of acquaintance, I have learned this about him. And he expressly asked for you to be there, as well. So, get your things on. We have to leave.'

John had to admit to being intrigued and even a bit excited as they set off from Hexford College and down through the thin canyons of the old town. They were going to *The Phoenix and the Carpet* on a Monday afternoon. This was the time that Henry and Reg had made their own. In just over a month it had become sacrosanct: one of the cornerstones of their new friendship. And today it seemed that John was required as well. He felt like he was actually being included.

The air was very bracing. A chilly wind was slicing through the city. Christmas was coming. Festive displays glittered in the dark shop fronts and there was a palpable feeling of suppressed merriment amongst the people that they saw.

Sometimes living in the college at the top of the hill made John feel too removed from the everyday people. It was tough, breathing in the rarefied atmosphere of the donnish life. But he supposed he was used to it by now, living with Henry. But he was always glad to get back into the life of the town and the thronging streets.

Reginald Tyler was sitting by the small fireplace in the pub's snug which the two Professors had made their own. He had already bought them a drink each. Three foaming tankards of a local brew sat waiting as they made their greetings.

The old man barely raised a smile as they sat down with him. The light through the distorting glass of the pub's bay windows was particularly bright and unkind. Tyler looked about a hundred years old. He was haggard with worry and both Henry and John noticed it at once.

'You must tell us what is ailing you,' said Henry, and John was touched by the warmth and kindness in his tone.

Tyler stared at them both. His shaggy brows were lowered over those flinty eyes. His lips were drawn thin and white, as if he was doubtful about baring his soul.

'You need our help,' John said, the words leaping out impulsively.

He nodded. John fancied he could hear the bones of his neck creaking like the wooden chairs they were sitting on. 'Yes,' he said. 'You see, they've vanished. Both of them. They've been gone all weekend.'

Henry was taking his first mouthful of ale and swallowed hard. 'What has? Who's vanished?' he spluttered.

Reg shushed him brusquely. 'The housemaid. And my wife. They have both… disappeared from my home.'

'What?' cried Henry, looking alarmed. 'But when? When did this happen? Are you sure?'

'Of course I'm sure,' said Reg through gritted teeth. He looked as if he regretted confiding in them now. 'I last saw them on Friday morning, before I set off for my office hours. When I returned Friday evening the lights weren't on. The house was in gloom. The kitchen was dark and there was no dinner prepared. Of both Brenda and Evelyn there was no sign.'

There was a short gap while Henry and John absorbed this and then they both started to beset the Professor with numerous obvious, urgent questions, which he weathered with a certain degree of patience. At last he burst out irritably: 'No, I haven't contacted the police. It's only been three days.'

'But...' gasped Henry. 'Three days! What might have become of them? Anything could have happened!'

'Yes,' said Tyler dryly. 'This is really what I require your help with.'

John spoke up, 'But has Evelyn gone off like this before? Without informing you?'

Tyler looked him straight in the eye and for a second John flinched as that grave visage studied his own. 'That is a very good question, young man. Very sensible. The answer is no, she isn't given to such gallivanting. She may seem... rather flighty. But she has never simply taken herself off like this.'

'And the servant too,' mused Henry. 'For her to go missing at the same time. This is highly unusual. Look here, Reg. Oughtn't you ring the authorities, do you think? I mean, something truly horrible might have happened...'

Tyler glared at him. 'I don't think the police can help us.'

'What?' barked Henry. 'But that's what they're for! Surely...'

Tyler sat forward abruptly. 'I suspect that there is more to this than the kind of explanation the police would be interested in.'

'Is there more to this, then?' asked Henry.

'It's not just the two women that have disappeared from my house,' said Professor Tyler. 'A number of my notebooks have also vanished. Portions of my magum opus have been taken from my locked desk.'

*

They accompanied Tyler back across town to his home. He rode off ahead on his rickety bike, leaving Henry and John to soldier through the hilly streets in his wake.

'Funny business,' John said, trying to get his friend to speculate.

'Indeed,' said he, puffing slightly in the frosty air.

'Do you think she's just had enough of him and run away?'

Henry laughed out loud. 'You can always make me laugh. I don't suppose our friend Reg has even considered that possibility. He's so bound up in himself.'

'What do you suspect, Henry?'

He looked at him shrewdly. 'Well, we've seen Evelyn at close hand. She's been having experiences similar to our own recent adventures in Darkholmes. It wouldn't surprise me greatly if there was something… unnatural about her vanishing.'

'Unnatural?' John laughed. 'You mean, she and the housemaid have run off to be together?'

Henry chuckled briefly too, but then grew grave. 'No, I mean that… these creatures and figures that we've all been encountering. From elsewhere. I think it's altogether possible that they have reached out a little further this time. And that they have… *taken hold* of Evelyn. Taken her captive.'

John swallowed hard, nodding. Henry had put his own thoughts into plain language, as often he did. 'And the Professor's book?'

'I'm thinking of the goblin men that the housemaid said came to her in the kitchen. Talking of *holes* in the world and how they are being caused by the book. Perhaps the goblin men came back, hm?'

And so they were heading to 199 Steps Lane to take a look at the evidence. Goblin footprints. Disturbed rooms. The kind of investigating and poking around that Henry and John hadn't done for a while. They were both rather eager, John felt, to embark on a little of that kind of work once more.

John was more than a little worried about Evelyn. She was a touchy character, sure enough. He had become quite fond of her, through their initial encounters. He would hate for anything dreadful to have happened to her.

*

'*Look!*' cried Tyler, flinging out his bony arm. 'Look at the chaos in here!'

Actually, his study looked about twenty times tidier than Henry's own work room. John glanced about at the orderly shelves and stacks of books. Only the desk had a few scattered items and crumpled sheets of foolscap, and the roll-top compartment had clearly been opened with some force. Jagged splinters hung over the empty interior and they looked rather shocking. It was all evidence of brutish violence in a room more frequently given to calm contemplation and composition. An ink bottle had been smashed and deep purple ichor smeared many of the surfaces. It wasn't quite dry yet.

'I wonder if there are prints,' said Henry, practically.

'What?' snapped Tyler.

'Fingerprints in the ink. You might be lucky. Perhaps we can identify the thief...'

Professor Tyler sat down heavily in his chair, on top of an opened ledger of some kind. 'Do you know how long I have spent writing my book? Hm?' He glared at them both in turn. 'Seventeen years. Seventeen years of my life. Every drop of my intellect and my energy that I could spare has been wrung into that manuscript.' He looked distraught and all at once John saw that the loss of his precious notebooks was weighing on him much more heavily than the loss of the two women. John was scandalized by this, but did his best to hide these feelings.

Henry was looking down at him sorrowfully. 'Of course you made copies of your pages...'

'No, I did not,' snapped Tyler. 'I felt that to make copies would be to somehow... dilute the... the magic.'

Henry stared at him in amazement. 'Dilute..? What...?!'

John decided that the best thing would be to get Tyler back downstairs and make him some tea. They all needed reviving. John wouldn't mind doing the housemaid's work and making them all a brew. They needed to put their heads together calmly and logically and think about their next steps. Tyler was going to go maudlin and catatonic, John could see it. There was a wave of depression surging through him and it was getting more powerful the longer he sat in this chair, in this site of his greatest loss.

Downstairs they sipped their tea from mismatching china and Tyler rallied somewhat. He paid particular attention to Henry's sensible question as to whether he and his wife had argued recently.

'Why, yes. On Thursday evening, there was, if I recall, a slight note of discord. I mean, there often is. My wife can be rather volatile. She is emotional and quickly becomes upset about the most trivial matters...'

Henry and John exchanged a glance. John knew they were both thinking that the Professor must be a rather challenging man to live with.

'Tell me about the argument on Thursday,' said Henry coaxingly. John was remembering just how good he was at these investigations. Yes, he thought, all at once. He had indeed missed being embroiled in their adventures. It was good to see Henry regaining his old focus.

'She began by expressing some interest in the progress of my writing,' said Tyler. 'Something which she periodically does, and which I find maddeningly intrusive. I always try to fob her off with something vague, telling her that I have been making good progress and have had some interesting breakthroughs recently. But really, it should be of no interest to her. My writing doesn't concern her. All she wants to know, however, is when I intend to publish my novel. She imagines that I will be able to submit it to a London publisher and they will accept it in a flash. She is under the illusion that somehow, the product of my seventeen years of work is going to make me – or rather, *her* – very rich. That's all she can think about. I have no idea how she has come by such a ludicrous idea. She has far more faith in the commercial viability of my work than I do. I, of course, find such considerations hideously vulgar. I am not sure I'll ever be ready or willing to approach a publisher.'

He was almost snarling as he finished this speech. He looked entirely scornful at the idea of someone bringing out his book. Henry – who was, of course, already a published author (and a modestly successful one) looked perplexed by the Professor's attitude. He looked as if he couldn't understand it at all.

'Do you know what she said to me?' Tyler said, slamming his teacup down. 'She said, 'What's the bloody point, Reg?' She actually swore at me like that. She said 'What on Earth is the point, if you don't bring it out as a book and make some money? What's it all been for? Why make up stories if you don't want anyone to read them?" Really and truly – that is what she said to me.'

Tyler searched the two men's faces, but John knew that both he and Henry had a great deal of sympathy with Evelyn Tyler and her frustrations. Stories had to be meant for someone, didn't they? You couldn't just write them and hide them away.

Henry paused carefully before asking Tyler his next question. 'Reg, is it possible, do you think, that your wife might have taken your notebooks with her? Could she have stolen them? In order to teach you a lesson?'

The old professor gave a triumphant shout. 'Yes! That's exactly what I think she's done!'

*

'I don't think that's what she's done,' Henry told John, much later that night as they sat up together in the Tylers' drawing room.

'You don't?'

He shook his head grimly. 'I think there's something altogether more sinister to this, John. I think you and I were correct in our earlier surmises.'

'Oh yes?'

The fire was dying down. Its fitful orange glow was the only light in the room. They were whispering to each other as they maintained their vigil.

Henry said, 'I think she's been nobbled by one of those... supernatural beings we've encountered.'

'Aha,' said John, not out of scepticism, but because he couldn't think, in that moment, of anything more sensible to say. Chances were, Henry was right. In John's experience he was generally right when it came to adventuring and investigating. John was in his hands completely, as usual.

All about them 199 Steps Lane was darkly slumbering. The house was chilly and it felt, somehow, neglected already. The women had been away only a couple of days and yet the heart had gone out of the place. The kitchen was strewn with used teacups, its surfaces covered with mess. Henry hadn't let John clear things up for the Professor: they had more important things to focus on.

While Tyler stumped off to his bedroom at round about midnight, Henry and his friend were determined to sit up the whole night downstairs.

'But whatever for?' Tyler had said harshly.

'Bear with me on this,' said Henry. 'I have a feeling. Just a strange feeling… that *they* will come back.'

'The women?' frowned Tyler.

'Go to bed, Reg. You look as if you haven't slept for days.'

Off he went and they never heard another peep out of him. Henry and John sat and kept up their watch, with a flask of Bovril on the dining room table. Really they should have had strong coffee, to keep them awake.

'This is to do with *that woman*,' Henry said, apropos of nothing, just as John felt himself drifting off.

'Hm?' he roused himself, and wished they were back in the comfort of their own rooms. That huge, lumpy, warm old bed. 'Who?'

'That devil woman. Catriona Mackay. She's behind this. Mark my words.'

John snorted. Not in a nasty way. Just joshing him gently. 'Watch out. You'll sound like you're turning into a woman-hater.'

'In her case I'd be justified. Just you wait, John. Wait and see. She's got plans, I'm telling you. Plans for us all.'

John tutted and shook his head. But still, he thought, it was rare that Henry's instincts were wrong.

They sat like that for hours. John jerked and sat up whenever there was a creak or a groan. Funny how some noises could take on such a terrifying aspect in the pitch dark. The staircase was being climbed by some ghastly beast. The curtains hung exactly so as to look like a creeping fiend. A fox in the undergrowth of the back garden made a sudden noisy pounce and nearby there was a cry like a banshee's...

The furniture in the Tylers' drawing room was bloody uncomfortable. With his usual shrewdness Henry had bagged the comfiest armchair and John was resting some rickety pew-like thing, and hugging a tassled rug around him. Some time before dawn, as Henry's snores were just starting to drive John demented (why did they sound so much worse here than they ever did at home?) he got up. There was no point in sitting here. If this was a vigil, then he might as well go and be vigilant. He may as well do something useful.

And so he poked around the downstairs rooms of the house, quite nosily.

The moon was full and peering into all the rooms at the front of the house. It was beautiful, milky light. He felt like a ghost, tip-toeing from room to room. The contrast with his first visit to Steps Lane – and that awkward academic party – couldn't have been greater.

Without quite knowing why, he climbed the staircase. Careful to be as quiet as possible. Wincing with every tiny creak. If Tyler woke suddenly and came bursting out of his room John would say he was heading for the bathroom. Of course. Nothing strange about that. John knew Reg was sleeping on the daybed in his study. In a brief, touching moment – one could tell it was a rare show – Reg had told the two men that he couldn't face the room he shared with Eveyln without her there. It would be impossible to lie there without her. He hadn't slept there since she had left him.

Left him? Could she really have done such a thing? The grey worry on his face. He was in shock. It was indeed the face of a man who realized he had pushed his wife too far.

Upstairs John went, and realized that he needed the bathroom after all.

And as he passed by the door he knew led to the Tylers' bedroom he saw that there was golden light within. A molten line of light showed round the frame. It wasn't natural light. It wasn't from any kind of light bulb.

Without even thinking he stepped across the cold landing and touched the handle. It gave and he shouldered open the door.

The whole room was illuminated brilliantly. Gold and white. He had to cover his eyes with both arms. He heard the door slam shut behind him.

When he looked again, the brilliance had died down. The light was almost bearable. It was light like in the desert. In a cloudless sky when the sun was at its zenith.

And the light was emanating from the shabby dressing table.

In this light all the furniture in that room looked broken and scratched. The room was dusty and drab. But from the dressing table there came this wonderful, healing warmth and light. It burst from the mirror, but that was not its source. As John took tiny steps across the gritty carpet to see, he realized that the source of the amazing sunburst was actually a trinket of some kind, which was set out on display amongst the make-up pots and powders and feminine paraphernalia.

It was a golden lion. About the size of his hand.

No, not a lion. A hideous thing. Lizardlike, with wings. Some kind of trinket or charm.

And now he crouched down to look into its blazing eyes, he saw that it was moving. It was alive, and returning his gaze.

*

'*Impossible!*' cried Henry. 'I think.'

They were frying bacon in the extremely messy scullery the next morning. John had taken command of the cooker, while Henry was buttering white bread too thickly.

'It's all quite true. I swear it.'

'I don't doubt you for a second, my dear fellow,' he coughed. 'What I meant was, it's *impossible*. It's another plainly impossible thing going on right under our noses. You should have roused me, though. I'd have liked to have seen this... this...'

'Basilisk,' John said. 'That's what the creature told me he was. A golden basilisk.'

'What else did he say?' asked Henry, buttering away like mad.

John flipped over the bacon rashers. 'Hang on. Let me get this right... its voice was very queer. Sort of rasping and faraway sounding... It said that it had seen everything. It knows where the two women have gone...'

'Astonishing!'

'It said, 'They have travelled over to the Other Place. And they are trapped there now!''

With a deft flourish John began transferring the bacon to the waiting rounds of bread. He switched off the gas ring and the wonderful sizzling died away.

'He said the 'Other Place' did he?' asked Henry urgently. 'He actually used that phrase?'

'Oh yes,' John nodded. 'I'm quite sure about that.'

'And this thing... this basilisk... it's still there?'

'On her dressing table. When the golden light faded away, it just sat there, lifelessly... like an ornament or...'

Just then Professor Tyler himself joined them. He looked very rumpled in his tartan dressing down and his face all bleary. He seemed bemused to see that they had commandeered his kitchen. But his interest was piqued by the wonderful aroma of the bacon.

'I'll make you a sandwich,' John told him. 'Go and join Henry in the breakfast room and I'll bring it to you.'

'You're too kind,' he said, sounding much milder than John had ever heard him.

'Come along, Reg, and I'll tell you the outrageous tale John has just told me, all about his adventures in the night...!'

*

As they ate bacon sandwiches and slurped sweet morning tea John realized that Tyler probably wasn't overjoyed to hear that he had been traipsing about his house in the night, and prying into his bedroom. If he was annoyed by the investigations he never said so. He kept his energy for disputing the actual details of what John had witnessed.

'A tiny creature talked to you? It came to life and actually spoke to you?'

John nodded firmly.

'Hallucinations,' he declared. 'A dream. Trinkets such as that hideous object my wife brought home the other week do not spring into life of their own accord and start conversing with house guests. That simply doesn't happen.'

Henry sighed deeply, dabbing at his beard with a napkin, and managing to smear it even more comprehensively with bacon fat. 'Open your mind, Reg. You have to start listening and believing...'

'Believing?' he cried. 'Why should I start believing anything?' All at once he looked angry. 'Why should I accept anything this young person says? This ruffian? Why, he could be anyone.'

'I will vouch for him,' said Henry firmly and solemnly. He met Tyler's furious stare head on and in that moment John was proud of him. 'Whatever John says I would believe implicitly. I would trust him with my life.'

Tyler sat there, twisting in his dressing gown, looking skinny and anguished. He looked as if he was choking on the bacon John had fried for him. He was just about to open his mouth, presumably to make more objections to the very idea of the basilisk discussing his wife, when there came a very loud banging on the front door.

'I'll go.' John thought it best to let the two Professors argue out the empirical truth of the basilisk for themselves. He would dispatch this early caller and then run up and fetch the ghastly creature from the dressing table himself. He wanted to get another look at it.

There was a very glamorous lady standing in the front porch. She was wearing a fur-lined cape and she wore her hair in a very precise, geometrical cut. There was something challenging, almost boyish, about her stance and the jut of her chin as she passed him two bottles of milk that must have been standing on the doorstep with her. She looked him up and down and smirked at his perhaps rather rumpled appearance.

'Yes?' he asked, taking the milk from her.

'I have felt a disturbance,' she said, frowning slightly. She took a step closer to him. 'I know that something has gone on. I know that Evelyn has disappeared. I must...' She seemed to be struggling to make her meaning plain.

'You know where Evelyn is?' John asked sharply. He realized that this woman hadn't introduced herself, and neither had he.

'I think she has gone to a place...' the visitor began, staring past him. 'To a place where I have always longed to go. And it's not fair... it's just not...' Then her eyes widened slightly as she saw someone coming into the shabby hallway behind John.

He turned quickly to see Henry stamping towards them, his face red with fury. 'You!' he bellowed. 'Get away from here! You are not welcome here! Nor are you welcome anywhere my friends are. Begone!'

John had never heard Henry talk like this. Not unless it was to a demon or a succubus...

He turned to look at the woman again. She was snarling back at him. Actually snarling. John almost dropped the milk. 'Henry, what on Earth...?'

'This is her, John! The one! The very one that Evelyn was telling us about! Catriona Mackay! She's behind all of this, you mark my words. What have you done with Tyler's wife, you harpie? Tell us! What have you done?'

John was shocked then because Henry's hands flashed out and grabbed one of her wrists. She had very white, elegant wrists. John had noticed them particularly as she'd held out the milk bottles. It was frightening to see them closed inside Henry's meaty fingers. John thought he was going to break them, or at least shake her into submission there on the Welcome mat. He was appalled at his friend's behaviour.

'Henry! Stop it at once!' John had never seen him behave like this. 'Unhand this poor woman!'

Henry's head whipped round and he shouted: 'This is no woman!'

Catriona let out a whimper of fear. John could tell it was involuntary. She struggled feebly against Henry's deceptive strength. She was very brave, John thought. Many would have screamed at being treated like this. 'Henry!' he yelled. He'd lost his wits!

'Ahem,' came a very dry cough behind them.

Professor Tyler was standing there, his dressing gown tightened about him and his demeanor so proper and censorious that all three of them fell quiet at once. 'Would one of you mind explaining to me what is the meaning of this fracas in my porch?'

*

Curious scenes ensued. It was something of a disaster, as it turned out. John had never seen Henry act so badly in public, nor had he seen him take against an individual quite so violently. Later, as they made their way home – him stumping crossly through the snow as it settled – John tried to get to the bottom of it.

'Don't you see, you young idiot?' he shouted. 'It's her. It's all about her. I told Evelyn just the other night when she was at ours... I warned you, too. This Mackay woman... she's behind everything. Many of the things we faced and defeated, even before we came here to Darkholmes...'

There was no echo to his voice as they stood in that suburban street. The falling snow muffled everything. It was as if they were standing in a bubble. In one of those festive snow globes, where nothing could penetrate, and nothing could get at them. There was a plainly stricken expression on his friend's face. It was a long time since John had seen him like this.

'Calm down, Henry...'

At this he seemed to lose his patiently entirely, and turned on his heel and started walking quickly again, down the hill towards the town and the bridge.

John was embarrassed: that was his chief feeling as he remembered how he'd carried on in front of the intriguing Catriona Mackay. Henry had hopped about and fulminated as Tyler showed her courtesy, allowing her to perch herself elegantly on a chair in his dining room. To Tyler she just looked like a beautiful woman, rather upset. A stranger he must offer refreshment to, and to whom he must listen. Reg and John both listened to what she had to say, even as Henry berated them for giving her the time of day.

'I know this is a bad time,' she told Professor Tyler. 'I know... a little about what has happened here.'

'You do?' he beetled his brows, stooping closer to her. He seemed... now that John thought about it, mesmerized by her beauty. By the snowflakes melting on her fur collar and in her glossy hair. John realized that he too was held a little under that spell.

'She hasn't walked out on you, Professor Tyler. You must believe that. She has not left you of her own volition.' Catriona sipped the mug of brandy he had brought her. 'She was taken from you.'

'Taken..!'

The woman Henry had described as a witch nodded solemnly. Tyler had locked Henry out in the hallway by then and still his noisy warnings battered at them. John was disturbed as he stared at Catriona's pale beauty. Had Henry lost his mind?

'I can't say too much,' she added. 'Otherwise, it will be known that I have interfered too much. That I must not do. However, you men must know this: that at this point, the very fabric across the boundaries between the worlds is stretched very taut and thin; in places its weft is frayed and falling into tatters. In places it is sheer like satin or thin muslin and any breeze can stir those curtains and blow them apart...'

'Hold on a moment, my dear,' said Professor Tyler. 'Let me stop you there and ask: what the devil are you *talking* about? What nonsense *is* this?'

'Professor, you must believe me. You of all men.'

He blinked at her. John saw his eyes. They were less kindly and less concerned than had been a few moments before. 'Just who are you, young lady?'

She smiled. A radiant smile. She turned it on both Reg and John and it was like the clouds parting. 'I am your wife's friend. Catriona Mackay. When I heard that Evelyn was missing I felt it my duty to come here and...'

'Catriona!' gasped Tyler. 'You're the one. The one she said wanted to join the... my Smudgelings?'

'The very one,' she nodded.

Tyler's lips turned white and very thin. '*Get out*,' he told her.

She tried to seem surprised, and she mustered an attempt at protest, but Tyler was staunch. In no uncertain terms, he invited her to leave 199 Steps Lane. Then he seemed to think again. He asked her: 'Can you help me find my wife and my servant?'

'I cannot,' she was on her way out, past the pent-up looking Henry. 'I must not,' John heard her add, under her breath. 'But when she returns, you must tell me, you must let her...'

'Out!' thundered Tyler, looking almost as crazed as Henry had.

John was appalled by both of them. She was a young lady, for goodness' sake! Possessed of dark magic or not, there was no excuse for not acting like a gentlemen.

But Tyler refused to discuss the matter further and Henry was furious all the way home to Hexford College. They made the journey unhappily, clad in yesterday's clothes.

Well, John thought desultorily. Some use we were in helping Tyler with his mystery. Really, we're no further on at all.

*

'Honestly, the Vice Chancellor's secretary?' John laughed. Poor Henry. He was cross because John couldn't stop laughing about this whole business. When John looked back later his own hilarity seemed somewhat misplaced. He wondered if some spirit of devilry had got into him? It was driving Henry crazy, but John couldn't stop laughing at his wild theories about secretaries being emissaries of the devil, and whatnot.

'Once upon a time you would listen to me,' he said glumly, slumped in his favourite chair. 'Can't you take my word about this, after everything we've been through?'

Ah yes. All those adventures. All that they had faced together. The monsters in the Fens, in those eely marshes, when they found themselves ineluctably drawn into some kind of prehistoric wilderness. And the terror in Cathedral Close in Norwich. The affair of the Hirsute Stabber. And the demented crime lord of Limehouse, Mumu, with his skull-like visage and his painted claws... Yes, they had come through quite a bit together. John had trekked in the Himalayas with Henry; he had journeyed to Peru and God knows where on account of Henry, and his forever needing help with another little escapade. They rarely talked about their adventures, even to each other. John sometimes kept a sporadic diary detailing their encounters, but it was all very discreet.

'She is behind everything,' Henry kept saying, steadfastly. '*Everything* that we have ever faced together.'

*

Sunday.

When it happened John was sitting perfectly still and quiet. One minute he was there, in the corner of the Tylers' parlour, and then... he wasn't. It happened gently. All of a sudden, snow was falling inside the room.

He felt it land on his hands and in his hair. Melting on contact, and then settling on the sleeves of his good new jacket.

Snowing indoors? In Reginald Tyler's sitting room?

Which was especially odd, because that Sunday evening the room was so warm. The fire was blazing away and all twelve of the Smudgelings were in attendance. John was the thirteenth, sitting closest by the door. His presence was tolerated. Henry had insisted that he be allowed to accompany him to this meeting.

John couldn't see what all the excitement and secrecy was about, if he was honest. The way they carried on. Like they were spies or something, up to subterfuge, or something that really mattered to the world at large. Really, all they were doing was reading long, long, terribly long poems and fairy tales to each other.

The vanished Brenda's tasks fell to him, as the only non-writer in attendance. He didn't mind. He balked at using her hostess trolley, however. He wasn't about to make a complete fool of himself in front of Henry and Reg's colleagues. He brought them trays of tea and biscuits, and didn't go to a great deal of trouble to keep them refreshed. He went through the scullery cupboards, looking for some seed cake or the like. He gathered that Brenda baked special cakes and things for these events, and the scholars young and old looked doleful and disappointed at the news that her absence was robbing them of their usual treats.

It was perhaps two hours or more into that Sunday evening that he felt the pinpricks of snow on his scalp and hands, and he blinked awake suddenly, having dozed lightly through some dullish screeds. Now Professor Tyler himself was reading. He had some loose pages upon his knee and he was regaling all the fellows with brand new words. He had been shaping and sculpting them all week, he explained. Only Henry and John knew that all his old words had disappeared with his wife and housemaid. Without something new, he'd have had nothing to contribute.

Still, the pages he read aloud were a continuation of the long, long story that he had been writing for so long. It was concerned with the pixie folk who were going to hell, or somesuch. A frightening tale of gentle creatures who were tasked with an impossible quest...

Despite himself, John found himself being drawn in.

And the parlour fire crackled and the men sat forward and the warmth was such in that room that John started to drowse once more...

The snow came falling quicker than ever and now he didn't question it at all, as the shadows drew forward and obscured almost all the details of the room barring the molten gold of the flames...

His eyes closed for several seconds in a row and he realized he must be falling asleep. He roused himself suddenly, hating to be rude. He woke with a shout, which he quickly suppressed. He opened his eyes and found that he was sitting in the middle of a forest.

He didn't jump up and start running about shouting. He didn't fly into a fit or go raving mad. He understood at once that he had been transported. He had been taken elsewhere.

He was still sitting in the rather fusty, nubbly armchair from the Tylers' parlour. One of its lace antimacassars had been knocked awry and snow covered it somewhat more thickly, but apart from that, it was no different at all. The armchair and John were just elsewhere.

Like the women. He knew it at once and the thought – strangely, and momentarily – almost made him smile.

It was the middle of the day. The startling flash of the silvery snow and the pearlescent light through the canopy of firs was almost painful. And then the cold hit him, all at once. He wasn't really dressed to be outdoors in the wintry woods.

He was sitting there alone. It took him several excited minutes for the truth to sink in that he had no way of returning home, nor of contacting Henry or Reg or anyone there.

So he would have to do something for himself. He couldn't sit there in an armchair all day as the gently sifting snow covered him up.

He stood up and walked tensely over the frosty undergrowth, as if testing out the sureness of the ground. The crackle and crunching of the snow filled his ears. There was nothing else to listen to. Just some distant pigeons, and hungry-sounding crows.

Could he be in the woods near the college? wondered John. But the ground wasn't hilly at all. He could be beyond the bounds of Darkholmes, perhaps, for there were miles of woodlands outside the city. They had observed these from the train windows when they had first travelled to their new home... But he wasn't convinced he was in the vicinity of the university town.

He had come to the *other place*.

And the thought made him shiver as much as the sudden chill had done. He set off – with rather more aplomb than he would have expected to, in such bizarre circumstances – through the woods. The armchair was left sitting there in a frozen glade, and he wondered if he would be able to find it again, should he ever need to...

When he came to a fast-flowing river, fringed by brittle reeds and crusted with ice, he decided to follow it. Surely it would lead him to signs of habitation before long. He congratulated himself on his reasoning. It was the kind of thing he had picked up from reading a hundred adventure stories in which characters realized the exact same thing. The light was starting to dwindle, and he would need to find shelter. Following the river was the most sensible thing he could think of doing.

John was heartened when he found tracks. Something that was very nearly a path. By then the sun was low, dropping behind the trees. Was it even the sun he knew? Was it another sun, on another world?

Idle speculations. He picked up his pace. The cold was getting to him.

And then, just as he was setting forth more briskly, he caught the unmistakable tang of wood smoke on the air. Someone, somewhere not too far away, had lit a fire. Unconsciously he started to run…

And that was when they jumped him.

*

It was a horrible little skirmish. Three of them, tall men, wearing rough clothes and each had some kind of sacking material over the heads. Dark eye holes poked in the rough material, just like the figure John had seen sometime earlier at home. He gained only a very brief glimpse of his assailants before they were upon him. They pushed him about, knocking him flat onto the ground and giggling as he went sprawling.

John leapt straight back up, spluttering with surprise and fury. He landed a few good punches on first one and then another, but they carried on laughing in this horrible high-pitched way, as if they didn't feel a thing. They rounded on him again, and he realized that they were forcing him sideways, off the path, through the rough grass. They were edging him towards the slow-moving river. He felt a pang of fear at this.

Just momentarily. They could shove him in the water and watch him drown and no one would be the wiser…

With a great roar he launched himself at the closest of these spectres. His body under the sackcloth was thin but tangible. His laughter stopped as John swung him round. Desperation and fright made John marshal his resources and it seemed the horrid person realized that he was quite prepared to do him some serious damage. His two fellows drew back, suddenly alert.

'What do you people want with me?' John shouted into the masked face. 'Who are you?'

Their smell was indescribable. It was like mould. They had a whiff of something that had been underground too long.

John reached out – not even sure why – with his free hand and wrenched the creature's mask off his head. It came away with a nasty tearing noise and he found himself face to face with the astonished, snarling face of a kind of animal. A weasel, perhaps. Its eyes were wide open in outrage. Its teeth were bared. He let go of the creature at once.

He cried out in dismay, as if warding them off. All three set to giggling again and he almost fell down in shock. What the devil were they? Monstrous rodents in the hooded garb of a secret order of monks…?

Then they were off. They turned tail and scarpered back into the woods, where the mist soon obscured all traces of them.

It took him several moments to get his breathing under control.

And then he hurried along the river path till he came to signs of what he hoped was more ordinary life.

*

He thought he was back in Darkholmes.

At the first sight of the bridge spanning the bronze river and the stone steps and the blocky buildings of the old town he was excited and relieved. Whatever had happened, and however he'd been transported into the winter woods and whatever those weaselish monks had been, he was home again. He was among the quaint, humdrum buildings and windy streets of the university town.

But as he moved closer he could see the subtle differences. The bridge was strung with festive and colourful lights. There was a crowd surging and mingling up there. Queer hurdy-gurdy music was playing from somewhere unseen. All of this was too busy and bustling for a Sunday evening in the town that John knew.

On the river itself he saw small boats and coracles loaded up with goods. Some were market stalls, tethered to docks. He could make out townspeople busying themselves.

He took the stone steps up to the level of the streets. The people he passed paid no attention to him, but he could hardly stop himself from staring at them. Half of them were recognizably human, even if they were dressed in rather archaic style, with the hoods and gowns and cloaks of another century keeping them warm against the frosty night. Others, partially obscured in their outdoor things, were less obviously human and his mind at first rebelled at the sight of them. He saw rabbity faces, mouselike-features, shrewd feline expressions. He even saw a tall heron picking its way delicately down the lichenous steps. It was holding up the queue of people wanting to go down to the market stalls under the bridge. It nodded its beak at John in appreciation of his patience as he let it go past.

John climbed up the steps and found himself in the midst of a cheery crowd. They were evidently Christmas shopping, or somesuch. They were buying presents and goods for whatever festival it was they celebrated in this world. He knew now that this certainly wasn't his world, no matter how familiar some of the trappings might seem. This was a world of animals and queer beings.

A dog-faced nanny pushing a pram with huge wheels went past him, snapping at him to keep back. She was looking after twins and when he looked he saw they were frogs, and the lace bedding was all green with slime. Part of him was revolted by all these nightmarish visions as he made his way up the cobbled street towards the town square at the heart of the island. But another part of him was excited, too...

For he suddenly remembered. Being a child. Drawing animals in human costume. Drawing vast pictures and panoramas of animals living alongside human beings and imagining stories for them. Picturing what their lives would be like. And now here he was: in a world the ten year old him might have made up. It was real. It existed. A marvelous world of curiously-shaped people, all going about their business.

John held down his panic. He kept tight hold of his need to react loudly to what he was seeing. He wanted to scream and whoop with delight and he wanted to do both in equal measure.

And then he saw a doorway and a shop front that he recognized. It was *Chimera*: the old bookstore he had found soon after he and Henry had moved to Darkholmes. It had its counterpart here, also called *Chimera*, in this dimension of animals.

He made straight for the place, glad to see its windows lit and what looked like a Christmas display in its window. It must be said, this shop seemed more spic and span here in the other world than it did at home, where it had fallen into a decrepit and shabby state.

Inside it was busy, which was another novelty. Some kind of baroque music was playing and the dense scent of dark coffee filled the air. John had to turn sideways to negotiate the closely-pressed stacks, and get past several browsing customers. A tall parakeet wearing a brown suit and pince-nez muttered something at his back. An antelope smiled at him.

Behind the counter at the very back of the shop he didn't find the strange elderly white-haired lady he was expecting. The contrast between her and this shop's owner couldn't have been more marked and he took a moment to absorb it. He was realizing that, as a stranger here in the land of animals, he had to practice being more nonchalant. Since no one here reacted to *his* presence with horror and surprise then he must endeavour to return that compliment. He must pretend that nothing he saw came as a shock.

But having said that, his first glimpse of the Mumbo-Jumbo did give him pause for thought.

*

Here he was in the bookshop he had already visited in another world, and he was standing before an elephant who, sitting awkwardly in a reinforced wooden chair, was still more than twice John's height. His slightly downy grey scalp brushed the ceiling. He was busy working away with two clumsy feet and his trunk, tying brown paper parcels together with tarred string. Books were spilling out onto his desk and he kept cursing under his breath about his ineptitude. His breath, as John approached, seemed to smell of cinnamon buns.

Without thinking about it John took firm hold of the pile of books the shop owner was attempting unsuccessfully to wrap, and kept them still while he rearranged the paper and string. They were books about bird watching and had slippery, shiny covers.

Those ancient, doleful eyes raised themselves to stare at John through softly-wrinkled skin. 'Thank you,' he said gruffly. 'I need to get these into the post this evening and I wasn't making much headway.'

The elephant's desk was covered with lists and memos of all kinds, as well as a great tangle of hairy string and crumpled rolls of brown paper. He certainly seemed to have his work cut out for him. Also, a queue of customers was beginning to form at John's back. It was clear that the *Chimera* bookshop in this world was a lot more successful than the one in his own.

'What can I help you with?' the elephant enquired, with a rising lilt in his vastly deep voice.

John wasn't exactly sure. He had gone in there because the shop seemed rather familiar. Perhaps he was trying to locate parallels or even perhaps points of contact between this place and the world he had left. He wondered about going to the uppermost floor of this house and finding the route into the world he had slipped through before. He thought about that strange, middle eastern-type bazaar he had found up there. Maybe that was a way back home? But before he could even pursue this thought he realized that the bookseller was studying him intently.

'There's frost on your clothes. And not just because of the cold.'

'Pardon?'

'World frost,' he nodded sagely. 'You're new here, aren't you?'

John leaned across the desk and lowered his voice. Absurdly, he was whispering into one of the bookshop owner's immense ears, which hung down, thick and rubbery. His ears were reminding John of shower curtains, or policemen's capes, perhaps. 'I've just arrived in this town, er, yes.'

'Daakholm,' the elephant murmured. 'We call this town Daakholm. And you come from somewhere similar, do you? Did you come here on purpose?'

'I...' Actually John had no answer for that. He had been transported when he wasn't expecting it. Also, he was investigating, wasn't he? He was in the process of hunting for the missing women. 'Are you saying you can tell that I've come from elsewhere?'

'It clings to you,' he waved vaguely with his trunk. 'The frost from the cold between the worlds. Not everyone can see it, don't you worry. But these eyes of mine have seen so many things and I *know*. I can see where you've been. I'm the Mumbo-Jumbo, by the way. That's what they call me here.'

John had to step back to let some impatient customers to the desk, and he watched as his new friend rang up their purchases on his clunky till. He pressed down hard on the keys with the tip of his trunk and the effort seemed to hurt him, because his brow went dark and his eyes welled up with tears. 'Oh, it hurts me to part with my precious stock,' he sighed. 'And the keys on that till scrape my trunk something rotten. Now, where were we?'

The customers – a lady fox and a tall man with long, blue-black hair, had taken themselves off, out of the shop, clutching their treasure to their chests. Now the Mumbo-Jumbo and John were virtually alone. 'You said you could tell I'm not from round here.'

'Yes, well, we're getting used to visitors in our provincial town,' he said. 'Of late, there have been all kinds of foreign folk traipsing through. The monks have been quite irate about it all. They see it as a kind of irreligious thing. They want it to stop.'

'Yes,' John said. 'They tried to do me in, down by the river, just now.'

'Do you in!' exclaimed the bookseller, looking alarmed. He raised his head and John noticed for the first time just how elegantly he was dressed. He wore a deep scarlet dressing gown over a paisley tapestried waistcoat. A blue silk cravat was tied neatly under his wattled throat.

'Oh yes, they certainly meant business. Those monks... did you say? Didn't want me here in... Daakholm at all.'

'You oughtn't to be here actually,' harrumphed the Mumbo-Jumbo. 'What if we all started traipsing willy-nilly between the worlds? What then, eh? There'd be an unholy commotion, I imagine.'

'You said others were here,' John said. 'Have you seen two women? One rather pretty, about forty, I'd say. A Professor's wife. She's called Evelyn Tyler, and she must only have been here a few days. She's with her servant, a rather unprepossessing, tall, ungainly woman called Brenda, who is her servant...'

'Her servant?' The bookseller frowned at him.

'Her maid. They both disappeared from their home, in the town I come from.'

'And you think they might be here, for some reason?'

'Do you know anything?'

He thought about this, and fiddled with the papers and oddments on his desk. 'I don't know you. You could be anyone, asking me questions.'

'I'm a friend of theirs. I only want to bring them home.'

'Might be easier said than done,' he sighed. 'And you know, those people who manage to find themselves into new worlds... sometimes they don't *want* to be found, you know. They don't want people to come and take them back. Some of these people walk away from their lives on purpose. They just slip out of the bounds of their ordinary lives and never look back.'

He knew more than he was saying. All at once John saw that he knew precisely where they were. He had met both Evelyn and Brenda. John was sure of it.

'Tell me where they are, Mumbo,' he said. 'I promise you, I mean them no harm.'

*

Under instructions from the bookseller John hurried out into the streets again and made his way up the hill. The crowds were thicker and it was darker by now. There were no signs of the excitement dissipating or the crowds abating. He had a small scrap of paper with a hotel's address scrawled in the Mumbo's distinctive hand. The hotel was called 'Woodbegood's' and it was only a few cobbled lanes away, apparently.

When he ducked through the small doorway he found a pleasant lobby and reception. The carpet and wallpaper were all swirling orange and green: hot jungle colours, he thought. Coats and hats crammed the alcove and he had to struggle a little to get to the desk, where a cat-faced young man blinked slowly at him and asked if he had a room reserved.

'I'm looking for a woman. Two women...'

The young man glanced up at him, his whiskers quivering with amusement. 'Oh yes?'

'I believe you have a Mrs Tyler staying with you? And her servant...'

'Of course.' He snapped his fingers and a small Scotch terrier came running out from under the stairs. 'Tell Mrs Tyler in the Crimson Room that she has a visitor. A Mr..?'

'Stannard,' John told him, stiffly. He was sounding pompous and he had no idea why. Perhaps he was acting all formally in order to maintain his own sanity in this ludicrous place. He watched the little dog dashing up the first flight of stairs, and could hear his busy feet mounting further flights above us.

'Perhaps you'd like to wait in our lovely conservatory?' the cat-faced man asked, still looking amused by John's expression. He was in a black uniform with golden braid. His lips were black, too, like a tiger's, and his fur was a browner, deeper gold.

John followed his glance and walked into the glass-walled room at the back of the hotel. It overlooked the river, he found, and a walled garden below. It was a wonderful view of the town's rooftops and the glowing strings of decorations that hung like cobwebs, ensnaring every chimneypiece and turret. From here he could see the bridge and the densely-swirling crowds.

He sat down in a comfortable chair at a table and lost himself in the view. This was perhaps the first moment of absolute stillness he had experienced since he had sat in Professor Tyler's parlour, much earlier that day. That same day? Did days continue over between worlds, like sentences could run on over pages, verso and recto? Did these things even work like that?

John felt quite ignorant in the ways of the worlds. He still had bright world frost on his shoulders and in his hair: that's what the Mumbo Jumbo had said. He could see that John was new in Daakholm. It sounded like another way of saying he was wet behind the ears...

He was glad of him, though, that formidable elephant. He was glad that he had known who John was looking for, and where they were. It seemed miraculous, really, that it was even possible to catch up with who you were looking for, when everything was so strange and opened out like this.

The Mumbo Jumbo had been more helpful than he might have been, perhaps, had John not told him the name of his friend. When he had formally introduced himself, and talked about what connected him to the distorting mirror-image town that stood in Daakholm's stead in his own world, he had naturally mentioned Henry's name. The elephant's dark and smudgy eyes lit up at the mention of Henry Cleavis.

'Goodness me!' he cried, and his trunk stirred a little, and gave a kind of trumpeting noise, which he quickly stifled. 'The Other Place! Hyspero! The man who wrote those books? He lives?'

'He lives with me,' John said, smiling, confusedly. 'We, that is, live together. Why, is he known here, then? You've heard of him?'

And then the bookseller spread his forefeet wide in a curious gesture, and made stabbing motions over John's shoulder with his trunk. He looked behind at the bookcase closest and, sure enough, there were multiple copies of Henry's first novel for children, 'The Other Place' in an edition John didn't recognize at all: a much more lurid paperback copy than the one he was used to. Also, rather perplexingly, there were two other titles bearing names that John didn't know at all: 'Return to Hyspero' and 'The Mysterious Mr Tweet'.

The Mumbo Jumbo had smiled at him. It was a clumsy smile, his teeth were large and stumpy and there was something almost foolish about his expression. 'You must return and tell me more about your famous friend,' he said. 'But in the meantime, let me write the address and some instructions for getting to the Woodbegood Hotel...'

John was gasping at these extra books by Henry. Were they things he had written that John didn't even know about? Could he possibly have kept other books secret from his best friend? And then there came a more tantalizing, impossible thought: could these be books by Henry that even Henry didn't know about yet? Could they have crept out and escaped from his imagination into another world and yet he knew not a thing about it?

John did not feel qualified or capable of outlandish speculations such as these. He was much more prosaic than dear Henry. He could follow directions to hotels even in foreign lands and he could locate missing females, and such meat-and-potato kinds of investigations were the things that he was more comfortable with.

As he sat there idly musing on the spread lights of Daakholm Mrs Evelyn Tyler silently entered the conservatory. Then she was standing before him, resplendent in rather old-fashioned clothes. It was a dress from his grandmother's era. A silken taffeta thing, with puffy sleeves. Rather glamorous, he supposed. And her hair was all knotted up on top of her head in a fashion that was most becoming to her.

'John..?' She looked amazed to see him. When he turned in his seat and hurriedly stood up, he gave a smart bow – aping the manners of an earlier time, too – and she burst into laughter.

'I'm glad to have found you,' he said. 'Evelyn, your husband has been so worried about you. We all have. You just...'

'Waltzed off,' she nodded, and rolled her eyes. 'Yes, I know that's how it must have looked to everyone. It must have seemed as if I'd left him in the lurch and done a bunk. But I really didn't, John. We were *brought* here, Brenda and I. We had no choice.'

'That's what Henry and I thought,' he nodded. 'You were kidnapped, then?'

She affirmed this quickly. 'Yes, exactly. It was awful. But they didn't hurt us. And now... well, to tell you the truth, John, we're both rather enjoying ourselves. We both find that we're... actually fitting in here rather nicely. So far, our sojourn has been like a welcome little holiday.'

*

The cat-faced boy eventually brought them coffee. A very fine pot and tiny cups and saucers, all of gold and eggshell white inside. John watched, amazed, as Evelyn thanked him and casually called him 'Eric.' Then the two of them were sitting together, taking refreshment as if they were in the Tylers' parlour, or John and Henry's rooms.

'You seem to be taking all of this admirably in your stride...'

Her gown rustled as she gave a becoming little shrug, as if to say, 'What else could I do? What choice did I have?'

And then she outlined to him the brief, shocking events that brought her to the town known as Daakholm. As John had already surmised, it was all down to the interference of those hideous goblin men that Brenda claimed had already interfered with her once, in the Tyler scullery. They came back in the dead of night and this time they had meant business.

'The first I knew of it was… Oh, this will sound absurd to you, John. But I have a golden basilisk, a kind of ornament, on my dressing table, given me by my friend recently…'

'And it was glowing? It came to life?'

'To life?' she laughed, surprised. 'No, but it was glowing with the most unearthly kind of light. Why did you say…?'

John nodded grimly, and explained that, in the course of investigating her disappearance, he too had seen the golden gee-gaw behaving very strangely.

'So you were very thorough in your searches,' she frowned.

'We took it very seriously,' he said. 'And we still do. But tell me more. The basilisk was glowing… Did it say anything?'

'Why, of course not! How could it talk?' She looked at him askance. 'But the golden light was enough to wake me. Reg sleeps like the dead, of course. He never heard – as I did then – the noises from our downstairs hallways and upper landing. The goblin men were back, and they had got inside our house. I received only the most fleeting, horrible image of them as I stepped into the hall, before they seized me roughly by my limbs. And I heard the muffled struggles of Brenda, too. And I thought – well, if she can't fight them off with all of her brute strength, then what chance to I have?'

'Indeed,' he said, appalled, as he pictured the scene. The two ladies in night things being accosted by creatures he couldn't even fully visualize.

'They drugged us, somehow… injected us with some kind of noxious stuff, just as we were carried out into the night. I don't think I've ever been so terrified, John, and it was a mercy to fall unconscious…'

They paused and sipped their coffee, allowing Evelyn to regain her composure.

'And you woke up in this curious place,' he suggested.

'In a room at the top of this very hotel. With our bill paid in advance, very mysteriously, and not a single sign of those horrid amphibians.'

'Even more of a mystery,' he mused. 'Someone here in Daakholm clearly wants you to be here. Bad enough to employ a band of rough kidnappers.'

'I don't have a clue what's going on. We've been here almost a fortnight, and no one has come to see us or spoken to us about who we are, or how we came to be here...'

'Hang on. A fortnight, you say? Surely it's just a week since you left home?'

She shook her head. 'I'm quite sure how long Brenda and I have been... incarcerated here. Oh, it's comfortable enough. Cosy, even. But underneath it all we know that we are prisoners.' She sighed and reached for the golden coffee pot. 'Though now, of course, we seem to have our very own rescuer!' And then she beamed at him.

'Time is moving at a different rate here than it is at home. Not hugely. But big enough. You've been away for less time than you yourself have subjectively experienced.'

'You look so solemn, John. Does it matter so much? Just a few days out?'

'I'm not sure,' he answered grimly, then tried to look more reassuring. 'But if it's afforded you a few extra holidayish days, then perhaps there's no problem, eh?'

As if on cue, Brenda appeared in the conservatory.

It was quite an entrance she made. She was wearing Victorian clothing, just like her mistress, but her garments seemed even more elaborate and over the top. She was dressed all in purple and black and looked, it must be said, bizarrely formidable.

But somehow, in the midst of all the garish multifariousness of life in this strange town, her impressively corseted and whale-boned figure didn't seem as peculiar as it might have done.

The other unusual thing about Brenda was, John realized, that her face was wreathed in smiles. It was quite astonishing, the difference it made to her visage. He was so used to seeing her downcast, looking at the floor, grey-skinned and overwhelmed by the miseries of the world. He was used to her cheerless monosyllables as she wheeled her hostess trolley about. But now she was grinning at him and her mouth was wide and her eyes sparkled. Her face was caked in make-up. Real clods of it were stuck on her skin. She was rouged up something horrible. But these were uncharitable thoughts to be having, John reminded himself and he stood in order to take her daintily proffered hand.

'I would never have recognized you,' he said.

She blushed – even through the rouge, you could tell – and grinned even more broadly. 'I am having the most wonderful time,' she told him. 'It's been just marvelous. We've got no idea why we have been brought here, or who it is wants us, but so far it's been just wonderful. Waited on hand and foot, all day long. I've never slept so soundly in all my life. I've been given the comfiest bed...'

Her words came spilling out of her, all in a rush. John glanced sideways at Evelyn and she just shrugged, evidently used to the changes in her servant by now. John could see that here, in this new place, they were no longer in their old roles. How could they be? Evelyn couldn't be justified in bossing her old maid around here. Not when they had everything done for them, and where they were both equally at the mercy at whatever forced had transported them. Here in Daakholm the women were equals for the first time ever and it was clear that, under these new and unusual conditions, Brenda was flourishing.

'I've come to take you both home,' he told her.

And all at once – though she tried to hide it – her face fell. 'Oh, really?'

*

They insisted – both of the ladies and the cat-faced person (who, it transpired, was called Perec (not *Eric*), though he didn't sound at all French to John's ears) – that he got himself rested and refreshed before they even started to address the quandary of how to return to their native dimension.

As he climbed the lavishly-carpeted stairs to the room that he had been appointed, he mulled over the easy way they had started saying such things. Returning to our 'own world', and so on. It was like being in a living, waking dream, but one in which they were all participants, and egging each other on in their queer follies.

But he was bone-weary, he realized, as soon as he stepped into the small, blue attic room. By now at home he would have been in bed for an hour or more. He barely looked at the contents of the room before he flung himself fully-clothed on top of what was a very inviting bed indeed.

He slept extremely deeply. Vaguely heroic dreams flashed across his mind's eye as his feeble consciousness attempted to make a kind of sense out of what he had experienced of late. He found himself fighting those disturbing, cloth-faced monks again, down beside the misted river, only this time he was rather more proficient at besting them. Several went spinning into the chilly clasp of the waters, with great, sodden cries of rage. He also dreamed about the thronging streets of the town known as Daakholm, and the grotesque faces he had peered into. The shining, dark eyes and elongated snouts and tufted ears of unhuman beings. The trotters protruding from the sleeves of expensive winter coats and the tails that dragged along the cobbles. In his dreams he looked at all those faces again, and heard once more the braying, barking, chattering noise of the citizens of this half-familiar town.

When he awoke Brenda was letting herself into the room. It was morning and the attic was brilliant with light. John could barely squint at it. He had a thick head like he had been drinking spirits all night and smoking the nastiest cigars.

The thickset woman was dressed in the outfit of a Victorian lady again. Really, she looked quite absurd, and he hoped he didn't give away his reaction too much. He didn't want to hurt her feelings, especially since she had arrived with a breakfast tray from the Hotel Woodbegood kitchen. The aromas from that ramshackle heap of crockery were delicious: he could smell eggs and bacon and freshly-baked brioches, and chocolatey coffee. Proudly, Brenda dumped the tray on his lap and, beaming, she started laying the dishes out and pouring him a bubbling, frothy cup of coffee.

'You are a tonic,' he told her.

She mumbled a few words, seeming very pleased.

'Really, though, Brenda, you don't have to wait on me. As you know, we're not at home now...' At the back of his mind, already, he was wondering how any of their party would be paying for their accommodation here at the Woodbegood. Had Evelyn even given it a moment's thought? She was the kind of woman who was supported by her husband, but Tyler surely wasn't short of a bob or two. Evelyn had probably never had to box clever with her money at all. And come to that, what currency did they actually use here in Daakholm? Notes and coins bearing the head of the King of England would be useless here anyhow, one presumed.

Even as John tucked into his marvelous breakfast, on his first morning in another land, he was fretting about these prosaic things. He imagined that was exactly what Henry would have said, if he had been there with him. Look about you! A land of talking animals! Amazing, wondrous, impossible things! And here you are, John – wondering how much it all costs! Yes, well, John thought: if you grow up poor then you're always worrying what things are going to cost because, sooner or later, someone's going to come along and tell you...

But Henry Cleavis wasn't there. There was just John and Brenda. And all at once he was aware of her studying him as he sat there, making a fried egg and bacon sandwich. When he looked up at her it seemed that she was bursting to say something to him.

'What is it?'

'When she says that we've been left alone here, it's not true,' Brenda said, all in a rush.

'What? Who?'

'Evelyn... Mrs Tyler. She says that we don't know why. Or who brought us. Or anything. That's what she said, isn't it? She's telling you that we're none the wiser. We don't know anything.'

'Well, yes, that's the impression I gained last night...' John chewed a mouthful of the most heavenly bacon. 'It's a bit of a mystery.'

'They *have* been in touch,' said Brenda. She was frowning and gurning spasmodically, dancing awkwardly on the spot. She must have felt like she was betraying her mistress, but she obviously felt she needed to confide in him.

'Just calm down, Brenda. Take a deep breath. Tell me. *Who* has been in touch?'

'*They* have. The high-ups. In the castle. They've been leaving notes. Mrs Tyler's been getting notes. Left at the desk, delivered to our room. She's been getting messages. Almost every day.'

'I see...' John wondered why Evelyn never said. Was she concealing this? Maybe she thought the notes weren't very relevant? Maybe they weren't indeed. Or maybe Brenda here had got the wrong end of the stick. But no. John didn't think so. He suddenly grasped the fact that Brenda was wise. Much wiser than anyone gave her credit for. She saw absolutely everything, and she understood its import. John hadn't realized this until that particular moment.

'She's been getting letters from the man in the castle above the town,' Brenda said. 'Mr Tweet is writing to her almost every day...'

CHAPTER FOUR

Evelyn was writing another letter her mother would never receive.

Often she didn't actually send her mother the letters she wrote because she realized, right at the last moment, that mother probably didn't want to hear about her daughter's life in quite so much depth. Evelyn had always been one for sharing too many details. However, on this occasion she didn't have the slightest clue how to go about posting this letter to Scotland and mummy.

I am, you see (she wrote it out and said it aloud to herself) *in a different world.*

Strange things have been brewing for some weeks...

I suppose it was only a matter of time until something completely outlandish became of me. Literally outlandish, as it happens.

She went on to explain how her housemaid and herself had been transported into a new world, and away from her comfortable home and the protection of her husband. They had been precipitated into another world that looked a little – but not exactly – like their own. Many of the buildings and landmarks of this town they called Daakholm were similar to ones they recognized, but almost everything else was different. Oh, how could she even start explaining?

Suffice to say that they were safe. No one there – beast or fowl – seemed to mean them any harm. Evelyn felt that most particularly. Brenda felt the same as she did. They had fallen into safe hands here, and had made themselves very comfortable in a hotel by the river. It was a less shabby place than its equivalent in their own town. In Darkholmes it was a travelling salesman kind of place. But here in Daakholm the Woodbegood Hotel was rather smart, as befitted Evelyn and her travelling companion.

She had absolutely no money with her. Well, a handful of coins. Less than was necessary for over a dozen nights in a place like this. The manager had just waved them in. They looked respectable. They looked high class. Their credit was good there. Evelyn decided that they seemed to find human females trustworthy.

In their first few days in Daakholm she and Brenda visited a shop or two. Department stores. Boutiques. Their heads in a whirl with fabrics and designs. Flibbertigibbets, Reg would have said. Here they were, in a world no being from their own world had ever seen before. Here they were dressing up. Excitedly fastening themselves into gorgeous garments, the likes of which Evelyn had never possessed, and certainly Brenda hadn't. But what else were they to do? Dragged here against their will with only the clothes they were standing up in?

The shops in Daakholm extended credit to them, too. They must have looked so respectable. They left, triumphant, with bags and bags of new outfits. Clothing from a different age, as Brenda kept saying. Things that women were wearing fifty years before. Her eyes were agleam as she said that. Evelyn had never seen her look so alive. Really, it was like a tonic, this unexpected visit.

Evelyn was battening down the qualms she was experiencing about the money side of things and the concept of actually paying for any of this stuff. Perhaps, when it came to it, the two of them could do a flit?

She didn't know. Several days into their Daakholm visit, her head was still fuzzy and undecided. All she knew was that they had had to find somewhere to sleep. They had had to find new clothes to wear. What were they going to do? Sleep under the arches of the stone bridge?

*

She couldn't tell Mother about the people in Daakholm. She would never have believed her.

In just a few days Evelyn and Brenda had grown used to walking about the streets and seeing the folk of Daakholm. Evelyn had learned not to stare. She nodded and smiled and greeted strangers affably. In a way, she felt more at her ease there than she did at home. But the faces that surrounded her and her companion as they gadded about the town were those of foxes and badgers and reptiles and ducks. Owls wearing top hats and kittens in bonnets. The two women moved – in their nice new clothes – through milling crowds of characters out of fairy tales or children's rhymes. And Evelyn was far too well brought up to draw attention to the fact.

Brenda seemed to take everything in her stride. How strange it was, thought Evelyn, that she was so quick to accept the plain fact of almost everyone here being animals. The woman was full of surprises.

*

Mother, she wrote, *this is the most absurd thing yet.*

I have received a card.

She remembered the tales her mother once told her. About the characters she had borrowed from her own childhood, and the stories she had learned from her own girlhood friend.

They were stories about The Goodnight Ladies and The Time Gentlemen and that curious figure, Mr Tweet. He was an old man who lived in a tall tower at the top of the town and when he looked out he could see into the windows and souls of everyone around. He kept in his tower a thousand and one birds, each of a different species, type and coloration. Each of these birds bore his messages to and fro, tied to their legs on labels covered in his tiny handwriting. He was like a benign wizard in all those tales, and he was one of the most vivid things Evelyn remembered from those late night stories her mother had told her. His was a face that rose up from the past, amid a generalised impression of strangeness and murky magic.

And now Evelyn had received a personal note from him.

It was delivered to the room she and Brenda shared at the Woodbegood Hotel. It was brought by one of the frog-faced goblin men who had kidnapped them from home. He grinned repulsively in the doorway and held out a silver salver on which there lay a cream-coloured envelope. Very tiny.

Evelyn had no coins with which to tip the goblin man. He left, muttering, and she tore into the card. Her heart was beating hard. Who even knew that she was here in this land? Perhaps she was about to learn the very reason for their being transported to this place? For four days they had been waiting to learn something, anything.

And now here was a card.

'Will you come and visit me, my dear? I live in the tower at the top of Vexing Castle. My goblin men will show you the way. I am most anxious to see you in the flesh.'

And this message was signed: Mr Tweet.

A figure from fairyland. From tales that she had heard from her own mother's lips.

Well, naturally, she went.

*

Brenda dogged her footsteps all the way, of course. Here in Daakholm the housemaid was more clingy than ever. She followed Evelyn out of Woodbegoods, through the market square and up the winding street that Evelyn knew led the way to the top of the hill, just as it did in her own town. There, facing each other across a grass square were the cathedral and the walled citadel which at home was Hexford, but here was known as Vexing Castle and college. Above it all rose the tower to which she had received this curious invite.

Brenda almost – but never quite – said, 'This will end in tears! You mark my words!'

She was at Evelyn's back all the way up the hill, through the narrow capillaries of quaint alleyways. All Brenda knew was that a strange man had asked her mistress to come and see him. As yet, Evelyn hadn't told Brenda that she recognized his name. She hadn't said she knew where that name came from... She didn't think the poor dear could have coped with that added element of oddity.

Evelyn managed to shake her off. On the green at the top of the hill, where they were lost in the inky shadows of those lofty, ancient buildings. She rid herself of Brenda's irksome presence in the simplest way she could. She pulled rank as her mistress and as her employer, sending her away with a flea in her ear. Evelyn didn't feel proud of herself, watching Brenda's hefty shoulders slump as she turned and walked away. Evelyn almost felt ashamed of her own behaviour, treating Brenda so when they had just started to become closer, almost like friends, in fact. They were in this queer boat together and Evelyn had no right to go ordering her about. Evelyn knew it. Brenda knew it. And Evelyn would have to try hard to make it up to her later.

Poor Brenda.

But Evelyn must steel herself. She knew she was doing the right thing, in responding to this summons from Mr Tweet.

A small, chattering yellow ape came bounding across the green towards her. He clung to her arm and practically dragged her to a wooden door in the wall, almost hidden under a curtain of honeysuckle. 'Mrs Tyler? Mrs Tyler?' he kept saying, and she had to go with him, through the wall, into Vexing College.

*

Evelyn thought she already knew all about Mr Tweet.

His stories were coming back to her. It was like that card he sent had made her catch hold of one thread in her memory and she had tugged at it. And the more she pulled, the more the thread lengthened and the fabric pulled short and tight. The stories came back into her mind... How could she ever have forgotten?

Mr Tweet was a magical old man, quite friendly, quite harmless. He was friends to all the birds in the world. He wore a cloak made up of feathers, kindly donated by every single species of bird the world had ever known. But they didn't allow him to fly, or anything magical like that, like one might have expected in a tale of fairies. No, he lived in his tower, at the top of the town, and it was a kind of aviary, with perches lining the dark interior, going all the way up to the pinnacle.

The birds roosted here and flew together in a marvelous swirl, forming a whooshing, flapping vortex under which Mr Tweet would stand and clap his hands delightedly.

His friends would carry messages back from the world. They flew out through little portals that lined the inside of the tower. They flew in and out, all day and all night, and from where Mr Tweet stood, it looked like stars going in and out all night long. Tiny, busy flickers.

When he stood there the birds came dashing down in hurried flutters, bringing him notes and tales and snippets from the world outside. Actually, now that she remembered right: their messages came from all the worlds. From an infinite number of places.

As the little ape dragged her insistently through a warren of crumbling brick buildings, across quads and down twisting stone corridors (it all looked so much like Hexford, she felt quite confused) Evelyn was thinking furiously: this couldn't be what she was expecting, could it? That this tower – Vexing Tower – the highest in all of Daakholm, was actually the tower belonging to the man in the tales? She stared up at it, cricking her neck and squinting up at the snowy skies and yes, there were birds massing around its spire. Perhaps more than one would expect. They were so far away they looked like a dark twist of smoke up there.

The ape urged her on, explaining as he went that he was just a porter here, but he knew who she was. He'd been very well briefed, and he knew where she had to be taken, with all due haste. This was unusual, he added. Visitors to Vexing College were never usually brought so informally and so quickly into the inner courts, and certainly never directly into Vexing Tower... Evelyn smiled weakly, trying to look as if she felt honoured.

But actually, she was beginning to feel a little sickly and wan. She wished she had insisted Brenda had come with her. Her stolid presence was reassuring. Evelyn had come to rely on her brutish good sense and strength. Why, while she was here alone, they could do away with her – and no one would ever know what had become of the silly, foolhardy Professor's wife...

Now she was alone in a poorly-lit room and waiting. The stone flagged floor was circular and there were splashes of bird droppings all over it, like horrid white scabs that no one had cleaned up for years, it seemed. When she went to sit on the single rickety chair at the foot of the spiral staircase – presumably set there for the convenience of visitors – she discovered it was just as befouled as the floor. Its tapestried cushions were crusted with years' of pale excrement, as was the carpet, the banisters, the newel post. She was starting to feel nauseous, when she heard footsteps on the creaking stairs above.

*

That night she tried to tell Brenda all about it. Brenda wore her most disapproving face as they sat opposite each other in their shared room at the top of the hotel.

'It's all right, Brenda,' Evelyn insisted. 'I was perfectly safe...'

'You didn't know *what* was in there,' she grumbled.

'You're not my protector, Brenda. I don't need you to come absolutely everywhere with me...'

Brenda looked very glum at this. Dolled up to the nines again. Wearing a hat with a little veil indoors. Evelyn was even starting to wonder by now whether their recent dislocation, and the strangeness of things, hadn't sent Brenda a little mad.

'Tell me, then. What was in there. What happened?'

'Well...' Evelyn smiled brightly. 'He was charm itself.'

'Mr Tweet?' Brenda shook her head. 'Stupid name.'

'I don't think it's his real name. It's an alias. It's a name from stories, from legends... and this person has stepped into the role, you see?'

'What does he do that's so great?'

'He explained it all to me,' Evelyn said, and wondered again why she was making her voice so sparkly and bright for Brenda's sake. Really, Evelyn was feeling perplexed underneath it all, but for some reason she didn't want her servant – her friend – picking up on that...

'Have you noticed how this place is so much more... peaceful than the world we know at home?' Evelyn asked her. 'It's harmonious, isn't it? There's a... a kind of happiness here...'

She shrugged. 'Is there?'

'Oh, yes, I think so.' My, but Brenda was sulking hard. And all for being left out of the afternoon visit to Vexing College. How ridiculous! Evelyn almost felt cross at her, for acting so. She was like a loyal and faithful dog, cross because she had been locked up outdoors. 'Don't you think, Brenda, dear? There is a contentedness here in Daakholm. I felt it at once.'

'Maybe.'

'What I learned this afternoon is that there is a reason for that. It's all to do with Mr Tweet and his work up in that Vexing Tower. He showed me. He explained it all to me. He showed me into the tower itself, where he's got all these birds roosting...'

'You make it sound like there's something magic about it. Something peculiar.'

'But there is, Brenda. It's all about magic. His magic.'

During her visit he stayed mostly in the shadows. He was friendly, affable, but distant. He kept a few paces back from her, and his cloak of many feathers rustled and whispered throughout the meeting, as if it was alive.

His voice, rich, resonant, slightly scratchy. Like scaly feet on metal bars. He spoke to Evelyn as an equal, and she was flattered. He explained his work. She didn't think she understood the half of it. He told her about his birds. About the messages he wrote on slivers of paper and attached to their legs.

'I had an uncle who kept pigeons.'

'Did you?' She could hear him smiling, even in the muted light and the slanting shadows as they climbed the staircase. 'This is very similar, I imagine. Just on a different scale.'

'It was so odd...' Evelyn went on. 'They went all over the world, my uncle said. And they always flew back to him, and his little shed. They had been everywhere, but the place they wanted to be was with him. He had a coop in his garden. He let me help, sometimes, putting them in baskets, and feeding them. I was only small. This was in Huddersfield. I don't suppose you've heard of the place...'

What was she saying? Babbling like this? To a man who came from another world. While she was ascending this tower... to see... *this!* To stand here and listen to this vast noise of birds, chirruping and calling to one another. The echoes were grotesque. Sweet, repulsive, menacing. She couldn't see them. They were just shrouded, bobbing shapes on ledges, obscured by smoky shadows. There was a bright disc of sunlight, way up above. Mr Tweet seemed pleased by how amazed she was.

'I wanted you to see this,' he told her.

'Why? Why me?'

'I'm not sure. I've been aware of you. Here. Since you arrived in my town. I know you come from somewhere special. Another world. Far off. Oh yes, I'm aware of the other worlds. My birds flit back and forth across those divides, easy as anything. Once upon a time... I used to do the same myself. But my time for journeys has passed.'

In the blueish light that poured down the interior of the tower Evelyn could see his features better, for the first time. She saw his thin, slightly bent nose. Those lavish, untamed eyebrows and beard. His hooded eyes. And she thought, all at once: *Reginald*. Surely... he was the spitting image of her husband, Reg?

He seemed to feel her scrutiny upon his weathered features and he drew back, further from her, into indigo shadows. 'I hope you will like living here, in your new town.'

'Oh!' she gasped. 'Well, I... that is, we... don't intend to stay. Not forever. This is a holiday, a small trip. Some time away from home. Of course we intend to return there...'

'Do you?' he said, and his voice had more sadness in it than menace.

Then they both fell quiet, and they watched the birds and listened to their horrendous songs.

After a while she realized he had gone and left her standing there, at the bottom of the tower. She felt a momentary stab of panic. Was she a prisoner here? She turned about and gasped, and couldn't find the exit. He'd tricked her..! He'd...

Then she felt a small, cool hand slide into her own. It was that same yellow ape who had brought her into the college in the first place, seeming hours ago. He chattered at her nonsensically, and led her away from the tower and back into the daylight, and sent her on her way.

Of course, she never told Brenda half of this. She gave her the bare sketchy facts. The old dear wouldn't have been happy dealing with the rest of it. She certainly didn't tell her how Mr Tweet reminded her of her husband. She wouldn't understand that. And to tell the truth, neither did Evelyn. What did it portend?

*

She went back. Two times, three times.

After a while he said she didn't need an invitation. Whenever she turned up at the gate of Vexing College he sent out his young helper and let her in. He would always be happy to see her, he said.

And she didn't know what was wrong with her, but she wanted to go back. She liked being there. She found his company quite calming. She didn't know why. All that fluttering, all that cacophony from his birds – it was hardly conducive to serenity. With all their racket it was difficult for the two of them to carry out a conversation. Yet still she was drawn to Vexing Tower and the company of Mr Tweet.

Brenda watched her narrowly as she got ready to make her visits. As week followed week, she remarked that Evelyn was going there almost every other day.

'What's it for?' Brenda growled at her. 'Are you in love with him?'

Her question took Evelyn by surprise. By now she had seen him a number of times and that initial resemblance to her husband she now realised was entirely superficial. He was quite different to Reg. Reg was all coldness and edges. When Reg looked at her she could feel his disapproval. She could feel him sneering at her, even when he smiled. This wasn't true of Mr Tweet. His features were similar, but they were rounder. Sweeter. When he smiled at her she could feel sunshine on her face. Oh, that sounded so silly and girlish, she thought. She didn't say any of these things to Brenda.

Up to the castle she traipsed, almost every other day. She became used to the sounds and smells of the spiraling alleyways. She popped into the little shops on her way, buying him tokens and trinkets – a pomegranate, a tiny mechanical sparrow, a box of peppermints tied up with ribbon. He told her she didn't need to take him gifts, but she could tell he was delighted.

He was a gruff, chuckling old man. He wore a fusty-smelling cloak made out of feathers. What on Earth was she thinking of?

'You're changing,' Brenda told her. And she was right. Daakholm – in just a few weeks – had done something to her.

And to her housemaid, too.

'I wish someone would tell us when Christmas is,' she grumbled, as they ambled round the marketplace in the square outside their hotel. 'These festivities. They're non-stop. When do you suppose they actually have Christmas?'

Evelyn told her what she thought – what she had been thinking for some days – that they *never* actually had Christmas. It didn't exist in this world. All they had were endless festivities to see them through the dark months.

They drank highly-spiced wine at busy counters. They tried pale cheeses and fragments of savoury pies. The river was frozen and they walked down the hill to see the icy sculptures and frozen waves on its surface.

'I am changing too, you know,' Brenda told Evelyn, puffing herself up. Self-importance. Vim. Those eyes of hers – much shrewder than Evelyn had ever realized before – dart sideways as they took in the sights. 'Oh, I am. You see, my memories are returning to me. All the years. All the things. My memories I thought were lost forever. Something has happened... something has gone *click*. It's like turning on an old boiler you thought was broken. And the water has started to run warm through the pipes again...'

Evelyn wasn't entirely sure what she meant. 'What are you remembering, Brenda, dear?'

'All kinds of things. My last few situations. My last few jobs. When I was in London, and who with. And all what went on.'

Brenda seemed weirdly proud of herself. The part of Evelyn's mind that wasn't distracted by thoughts of Mr Tweet mulled over Brenda and her memory for a few moments. Brenda had come to Reg and Evelyn a decade ago with no history at all. Crucially, no references. Evelyn knew that she had been in service for many years, had been a servant and a maid in all kinds of places – but there were no actual facts or hard evidence that she could produce. She was shame-faced, humble, terribly apologetic. The Tylers both took pity on her. They decided to take a chance on her, alarming though she seemed at first, in her bulk and her glowering, scowling looks. It was the right decision. She might be a mystery, but Brenda was a domestic godsend.

Now: 'It's coming back. In bits and pieces. Slowly. Surely.' She looked up at the ink dark sky and breathed deeply, satisfied. 'This place. It's doing something to me.'

'Yes.' Evelyn could appreciate that. 'It's a good place. It has a healing effect.'

They were both agreed on this. They both felt it in their bones. And Evelyn knew that it all must have something to do with the man she was visiting several times a week. Up in his tower. Watching over the town. Just as in mother's stories of old. Mr Tweet guarded over his town and made everyone better. He looked after them.

Your tales, Mother. Catriona's tales.

For the first time it struck Evelyn that this place might be one wholly invented by her friend. She had found her way into one of the stories that Catriona said she had written.

The nights weren't as cold. The weather was mild for several days and the snow turned to slush, the river partially unfroze. The air felt balmy and bracing when she walked to the top of the town.

Evelyn's conversations with Mr Tweet took a metaphysical turn. (*Really!* she thought – *me! Metaphysical!*) But somehow he made it all right for her. He made her feel she could talk about and understand anything. Unlike Reg, whom he only *partly* resembled in her eyes by now. Reg made her feel a complete idiot. He was keen to make light of her silliness and lack of understanding of anything other than the material, the physical, the 'gross and earthly' – as he put it. But Mr Tweet thought her capable of so much more.

'Look at this,' he told her, and showed her a strange wooden cupboard, hidden away under the spiral staircase that led to Vexing Tower. The hinges shrieked in protest. He had to wind up bales of shaggy cobwebs to show her what was inside. A hot-tempered spider – as large as a toddler – unfurled itself and glared at them both. It gaped horribly at the damage Mr Tweet had done to the webs. 'They were stale, old webs, Sebastien. Be off with you. Go and spin something new, won't you? Who said you could curl up in my Astral Cupboard anyway, you leggy fool?'

Evelyn laughed out loud at this, as the creature scuttled away, bad-naturedly. Listen to me! she thought. Chuckling with amusement at a creature that would previously have given her nightmares or the screaming ab-dabs.

Then the interior of the cupboard was revealed. She was left staring at an array of switches and pullies and queer rubber hoses that hung down like elephants' trunks. Speaking tubes, she realised. That was what they were. You saw them in servants' halls in grand houses. Still sticky with webbing, still coated in dust. Each mouth-piece and flex of hosing was labeled. Strange names.

Mr Tweet told her: 'This is how I used to do it. Not any more, mind! My travelling days are long gone – but via these magical tubes was how I used to communicate, so easily, with life in other worlds. It's one of my most precious secrets, Evelyn. I wanted to show you this. My most magical, secret thing.'

*

Her head was spinning wonderfully for several days. She was flattered, naturally. Here was this astonishing, well-nigh cosmic being. This mysterious man. A fairy tale man. And he was telling her secrets about the things he could do. This was his inner sanctum. This strange cupboard with its arrangement of levers and tubes and whatnot.

Her mind couldn't help but draw comparisons with her husband. Reg, of course, never shared any of his secrets with her. He kept all his things private, sometimes under lock and key. He didn't think she would have any interest in his manuscript, or the worlds he was building. Or if she did, they'd be of the vulgar kind. But why shouldn't he sell his book and be a bestseller? But why shouldn't she want him to be rich? He should be glad she had such faith in him.

But Mr Tweet let her see everything, all his secrets. He even told her things like:

'The birds, my birds, they travel between the worlds, too. That is where their messages are going to, and that is where they bring messages back from. To me. So I know what's going on, in the other places.'

He turned to her, smiling gently, sadly. 'That is how I knew all about you, Evelyn Tyler.'

He had been keeping tabs on her.

'C-can you send me home? Me and Brenda?' She got up the strength to ask him, one Sunday evening.

'You wish to go back there? To the place where no one respects you or gives you the time of day? To that chilly house and that even colder man?'

She nodded, uncertainly. Then more firmly. Of course she wanted to go home. This was just a sojourn. This was just an interlude in her life. 'I have learned so much… about the wider worlds. Just being here a little while. But I must go back, don't you see?'

He nodded. 'I can send you back. Yes, of course. But you must promise me that you will return here.'

Evelyn agreed. But a change had come over him. Not just sadness. A hardness, too. All at once she knew he wanted something from her. And now he was about to say.

'Bring me the pages you took from him. Would you?'

He asked it lightly, like it was simply an afterthought. A momentary whim. He fixed his eyes on her and they had that gleam like a blackbird's eyes, or a magpie's. She saw that this was what he'd been after the whole time. Every visit had been leading up to this request. Her being brought here, with Brenda, was all about this. Reg's pages. The portion of Reg's manuscript that she had stolen.

It was in a little overnight case, under her bed at Woodbegood's Hotel.

'I should never have brought that. It's Reg's property. It's his precious...'

'Evelyn, look at me.' Now Mr Tweet's voice was kind again. It was like honey on toast, with butter melting, and late afternoons in autumn when one comes in from the cold and wet and wishes that someone special was sitting there with one. It was just like that, and his eyes had softened and gone darker and sweeter. He touched her face with his hard, almost claw-like hands. 'You would be doing everyone a favour, you know,' he said. 'Your husband is creating something very dangerous with this book of his. He doesn't even know what he is doing.'

'B-but... that's nonsense!' She pulled herself away from him. She stood much taller than this man. He was a pathetic little thing, really. A stunted, winkled old creature. Being so earnest and conniving. None of this was really about her, was it? He never wanted to see her just for herself. Suddenly she wanted to go. She looked around for the little ape who would lead her back out of the college.

'Please, bring me the pages, Evelyn. Remember, I can see what happens on so many worlds. My birds tell me the rest. And things are breaking down. *Holes* are appearing...'

'Let me go.'

'And it's all because of Reginald Tyler. He is reaching into the very heart of things. Somehow he is intuiting things he never should be allowed to. His imagination, Evelyn... it's tapping into dangerous forces. The very stuff of life...'

She whipped round angrily. 'Just put a sock in it, would you?' Her voice sounded shrill and awful. Common, even. She was like an old fishwife raving at him. 'You horrible old seducer! You vile, dirty old man! Leave Reg out of it! He's not doing anything wrong. And neither am I! You can just go and whistle...'

Mr Tweet simply smiled enigmatically and folded his hands together over his feathered cloak. 'Bring the pages to me, Evelyn. Let me put an end to the dangers your husband has created.'

She got herself out of there as quickly as she could, but the things he had been saying continued to play upon her mind. He sounded so sure. He was certain he was right.

*

This was the night that the young man came to them.

He joined the two women in Daakholm, just at the point Mr Tweet had made his demands plain to Evelyn. Just when she thought she knew what their being transported there was all about.

Brenda and Evelyn dressed up in their fripperies. Thinking that this sideways trip into another world was anything to do with them. Thinking that anyone even cared that they were happy or comfortable or settled.

The cat-faced boy said something when Evelyn came back to the hotel, as she passed through the foyer. Something alarming about settling the bill. He alluded to the costs incurred and how and when she might like to pay, and when they were thinking about leaving. He said it very politely. A little murmured question, very discreet. But the edge of threat was there in his voice, like he could lash out at any moment, just like the cat he resembled.

Evelyn knew this was tied up with the old man in the castle. Yes, he could make their lives uncomfortable. He could turf them out of this place. He controlled everything there, in fact, as he gazed down on the rooftops from Vexing Tower. Evelyn had looked out of the windows of his tower and it really seemed like he could see all.

She muttered something back to the boy at the desk. Yes, they would pay up soon, and they would be on their way. He nodded and seemed as if he believed her. Wry little smile. She didn't know what she was going to do. She and Brenda must do a moonlight flit, she decided. They must roll up Reg's manuscript in smallish portions and secrete it somehow about their persons, under the layers of the ridiculous, flouncy clothes they had bought themselves on tick...

It was just as these troublesome thoughts were going around in her head that she learned about John Stannard.

Brenda, up in their attic room. Two livid spots of red on her cheeks. She looked hectic. Excited. 'You'll never guess!'

It seemed that John had come across the great divide into this alternate town as well. Both Evelyn and Brenda sat on the bed and wondered what this might mean.

'He must be here to rescue us!' said Brenda firmly. 'He's a strapping chap. That young man. All muscle and spunk.'

Evelyn readily agreed. It did seem like the foolhardy, well-meaning thing that this particular young man might do. He might well force his virile way through the gaps in the worlds and come here looking for two silly women who just happened to be lost. He'd come here with pluck and more knowhow than they would ever have. He had come to take them home...

'Reg must have sent him. Reg and that Professor Cleavis. They've found a way, between themselves, to send John through after us...'

Typical of them to use another as a guinea pig! But then Evelyn thought about John. There was no way he'd let anyone else go ahead of him. He'd be the bravest, the most determined. Of course he would.

That evening. The stupendous coincidence that he too had been directed to Woodbegood's Hotel. More of Mr Tweet's machinations, of course. Mr Tweet must know that John was there. He was – for some reason – throwing them all together.

Was Mr Tweet was playing with them, then? Easy as anything he could have sent in his goblin men, or anyone stronger than ladies, and wrest those manuscript pages from them. He could take the precious stuff from them no bother. But he was playing games, wasn't he? He liked to see what they did. He wanted to see them wrangle and squirm and carry on.

That Sunday night there was a reunion in the conservatory at the back of the hotel. They had the room all to themselves. John was looking fresh and frankly astonished. His eyes were out on stalks. He'd seen the animal heads and the freakish things that Brenda and Evelyn had had several weeks to get used to. It was all new to him and he looked dazzled by everything.

He looked wonderful, sitting there. Gleaming and fresh and young. A sight for sore eyes, as the saying goes.

They gabbled and laughed and they were so pleased with themselves, for being reunited in another world. They felt like proper adventurers; like peculiar travellers. And they tried to act sophisticated and casual, like they were meeting up, say, in a pension on the continent, or a skiing lodge. But then they would remember how incredible this actually was and they would laugh and shiver all over again. They were meeting in another world. What were the odds against that?

It was soon established that the young man had not been sent by Reg and Cleavis. Not directly. Not on purpose.

Evelyn felt crestfallen to hear that. 'I thought they had found a way. Some magical way, perhaps. It sounds silly now, to say it...'

'They don't know I'm here. How could they?' John shrugged and smiled. Looking brave. Looking like he was hoping for the best. He looked like he felt sure in the knowledge that if he always did his best, and always meant well, then good things would happen to him. The world would never let him down. He seemed quite naïve in that respect, Evelyn thought. But then, that was one of the things she liked about him. He was so young there wasn't a scrap of cynicism in him. Not yet.

'How are you here, then?' Brenda asked him. Her face was dark with foreboding. As often happened with the Tylers' peculiar housemaid, her mood had shifted and it was like clouds that came out of nowhere and covered up the summer sun.

And then he told them a tale of sitting in an armchair. Those Smudgelings were meeting in Evelyn's parlour on Sunday evening...

'My parlour!' she heard her voice turn shrill. 'Just another meeting? Just business as usual?' She was hurt and confused for a moment. Reg was simply carrying on? Having one of his get-togethers and handing round the shortbread and the sherry. Listening to those interminable stories and poems. Pretending that nothing untoward had even happened...

John told them more. How he'd fallen asleep in the armchair. And woken here. The armchair had come with him into Daakholm. Even now it was sitting under snow in the woods just beyond the walls of the town.

'One of my good chairs!' was all Evelyn could think to say.

*

John was quite determined to set about getting them home. Oh yes, this was indeed a most fascinating new world. Oh, terribly. Terribly fascinating. But now it was time to get home.

Evelyn had to admit, she enjoyed hearing a man being so decisive. But what on Earth was he going to do? What could he do?

He and Brenda had little conversations together. Evelyn knew they were doing it. She wasn't sure why they would elect to confide in each other, but they did. Brenda took him on elaborate walks about the town, while Evelyn was busy at Vexing Tower. They explored the inner courts and the indoor markets. They wandered out onto the icy river, the day it snowed heaviest and had an entrancing time, they claimed. They wore wooden snowshoes and sat in a coffee pagoda that was carved in the ice, right in the middle of the river. An old baboon brought them piping hot cappuccinos, heaped with cream and chocolate, and dainty little cakes. They sat there in the swirling crowds and admired everything around them.

'John says how lucky we are. To be afforded this. This glimpse, he called it. Of an alien world.'

'Did he?' Evelyn was combing out her hair, sitting at the end of the bed in their attic room. Her hair felt lustrous. Honey-coloured. It was in fine condition. Maybe the water in Daakholm was especially good? Her complexion, too, was clear. Her eyes were sparkling, when she caught her own glance in the mirror. Even Brenda, who was never much to look at, seemed rude with health of late.

On the counterpane beside Evelyn – the small valise. Reg's manuscript pages were spread out. She had been studying them. To no avail whatsoever.

'John will find us a way home. I just know it.'

Evelyn wished she shared her faith. She was as fond of the young man as Brenda was. But she couldn't really see how he could do what she said. He seemed to Evelyn to be very caught up in the strange excitements of Daakholm. He had returned to a bookshop he had found here – managed by an elephant, he said! – and he had bought books written by Henry Cleavis himself. Books that Cleavis hadn't even written!

'Yet,' John gabbled excitedly. 'He hasn't written them yet. Do you see? This might mean that this world exists in the future of our own place…'

To be honest, it made Evelyn's mind spin dizzily on its axis. She didn't even like to touch the pastel-coloured dust jackets of the book he had brought back from the shop. The shop he said was owned by a Mr Mumbo-Jumbo.

Were they all mad? Was that what had happened to them?

Evelyn's mind kept skidding over the surface of things. Like now. Trying to make head or tail out of Reg's writing. Her eyes couldn't quite focus on the letters and words he had formed. It took her a little while to realise that they weren't written in straightforward English. Her husband used a kind of code or cipher, it seemed. She was relieved to realise it. She thought perhaps she was seeing things, or had lost the ability to read.

It struck her, as she combed out her hair: well then, what use could Mr Tweet even make of this manuscript? Even if she took it to Vexing Tower, as he kept requesting. This cipher would be as mysterious to him as it was to her, surely?

She noticed Brenda staring curiously at the pages spilling out of the valise.

'I wish he'd never written the dratted thing,' Evelyn said. 'I wish we knew nothing about it.'

And then she thought: I could give it to Mr Tweet. Then we'd be shot of it. The thing was more bother than it was worth.

Strange, treacherous thoughts like that. Evelyn had been having them rather a lot of late. Disloyal thoughts. Unaccustomed thoughts.

But Mr Tweet was paying her attention like no one had, in such a long time. Certainly not Reg.

So she went back the next day, and she gave him the bundle of papers.

She didn't tell Brenda she was going to do it. Brenda was going out with John that day. They had plans. Evelyn hardly knew herself what she was going to do, until she hurried off up the winding street, clutching that valise to her pounding chest. Only when she passed the whole thing over into Mr Tweet's grasp did it hit her – the magnitude of what she had done.

'My dear lady,' he said, blushing and hugging the case to his own chest. All the feathers in that strange, iridescent cloak rustled noisily.

'But it's unreadable,' she warned him. 'It's in a type of code. I think it's a code only Reg knows the key to...'

'That hardly matters,' said Mr Tweet. 'It's the properties inherent in the pages. That's what's important. It's about the doors they've already opened, and the *holes* they have scratched into the world. Not the actual sentences. Not the *sense* of it. Do you see?'

'N-no,' she admitted. 'I don't see at all.'

'Never mind,' he said. 'That's not very important.' Then he turned as if to hurry off into the darker recesses of the tower.

'So,' Evelyn said, rather pointedly. 'What happens now?'

'Hm?' He gave her his most genial smile. 'Now I'm rather afraid I have work to do, my dear. Lots and lots of work. So much work. I shall be very busy for quite some time. You can find your way out, can't you? You must surely know the way by now.'

All of a sudden she felt rather foolish. She was being rudely, brusquely dismissed by him. Now he had what he wanted from her, that was it. Now she must go. He had no further use for her.

And now she could see again how much he resembled her husband. Now that his attention was fixed elsewhere.

'Shall I come back here?' she asked, sounding a bit pathetic, she realized.

'Yes, yes,' he said, though he didn't sound very enthused. 'Of course. Whenever you like, my dear. Whenever the fancy takes you. Now. Off you pop. I must get to work...'

And then the monkey had hold of her hand. She hadn't even seen him approach, and jumped at the clammy clasp of his fingers. He pulled at her, and she followed him.

*

After that she had several gloomy days in a row. Mr Tweet didn't want anything more from her. All she had been was a means of getting those pages into his hands. She should have refused him. She should have burned them. She should have told the goblin men that she had no idea where Reg kept his manuscripts.

But instead she had given in and done exactly what she had been told to. Like a good little girl.

Dear Mother, she wrote, *I don't suppose you'll agree with this, but I have been a good girl all my life and I've always done what I've been told. Even when I didn't know the reason I just did what those in authority bade me do. I was a good daughter and I've been a good wife. That is, until I stole my husband's precious book and took it to another world.*

Oh dear. Reg was going to kill her. He would strangle her. She could already feel his hands on her throat, throttling the life out of her. Perhaps it wasn't the whole book, though. Perhaps it was even a copy. Perhaps she hadn't really thrown away seventeen years of his life and work?

Next morning, they were having breakfast in the conservatory. Brenda was tucking heartily into runny eggs and soldiers. Evelyn couldn't eat a thing. John seemed shifty, somehow. His appetite was off, too. He tried to smile and chat breezily, but Evelyn noticed that his eyes turned downcast and he clammed up whenever the cat-faced young man came in to see that everything was all right with his guests. Evelyn wondered what had been happening there? Had the young man been asking him about money, too? Or had there been something else going on between them, perhaps?

But her mind was more full of her own concerns.

That morning she was thinking about the bookshop her companions were telling her about. *Chimera*, it was called, which sounded somehow familiar. Also they were telling her about the bookseller, who was an elephant.

'You actually managed to get copies of these books? Of Henry's?' She was firing questions at John as she poured fresh tea.

He nodded, still looking discomfited. 'Yes, three of them. Only one is familiar. I've checked the publication dates, and I can't make head nor tail of the way they number years. I've begun reading odd bits… and, well, the bits I've looked at all seem to *sound* like Henry, if you know what I mean. Sort of like his style, and the kinds of things he would make up…'

'I see.'

Brenda was chomping away on crunchy toast, but she was giving Evelyn a fixed look. She was trying to work out what she was thinking.

Evelyn was thinking that she would like to visit this bookshop herself.

*

And so later that morning, as the snow fell heavily over Daakholm, they hurried down the cobbled lane to the shop that John had described so precisely.

Evelyn was no great bibliophile. Years of marriage to Reg had turned her off their musty charms. She did enjoy her romances and her murders and her movie magazines, of course. But she

151

didn't like to dwell for hours in the close confines of bookshops. However, having said that, this place had something rather special about it. There was a kind of calmness. There were no other customers that early in the morning, apart from a large goose in a headscarf, who waddled past, all businesslike, with a brusque 'Good morning.' John held open the door for her.

He showed Evelyn to the back of the store, as if he was already quite at home there, and he introduced her to the Mumbo Jumbo.

Even after all those weeks in Daakholm she was momentarily struck dumb by the awe-inspiring bulk of him, crammed into the alcove by the cash desk. His elegant tailoring and his dextrous, slightly furred trunk and the tiny pair of spectacles flashing in the glare from the desk lamp: he was an incredibly impressive sight.

Clearly, between them, John and Brenda had already told him much about Evelyn. He seemed glad to make her acquaintance, and said so in a voice that rumbled out of him and vibrated the wooden shelves and walls all around them.

'I wonder what I can help you with,' he said, looking quizzical. Evelyn stared straight back into his eyes, determined not to be put off her stroke. She didn't want to seem frightened or intimidated by him. But when she looked into his eyes she was shocked by the great wisdom and the great age that were apparent there. Her breath caught in her throat. She knew at once: he could see right through her. He could see straight into her soul. This creature – this being – he knew every single thing she was thinking.

But that was nonsense, she told herself. No one could do that.

The other two were looking at her, too. They wanted to know what it was she'd like to ask the Mumbo-Jumbo. Why was she so keen to come here this morning?

'Do you have a book by my husband?' she asked him.

'I have many books here,' he rumbled, still staring straight into what felt like her soul. 'I have just about everything in stock somewhere here. Could you give me more to go on?'

'Reginald Tyler,' she told him. 'My husband's name is Reginald Tyler.'

He frowned, and his face creased up. The lines looked like contours in a map of a very complex land. 'Hmmmm. And the title?'

She was aware of the eyes of John and Brenda upon her. She hadn't told them that she would be asking for this. She took a deep breath, as if Reg's book's title was a secret. In a way, it was. 'It's 'The True History of the Worlds.''

The Mumbo Jumbo grunted and eased back in his specially-reinforced chair, which creaked and groaned in protest. He looked as if he already knew what she was going to say.

'Do you have it?' she asked.

'Don't you have your own copy?' he mumbled, sounding kindly, but the light in his eyes had become hard.

'No. No, I don't.' She didn't confess to what she had done with the only bit of it she had. 'In our world... where we come from... it isn't even *written* yet. He hasn't even finished it, I don't think. No one has read it. But I thought... I just thought... since you sold copies of Henry Cleavis's books that seem to come from the future...'

John gasped at this. 'I didn't say that for definite,' he put in. 'It was just an idea...'

'The future?' smiled the Mumbo-Jumbo. 'So you think I am sitting here selling books that haven't been written yet? What a very intriguing idea.'

'Can you help me?' she asked.

'No.' He said it quite flatly. He didn't like her. All at once she could tell. He didn't like her at all. 'I cannot help. Your husband's book does not exist. He never wrote it. He never will. The book you have mentioned will never be read by *anyone*. Good *day* to you.'

*

Her friends were embarrassed for her, and she felt rebuked.

The Mumbo-Jumbo went back to studying the ledgers and files on his desk, dismissing them from his thoughts.

Evelyn just wanted to get out of the shop. She could feel the dust and mildew cloying at her. She was blushing ferociously.

But John had other ideas. He urged the two women to stay here, and to explore the upper storeys of the shop. Everything was higgledy-piggledy and rather nasty. No one had done a good tidy up for years. Evelyn could see Brenda looking about at the skewed shelving and the tottering stacks as they ascended into the upper landings. She could hardly keep herself from giving the place a good dusting-round.

'What are we looking for?' Evelyn grumbled.

But John seemed deadset on what it was he was searching out. He led them into the very attics, where some of the rooms were so gloomy Evelyn got chills just stepping through. Then he brought them to the farthest room, which was less cluttered than the others and had gorgeous, golden sun spilling through the skylight. Surely it wasn't the snowy light from outside? Had the weather changed while they had been in here?

He pulled back a velvet curtain and Evelyn was reminded, all of a sudden, that *Chimera* was the name of the junk shop she had visited weeks ago with Catriona. The day that Catriona bought her the golden basilisk. Another such moment was about to occur, Evelyn could feel it.

John smiled excitedly at the two women. 'Yes. I was right. It's almost the same.'

'The same as what?' frowned Brenda.

'As home,' he said but declined to explain further.

They stepped through the frayed curtain. Evelyn could hear its nap brush against her sleeve. Her nerves were strung so tautly that it made her shudder. But it was at that very moment she suddenly started to feel unnaturally warm. Now, this was very curious. She must be unwell. She must be having some sort of flush. But... but it wasn't unpleasant. She was wearing winter clothes. A hooded cape and furred gloves which she had kept on because the upper reaches of the shop were frosty... but all at once there was this arid heat. It was like she had been timing meringues in the oven and suddenly opened the door...

John looked round at them and grinned. They were in the confined space beyond the curtain. There were some darker drapes in front of him. He took one step forward and whisked them apart.

The sunlight was too intense. The heat was blinding. Someone shoved Evelyn. Jogged her elbow. Pushed her forward. Noise rushed into her head. Chattering, hooting, laughter and the rumbling noise of many bodies pressed together, going about their daily business...

Brenda was standing right at Evelyn's side and she laughed. She told her friend to open up her eyes. Evelyn hardly dared to.

'A-are we somewhere else?'

'Somewhere else again!' Brenda chuckled, and took hold of Evelyn's arm, very gently, and helped her ease off the furry gloves. 'Yet another world within a world,' she said. How gentle her voice sounded. And how clever. She usually spoke in such curt, clipped sentences. It was like she could only string so many thoughts together inside a sentence. But not now. Perhaps, thought Evelyn, she was always different deep down?

Evelyn was wondering about the way her maid was talking merely as a means of distracting herself. For she was standing in the middle of a crowd in a marketplace in a place that looked like the *Arabian Nights*. She was sweltering in furs and so was Brenda. Ahead of them, John was shrugging off his duffel coat and stripping off his heavy woollen jumper. He said, 'I came here once before! By accident. Just for a few moments. This is a different part of the marketplace to the one I visited before...'

'Which world is this?' asked Brenda. Her mistress gaped at her. How could she know what questions to ask? How could she sound so calm and au fait with it all? Evelyn turned to see the red velvet curtain and the darkness within and she wanted to scream. It was all too much. It was too disorienting. She turned back into the curtain and there was absolutely nothing beyond it anymore. Just the darkness. There was no way back into *Chimera*'s attic.

John was gazing at the stalls that were closest. This was just one corner of a marketplace that extended for quite some distance in every direction. The babble of noise was incredible. People were selling glazed pots and vividly-coloured rugs and queer-looking vegetables and fruits. The people themselves were a little like those in Daakholm in that they tended to the animalistic in shape and form rather than the human, but in this new land the animals were more difficult to identify. For example, there was a kind of reptile person pouring coloured oils into jars, working busily at the stall close by. He was a kind of cross between an iguana and a pelican. There were other, even more bizarre hybridized creatures, milling about. Monkeys with neatly-folded angel-wings. Porcupines taller than the canvas roofs. Ostriches and something that looked – at first and then second glance – very like a unicorn.

John was urging Brenda and Evelyn to follow him. 'I think I recognize this now,' he said. 'The first time I came, I didn't. But now I think I do. Having read one of the books that's supposed to be by Henry...'

He surged ahead, and so did Brenda, and Evelyn flapped along after them, helplessly, with half a hundred questions in her head. The bright blue sky beat down on them, through the narrow gaps in the sun-baked buildings. Evelyn was squeezing past armadillos, flamingos and hairy-faced men. Luckily her weeks of experience in Daakholm had accustomed her to the sight and the proximity of outlandish people. But this was even more disorientating. This place didn't look at all like home. Not in the slightest.

John found them a cool café to sit in. It was at one side of a busy public square. Here he chose a table surrounded by flaunting, butter-coloured lilies and ordered some iced tea, which arrived in a giant pitcher tinkling with ice. They sat there and caught their breath.

'Are you saying this is a place from Henry's books?' Brenda asked John.

'It feels very like what he describes. I've been stewing over those books for days...'

'Are you saying he's been here too?' Evelyn said, sounding sharp, even to her own ears. 'Or he will do in the future?'

'I'm not sure,' mused John. His eyes were seemingly drinking the place in as he stared at the square. 'I'm not at all sure. But this looks and feels to me like the world in more than one of his books. I truly believe, ladies, that we have found our way to Hyspero.'

His words sank in as the ice melted rapidly in the wonderful tea, which was flavoured with some delicious kind of fruit. Had they left Daakholm forever? Evelyn wondered if they would ever be able to return to Woodbegood's again, or whether she would ever see Vexing Tower and Mr Tweet ever again? She thought about her new clothes in the hotel. And about Reg's pages in the possession of the master of the birds.

Were they going to go through one world after another, like this, forever?

*

As they drank their tea John took out the books he had bought some days ago at the Mumbo-Jumbo's shop. Evelyn found it almost touching that he had been carrying them with him the whole time. There were three. 'The Other Place.' John placed the first one under their noses. Its paper cover was faded and worn. 'This is the book Henry published at home, in our own world. It already exists. But not with these illustrations, and it's obviously not decades old yet, as this copy is.'

Brenda leaned over the copy, breathing heavily, clearly fascinated. 'So there is a time factor involved...' she muttered, more to herself than the others. Evelyn wanted to say, 'Excuse me? Brenda? You don't *talk* like this! You simply don't say mysterious and peculiar things like this...'

But John was taking the other books out from his bag. 'And this. 'Return to Hyspero.''

This one was without a cover. Its cloth binding was scarlet. It was very battered and worn, as if it was a book that had been read hundreds of times and well-loved. There was Henry's name stamped in gold with the title down the spine.

And the third book? John slid it across the coloured tiles of the café table, careful to avoid the pools of spilled tea. 'The Mysterious Mr Tweet,' he said, and Evelyn's heart did a curious thing. It felt just like a gramophone needle skipping over several grooves and skidding out of control.

'Mr Tweet?' she said in a strangled voice. 'He wrote about Mr Tweet?'

She stared down at the cover. There was a drawing – pen and ink, washed with faint colour – of a castle with a crooked tower lancing into the stormy air. A spiral of birds twisted in the skies and all around the title. At the bottom of the drawing there was a familiar yellow monkey staring out and grinning at the reader.

'What's the matter, Evelyn?' asked John. 'Are you q...'

Just then there was a horrible whooshing through the air and a clatter of sharpened metal: like a guillotine coming down onto their table.

The glasses and jug smashed and sloshed everywhere as the table shattered between them. The books flew upwards and John made a hasty grab for them, even though someone was wielding a great big horrible...

Scimitar.

That was the word for it.

It was being held by a masked man. Vastly tall and infinitely muscular. Wearing some kind of leather armour. His eyes blazed down at them as he hefted the sword up again. Brenda was still screaming and John was scrabbling on the floor, shouting, trying to salvage Cleavis's books.

Evelyn was the calmest one there. The guard was shouting at them. He was directing his men to gather them up and take them prisoner. Everyone was making noise and busying about. The other café customers were crying out and whimpering and moving away as fast as they could. Only Evelyn was calm. She was frozen there in her wintry outfit. Numb with shock.

But it was Brenda who recovered her senses first. 'Leave the books, John!' she bellowed, grabbing hold of his arm and yanking him to his feet. 'Run!'

Suddenly it made complete sense to Evelyn. They couldn't hang around. They couldn't be so ridiculous as to let these... brutes take them prisoner. They might do away with them or whisk them off to just about anywhere. We are British subjects, thought Evelyn, and they can't do this to us!

John jumped to his feet and miraculously the three of them managed to slither out of the grasp of the cumbersome guards. The sight of those flashing blades gave them something of a prompt and, next thing, they were back in the market place and running for their lives.

Brenda could put on quite a turn of speed when she wanted to, Evelyn noticed.

'The books!' John was in despair. 'I could have saved them...'

From behind came screams amid the stalls and shady alcoves as the guards stormed straight through, shoving past everyone while those they pursued were zig-zagging furiously, doing their best to shake them off.

'What can they want with us?' Evelyn shouted to the others. 'How can they even know who we are?'

'They don't,' said Brenda. Her face was crumpled in anger. 'We could be anyone. We're just strangers here.'

All at once they seemed to have come to a dead end. A brick wall rose fully ten feet in front of them. They had clearly taken a wrong turning somewhere.

When one of the guards spied them he came running with a triumphant shout, but Brenda intercepted him. She laid him out stone cold with one single punch in the face.

'Brenda!'

She glowered at Evelyn. 'Let's get over that wall before his friends come after him.'

John was already piling up old wooden crates into a ramshackle staircase.

It suddenly looked like they were going to make good their escape. They sent Evelyn up first – out of gallantry perhaps. Though she didn't see what was so gallant about it when none of them knew what dangers might lie over the other side…

There came more cries from the marketplace as the soldiers bullied their way through the crowds. It could only be a matter of seconds before another of them discovered their panicking quarry.

'Hurry!' John hissed. Evelyn was so hopelessly awkward and uncoordinated. She was cursing herself, getting stuck trying to haul herself over the crumbling brick wall…

And then the most bizarre thing happened.

'Evelyn..!' Brenda urged. 'Hurry!'

A dowdy brown bird appeared seemingly out of nowhere and alighted on the wall beside Evelyn. She was so surprised she just rested there, panting, staring at it.

For a second it felt almost as if it had come to help her.

The bird chirrupped at her. A light stream of song. Like he was trying to tell her something of vital importance.

And that was when she noticed that he had something fastened to one of his spindly legs. A small white sliver of paper.

Evelyn reached out, very slowly, ignoring the increasingly panicked cries from her friends. She reached out one hand – balancing herself precariously atop the wall – and took hold of the scrap of paper very delicately. Putting on hardly any pressure at all for fear of scaring or injuring the bird. But the bird simply went on singing.

There were others there. Other birds in the alleyway. Wheeling about in the dingy canyon. Swooping around Evelyn. All of them were singing the same plaintive song. All of them had little notes attached to their legs, fluttering about her.

'Evelyn!' John cried. 'Please! *Come on!*'

There were small black letters on the strip of paper on the sparrow's leg.

All at once Evelyn recognized her husband's scratchy penmanship.

Was it in his queer cipher?

She screwed up her eyes to focus. And she managed to read two words in the very instant before the bird took panic at the sudden hullaballoo of soldiers surging into the alleyway. The bird spiralled up into the air, away from her, but she had already seen what his message was. At least two words of it.

Come home.

Just as Brenda started screaming again and turning to take on a whole phalanx of armoured men with scimitars, the world around them began to drain and fade away – with astonishing speed. All the colours and smells and the heat of the land that John had told them was called Hyspero - all of it simply faded away.

And then...!

The three of them were sitting together in Evelyn's parlour. It was bright and airy, with the French windows standing open, and the clock on the mantle was chiming a quarter past ten.

CHAPTER FIVE

Brenda was glad to be back in Darkholmes with everyone safe and sound. She and Evelyn were back at 199 Steps Lane and going about their everyday business. Evelyn had been in rather a gloomy mood since their return. John was back at Hexford College, in his rooms that he shared with Professor Cleavis. Brenda hadn't seen hide nor hair of him since Monday morning.

For whatever reason the three of them had decided to keep quiet about the experiences they had shared in recent days and weeks. Not that the choice was Brenda's. She was back in her monosyllabic servant role, of course, now that they were home. Not that she would be shouting it all from the rooftops, but it would be nice to be asked about these things.

She was back in the kitchen, banging utensils about, shoving pots into the cupboards and slamming them into the oven. She was making up beds. Rubbing washing with her bare hands and wringing it through the mangle. But still, she felt wonderfully rested. She didn't think she'd ever had a holiday like the secret one she had just enjoyed in Daakholm.

Evelyn and her husband the Professor weren't speaking. Though time moved differently between the two worlds – this one and its shadow – it wasn't different enough, and a significant couple of weeks had elapsed in their absence. Professor Tyler was naturally curious – more than curious! Furious, in fact – to know where it was they had been to.

'At my mother's,' was all Evelyn would tell him and Brenda thought he knew it was a blatant lie. They hadn't been in Scotland and he knew it.

'Then why did you take Brenda with you? And my manuscript? So help me, Evelyn, where is my manuscript? What have you done with my pages?'

Their arguments raged above Brenda's head as she worked her way through the mountains of socks and pants and shirts that need rubbing with soap and hot water. She listened to their clashing doors and their thudding footsteps.

'I sent them away!' Evelyn screeched at him.

'What? Sent where?'

Strange that the old man hadn't asked a word about the old-fashioned clothes they were both wearing on the day they turned up in the dining room. Perhaps he never really noticed the things that women wore? His neglectfulness was the thing Evelyn always said she felt most keenly. She had told Brenda this. During one of their many long chats in the other world. She told Brenda a lot of things that she didn't think she would ever tell anyone here.

'Where did you send those pages from my book, Evelyn?' Professor Tyler raged. 'Seventeen chapters are missing – and I know you took them!'

She screamed through the door at him: 'I sent them to a literary agent!'

And a dreadful silence fell.

Brenda knew she was lying. She knew she'd had those chapters with her in Daakholm, in a little valise. But Brenda didn't know where they were now. Definitely not with some fancy London agent. Brenda thought Evelyn might have lost them forever and was covering up this fact. She was going on the offensive, as she often did. And then both Tylers weren't talking to each other, and days passed.

*

There was something else that had put the Professor on edge, though.

Brenda knew what it was, at once, the first day she set off with her wicker basket and headed out for groceries. She had seen him get like this before and she knew what was behind it. When she saw the ramshackle collection of caravans and trucks on the Gipsy Green. When she paused and stared in the freezing breeze to watch the tents going up and the rough workmen milling about. She could hear the shouts of the fairground workers and she could hear other noises, too, above the hammering and the revving of engines. She could hear the discontented roars of caged animals kept in the dark.

There was a circus in town. A fair was being set up on the green. Sideshows. Exhibitions. All kinds of fantastic stalls and rides. Each year they came, but it was usually in the spring. So why were they here now? Hadn't they already been this year? Back in Whitsun week?

So what was this? Right before Christmas? A winter fair?

By the next day they were all prepared. Lights were strung all over their tents and their peculiar attractions. Brenda didn't go as close as she did the first day. She veered around the edges of Gipsy Green. These people were all strangers to her. They weren't the travellers they usually got in Darkholmes. She lugged her basket of bread and parcels of meat and vegetables , and she kept a look at the messy encampment out of the corner of her eye.

The thing was... it stirred something, deep inside her.

She wasn't sure what.

The fair people looked like they had come from abroad. They used a horrible, strangulated dialect and she didn't know what it was they were shouting at each other as she went by. They might have been shouting about Brenda herself, these bulky, bearded men in their vest tops and dirty-looking trousers. There was a curious music in their language. Slippery and guttural at the same time.

Gaudy banners were going up. From the edges of the green Brenda couldn't see what they said. But they rippled and pulled in the wind as it gathered force on Tuesday evening. It was a severe Northerly wind, bringing the dusty smell of ice and snow with it.

Who really would want to visit the fairground and sideshows on nights like these? With snow threatening to fall and the green itself matted and crusted with frost...

The freezing winds brought with them flyers that slipped through letterboxes like messages from beyond. Everyone in Darkholmes received a personal invitation on shiny dark paper. Golden letters spelled out the name of the travelling show. Further details followed. There was a heavily stylized drawing of a woman in a revealing golden swimming costume with feathers sprouting out of her head. She was whipping a blazing orange tiger into orderly shape.

Brenda stooped to pick the flyer off the mat in the hall. Her knees made a noise like shots going off at the start of a race.

Then all the breath went out of her in one horrible rush as she saw the name of the travelling show. It was:

'*The Carnival of Doctor Diodati!*'

*

Naturally Brenda didn't say anything about recognizing the name.

Diodati. Diodati. It sounded foreign. She couldn't quite grasp hold of all the associations it held for her...

Did she ever go abroad? Was she ever on the continent? She must have been, she mused.

Late at night, that week. When the tents were up and the sideshows were awash with light and the carnival was in full swing. Evelyn Tyler would wait no longer. She was keen to be out of the house and seeing the spectacle for herself.

Tuesday night Brenda was drying up the pots and pans in the scullery and Evelyn came dashing breathlessly to tell her that she must go with her. They were to make a foray into the night and Brenda didn't even have time to brush her hair. 'Throw on a headscarf,' Evelyn urged her. 'Pull on a shawl. I'll go crazy if I don't get out of this mausoleum soon, Brenda...'

By then they had been back more than a week. Evelyn was feeling her confinement keenly. She and her professor were barely talking.

Brenda couldn't help herself. She was thrilled that they were going out on a midnight adventure together, right under the husband's nose.

Outside the winter winds were plucking the tall trees this way and that way. The two women slipped out of the back garden through the door in the red wall into the side passage. The quick, quiet route to Gipsy Green. Wordlessly they made their way across the clumpy, sodden grass, hearing the hurdy-gurdy music itching over their skin and inside their bones before they could pick out the tune... before they could see the dancing lights like will o' the wisps in the misty gloaming.

Evelyn took Brenda's scarred hand in her own tiny one and off they trotted.

It was all very noisy and busy by now. There were townsfolk bundled up against the weather, looking excited and shifty as they moved between rides and stalls. Brenda noticed that there were a lot of students from the university, their faces bright with excitement as they braved the wildest rides, striped scarves streaming behind them...

She and Evelyn both agreed that they would never go on any of those dangerous contraptions: the kinds that spun and turned upside down and rattled one's bones until one felt sick. Though they stood for some time to admire the prancing, flaunting, painted horses of the carousel. For a few moments those golden creatures seemed as if they were alive and they toyed with the thought of jumping into saddles the next time the merry-go-round slowed down... alas, it never seemed to and all the mounts were taken...

They moved on, into a relatively more sedate part of the carnival grounds, where barkers were standing in front of their tents and calling out to passersby... There were a great jumble of enticements and elaborate alliterations pronounced in strange accents. The crowds heard about alligator men, mustachio'ed ladies, jelly-faced freaks and badger boys... Siamese twins who could play the piano and a family of mice so bright they could answer any question anyone cared to set them. This last one sounded the least alarming and Evelyn and Brenda stood at the periphery of a crowd to watch ten white mice sitting at long desks, paws on buzzers as a question master rat read questions to them from a stack of tiny cards. He spoke in such a high, scratchy voice, no one could make head nor tail of it and the crowd started to drift away in disappointment. The mice – and their owner – keen to show off their intellect, seemed very dismayed at this.

'But it's the The World's Greatest Mouse Quiz!' the owner shouted, throwing out his hands, pleading with them to return and give it a little more time. 'What more do you expect? They're doing their best. Look at them! They're so well behaved. Waiting for their questions so patiently…!'

Brenda found herself lollygagging, watching all this going on, lagging back, even though Evelyn was keen to follow the rest of them, to find more spectacular amusements. Elsewhere there were shouts of mermaids and abominable creatures from the dawn of time. The leopard boy, the vampire fox and the princess made from gold leaf and beaten biscuit tins. Brenda was feeling sorry for the young man in charge of the Mouse Quiz as he bent over their small table, dousing their spotlights, and telling them they might as well give up for the night.

The young man noticed her standing there. He frowned and rubbed at his dark beard, eyeing her suspiciously, like she had come to make trouble for him.

'I'm sorry nobody stayed,' Brenda told him. 'I wanted to see the mice.'

He shrugged. 'It's a stupid act. I was better off before, with Jasper the cat. Now *there* was an act. But he's gone now.'

'I'm Brenda,' she said impulsively, stepping forward.

He looked surprised. He scrutinized her face in the chalky fairground light. She remembered Evelyn never gave her time to put on her make-up before they left The Steps. She must look a fright. The harsh light would show up the scars round her neck and her temples. She pulled her headscarf tighter round her face.

'Diodati,' he said, with a shrug. 'Tony.'

'Oh! So… you're the owner..?'

He grinned. 'One day. If the old man eventually pegs it. If he'll ever trust me with his precious show. If I even want it.' He sighed, and stooped over his mice, who were out of their little chairs now and seemingly remonstrating with him in high-pitched voices that he gave every appearance of understanding. He turned to Brenda again. 'I'm not really sure this is the life for me. I don't really have the show in my blood. Not like he has. The old man. He's been at it all his life.'

'Yes,' Brenda said. 'Yes, I think… I think I remember.'

'Why am I telling you this?' Tony smiled. 'Who are you, anyway?'

She shook her head to clear it. Bells were ringing. They were ringing loudly in both ears. It was the call to the Big Top. It was time for the main attraction. The elephants and the monkeys and the lions and all that. It was time for the clowns and it was the clowns ringing the bells, of course and stirring the drifting crowds and drawing them towards the largest tent. But the bells were ringing inside Brenda's head, too, and she knew that she had been here, right here, amongst these people and their ilk before.

'Do you think I could see your father?' she asked Tony. 'Talk to him?'

'He's busy right now,' scowled the young man. 'Cracking his whip and shouting and showing off to everyone. He's in his element. You'd better hurry along before you miss any of it…'

Brenda turned to follow the crowd and her last glimpse of Tony was of him shoving his disgruntled mice into each of the pockets of his patch-worked coat.

*

Evelyn was not best pleased that Brenda had lost her in the crowd. She grimaced as they felt their way along the bleachers. Below the rickety bank of seats were the cages where they kept the lions and tigers. They were both alarmed to look down and see angry green eyes staring up at them. It was like being Christians in the Coliseum, Evelyn was hissing at Brenda, fetching out a bag of sucky sweets.

The lights dimmed and the crowd murmured excitedly (so many! Brenda had hardly thought there would be so many in such a highbrow town; so many keen on gaudy amusements like this!) When the clowns came running out they weren't really the kind that made one want to laugh. Not Brenda, anyway. Their make-up and their apparel were monochrome. There was nothing silly or jovial about them. They dashed about, calling volunteers from the audience, and flinging them about like rag dolls, making everyone roar with laughter.

Out came the ringmaster. Doctor Diodati. In golden jodhpurs and a scarlet waistcoat. His black beard was waxed and forked. His stovepipe hat was standing two feet tall, proudly, on his oily hair. *Yes, yes*, Brenda thought: *I do remember him*. She could barely repress a shudder. And, through all the spectacles that followed – the troupe of camels, the whirling elephants, the prancing llamas, she could barely take her eyes off the man who owned the show.

Evelyn was agog at everything, of course. To Brenda, the show was fairly tepid, generic stuff. None of this was exactly new to her.

Brenda only sat up and paid keen attention when the Carnival of Freaks appeared. Led by the Gold Leaf Princess, this shambling parade drew all kinds of responses from the crowd. Some hooted with derision, others barked out with laughter. Others were silent in their appraisal of the band of strange siblings. The freaks shuffled, lolloped and even skipped about the main ring as Doctor Diodati cracked his whip. They made one slow circuit so that everyone could catch a glimpse of them in their finery. There were about twenty. All shapes and sizes. A chicken boy. A man covered in green, shiny scales. Siamese twins who had clearly fallen out with each other. Two dwarves were carrying a black lacquered coffin between them, as part of the procession. Beside them skipped a fox-faced man with ginger whiskers and pointed ears, swirling a jet black cloak with scarlet lining.

Evelyn cried out at the sight of them. 'What a terrible, tawdry bunch!' And Brenda wondered: had she forgotten, already? In Daakholm she became quite adept at accepting the strangeness of the people they lived among. After just a couple of weeks she had hardly ever turned a hair, no matter how outlandish the people were. Yet here she was, crying out in delighted shock and dismay at the carnival freaks Diodati presented. Brenda felt obscurely disappointed with her mistress.

This made it somewhat easier, when the lights went down, to slip away from their seats above the cages, and leave Evelyn sitting there alone, and to exit surreptitiously from the tent.

*

There was no fuss when Brenda took her place among them.

It was like they hardly noticed she was there. The performers were resting after their moment in the spotlight. They gathered at the back of one of the caravans, perching on crates and fold-down chairs, passing flasks of rough spirits and bottles of beer. Around them the fairground continued its business, and the crowd in the Big Top were roaring at the big cats, who in their turn, roared back at them. These few were precious moments when the sideshow stars were allowed to gather and mingle and congratulate each other on their brief but magnificent appearance tonight.

Brenda slipped among them. And she was wrong. It wasn't like they didn't know that she was there. They simply didn't remark on her presence, and she understood with a shock that they felt that she belonged.

It was a sensation she hadn't felt for a long time. Someone passed her a bottle of black stout and urged her to drink. It was like a little party was going on back there.

'See?' said the foxy-faced man. 'I told you it would be fine. We went down a storm, didn't we? I knew they'd love us.'

With a shivery tinkling noise the Gold Leaf Princess shrugged and smiled at him. 'I thought they'd be too sophisticated in this town. Too highbrow. I didn't think they'd be interested in seeing the likes of us.'

Brenda was staring at her. Was she a real girl underneath? Or was she really made entirely out of thin, overlapping layers of precious metal? When she moved the metal within her tinkled and grated and there was even that rattling noise one got from biscuit tins, from the grains of rice trapped inside the perforated lid to keep the contents fresh. Her body and face were less Gold Leaf than painted tin, as if the gold had rubbed away with the years. Her features were labeled all over with the names of famous biscuits.

Brenda sipped the dark ale and took them all in. All of them. The jelly-faced man. Guido, someone called him. The disgruntled Siamese twins, who talked animatedly to each other's neighbours, but studiously avoided each other's eye. They were sitting on the shining coffin that the dwarves had been carrying round the circus ring. Who or what was inside? Brenda wondered.

One of the dwarves pulled at the sleeve of her coat. 'Hey, you. Who said you could come and sit with us?'

'Leave her alone,' muttered his friend. 'She's all right.' They were rough-looking dwarves, Brenda thought. With straggly beards and bits of armour all buckled and worn. Savage little faces, too, like they had known hard times.

The Foxy-faced man came to sit beside her, taking the bottle out of her hand. 'What is your name?'

She told him. He really was a fox, she realised. With those extremely pointed teeth. In an opera cloak. She found herself saying, 'I've had a number of different names. I've forgotten them all. These days I'm known as Brenda. And I'm nothing, really. Nothing significant. Nothing worth putting in a show. I'm not worth looking at.'

His beady, beastly eyes were boring into her. 'Oh, I wouldn't say so, Brenda. I think you must be uniquely talented.'

'Do you?' Her voice came out a bit weakly, like badly-brewed tea and she was cross at herself. 'W-why would you say that?'

'Charles. I'm Charles.' He smirked at her. 'I say that because you've been *clocked*, Brenda. You've been recognized. And that's what you want, don't you? You want us to see you, and remember who you are.'

'N-no,' she stammered. 'That is, I don't know. I was drawn here. I don't know why I came out to sit with you. It's just… everything is churning around in my head. Everything is…' She looked at him helplessly and saw, all at once, over his shoulder, the concerned faces of his freakish friends. They were all eavesdropping. They were all paying heed.

The Gold Leaf Princess stepped awkwardly, jerkily towards them. Her face was creased into a smile. 'She's lost her memory, haven't you, Brenda? You don't remember us at all, do you?'

Brenda wanted to be polite. She wanted to say the right thing. But when she looked at them, she wasn't sure. They crowded her in. They pressed around her. Suddenly the fumes of the booze and the sawdust and sweat and sweet, sticky make-up were getting a bit much for her. Her head started to whirl. She thought she was going to pass out.

'You're discombobulated,' someone said, just as she toppled forward onto the scrubby grass.

*

Was it an awful thing to say? It was just that they had about them the sweetish, brackish stench of those without regular access to hot running water. They smelled like they didn't have anywhere to wash their stage clothes and they just dabbed off the worst bits of dirt and grease. Just a lick and a promise. When Brenda came to, it was the first thing she smelled. Underlying the hot, exciting scents of the circus, she could smell the poverty and the grime.

She had become too accustomed to comfort. She shrank from the aroma of their tougher lives.

Someone had fetched her a chair. Now they were all inside one of the caravans. It was so poky and dim. For a second she almost panicked, thinking she had been kidnapped.

'No, no,' said the Gold Leaf Princess, pushing a cold flannel onto Brenda's forehead. 'Please, be calm. No one here means you any harm, Brenda.'

Behind her stood Foxy-Faced Charles. 'It must come as something of a shock. Remembering.'

He said it with such certainty, too. Like he knew what it was like when patches of Brenda's past returned to her.

'I know you...' Brenda said, and her voice came out gruffly.

'Not personally, no,' admitted the vampire fox. 'But I have heard so much over the years. I was too young to meet you. You had left Diodati's circus long before I came aboard.'

'H-had I?'

'I remember,' said the Gold Leaf Princess, biting her lip thoughtfully. The thin foil of her skin crumpled under her silver teeth. 'I'm the oldest here. I'm one of the few who were here when you were with our show. But the story of you survives, Brenda.'

'Brenda the Discombobulated Lady!' said Charles the Fox. He sounded almost mocking, but Brenda realized that he wasn't unkind.

'Bring her over here,' said a queer, wavering voice that seemed to come from everywhere at once. 'I want to get a good look at her.'

Then the two friends helped Brenda to her feet and walked her to the corner of the dingy van, where a certain someone was sitting atop a tallboy in a kind of display cabinet. Oh, Brenda thought. *I remember this.* It was another freak. Another star of the show. She never did very much. She just lay in a dry tank, letting people look at her. Half pike, half monkey. She was touted as a genuine mermaid and folks paying for tickets, handing over their hard-earned cash, stepping trepidatiously into the freak show tent, expecting to see a lissom young madam combing golden locks or polishing her shimmering green scales were invariably disappointed. Often horrified. Appalled by the sight of this stitched-together, makeshift, mongrel creature. The *Nonesuch.*

'Do you remember me, my dear?' it said in its quavery, ancient voice.

Brenda nodded.

'Step closer, so that I can see you, darling Brenda. These glass eyes of mine won't swivel anymore. My eye sockets are so dessicated these days I fear if I roll my eyes they would crumble away and then where would I be? I can only see things that are straight ahead and under my very nose, so to speak...'

Brenda stepped closer to this horrible tribute to the artfulness of a twisted taxidermist. She must have been over a hundred years old. Matted and scabbed and faded to the colour of old cardboard. She reached out with one bony paw to clasp Brenda's hand.

'It's wonderful to see you. It truly is.'

'Her memory has only just started to return,' said the fox.

'She'll be very confused,' noted the Nonesuch. 'She was like this before. She ran away once before, when Diodati's Show was in Paris. You had a little adventure then, down by the Seine, do you recall? You were hobnobbing with Phantoms and Hunchbacked men down in the catacombs, my dear. Messing about with the undead, as you were wont to do. And then Doctor Diodati found you, recaptured you, and brought you back to your friends. It was a long time before he let you out of his sight again.'

This monkey-faced effigy was gabbling away like mad, and Brenda wasn't really following what she was saying. Half-summoned memories rose and fell and frittered away. She couldn't remember being in Paris. She didn't really know what this creature was talking about.

'But the second time you ran away. That was in the North of England. That was with Joseph. And the two of you were successful. So successful that you eluded our master's grasp. Oh, he was fuming. He's been fuming for a full thirty-five years, Brenda. He'll be everso delighted that he's managed to find you again and draw you back...'

Brenda's hackles were up. Her heart was thudding. Even before the sense of what the Nonesuch was saying sank into Brenda's thick old noggin, she had realized that she was in a trap.

And yet at the same time Brenda was thinking: *Joseph.*

She escaped from the freak show with Joseph.

She knew that name. She remembered him. She knew who he was, didn't she?

The Nonesuch was laughing by now. Her dried-out fish scales were crackling as her sides heaved with unaccustomed mirth. Her skinny fingers clutched her bulbous head, clawing at the scrappy fur. 'He punished us, Brenda. He punished us all because you got away and got your freedom. The two of you. Running about, free as you please. Devil may care. You never spared a thought for us, did you? You never cared a hoot for all the freaks you left behind. We were at his mercy, Brenda! And *Doctor Diodati has no mercy...*'

Just then, as the dessicated monster's ranting reached a crescendo, there was a vast roar of applause from outside the van. From the Big Top, of course. The show had reached its climax and the audience were demonstrating their approval. For one bizarre moment it felt like they were responding to the Nonesuch's performance.

Brenda stood up abruptly. She couldn't stay there listening to this all night. 'I have to go. My mistress... Evelyn. She'll be leaving the tent, if the show is over. She'll be looking for me.'

'Of course,' Foxy-faced Charles gave her an ironic bow. 'You must hurry to your mistress' side, at once.'

'You'll never get away,' said the Nonesuch weakly.

'Brenda,' said the Gold Leaf Princess. She sounded kindly. Her voice chimed like the workings of a carriage clock. She took Brenda's work-scarred hands in her own smooth ones. 'I didn't expect her to say those things. I didn't mean for that to happen. I thought it would be a pleasant reunion. Of course none of what she says is true, you know. It isn't even the same Doctor Diodati. The old man died many years ago. They aren't looking for you. Almost everyone – apart from we oldest performers – have forgotten who you are.'

This made Brenda feel a bit better. She told her so.

'You are quite safe,' she smiled, shuffling elegantly towards the door and leading Brenda back into the hurly-burly of the dark, where the crowds were streaming out of the illuminated tent. 'You are safe in your new life, Brenda. No one can spoil it. Nothing from your old life can come back and haunt you. I promise...'

*

When Brenda found her mistress Evelyn again she looked at her strangely, but Brenda didn't tell her anything about her absence. They wove through the murmurous throng back to civilization, back to the illuminated streets that they knew. All the way Evelyn told Brenda about the climax of the circus extravaganza, which she had missed. 'They made the elephants dance, Brenda,' she said. 'It was the most amusing thing. Dance of the Sugar Plum Fairy. And there they were, these behemoths, turning pirouettes on their tippy-toes...'

Brenda couldn't help scowling. She was glad she missed it. 'I always thought it was cruel. Making animals act like fools.'

Evelyn studied her briefly. 'Oh, we are in a bad temper, aren't we? What's the matter with you, dear?'

Brenda shook her head. She needn't be rude to her mistress. They had reached a new level of understanding of late, and Brenda oughtn't take it for granted or jeopardize it. 'I'm just tired, that's all. It's been a very long day.'

'Aha.' Now they were back in the walled lanes that looped about each other between the tall, gracious houses. They walked under the leafy canopy and linked arms against the dark. 'It isn't really cruelty, you know,' she told Brenda. 'They are only beasts. They don't know any better, I'm sure.'

Brenda knew she was wrong about this. She gritted her teeth, and didn't say anything.

Just then they were overtaken by a figure who bustled past. Strangely, they never heard his footsteps at their heels. They both gave a little jump. And then another as he overtook them, wading through a pool of lamplight, and they saw that he was wearing one of the rough cowls and cloaks of the monks of Daakholm. Evelyn gripped her arm. 'Brenda!'

But the monkish figure didn't stop to bother them. It hurried on ahead and was lost in the swaying darkness.

'It's all right, he's gone...'

'But they're following us,' Evelyn hissed. 'They are following us from the Other Place...'

Brenda nodded. Yes, it seemed to be so. Someone was keeping tabs on their doings.

And then, all at once, they were beside the ivy-shrouded door in the wall at the back of the Tylers' garden. Home again.

*

The next day it was clear that the old Professor knew where they had been to in the night. He was quietly furious over breakfast, hacking away at his soft-boiled egg with more force than was required. Brenda hovered around in the breakfast room, aware of the crackling tension between his Nibs and Evelyn, who was trying to remain serene and ignore his bad mood.

Eventually, mouthful of runny yolk, he couldn't hold himself back any longer. 'To be frank, I thought you had run away again.'

'I beg your pardon, darling?' Evelyn buttered a tiny triangle of toast.

'I sat there for hours in my study. Listening for the door. Hearing nothing at all but the creaking of the house. I realized I was utterly alone.'

'But that's how you like it, isn't it? Lots of lovely hush. And then you can concentrate. That's what you always say. You can't have it both ways, Reg.'

His face contorted with anger. Then he deliberately calmed himself and stared hard at her. 'Where did you go?'

She returned his gaze. 'Just out and about.'

Brenda started to collect up their dishes. Clattering noise. Bustling. Anything to break the tension between them. She could have cried out *Allelujah!* when there came a hearty knock at the front door. She hurried to answer.

Why was Professor Tyler so dead against the fairground folk? It was a rum do. When they visited in the spring – the usual, more conventional show people – he was never exactly chuffed as muck. But he was never like this. Brenda wondered what he knew about Doctor Diodati and his show folk? And what he could have had against them.

How she wished she could remember more. The previous night's stirrings of memory were quite alarming. Things had started to return to her. But as soon as she stepped away from the Gipsy Green, her unconscious (was that the correct term..?) stopped its bubbling and its belching. Nothing else came back to her. And the bits already back seemed far too outlandish to be real. By the following morning Brenda was already doubting the scenes she had been privy to, and also the people she had met. That elegantly fanged foxy person with the rancid breath. The friendly girl made out of crumpled gold leaf, wearing thin. 'Family Assortment' printed in blue letters down her face. Had all of that actually been real?

Snow had been falling ever since Brenda had served breakfast. It lay evenly on the front garden and the street beyond. It had settled on the shoulders and hats of Professor Cleavis and John, who had set off early, it appeared, to pay the Tyler home an unannounced visit. Brenda couldn't help but be delighted to see them again, especially John. She felt like they were veterans and colleagues from an adventure. Yes, that was exactly what they were.

'And good morning to you, too, Brenda dear,' grinned Cleavis, stamping his feet in the hallway and unwinding his snow-crusted scarf. John followed him into the Tyler household, looking sheepishly friendly as ever, his cheeks gleaming red with healthy exertion. Oh, Brenda did like these two. There was none of the snappish back-biting and tension she was used to with the Tylers. She wondered if they would let her come and work for them instead?

'In the dining room, are they?' Professor Cleavis surged up the hall, quite at home barging into Brenda's employers' breakfast time. 'Reg? Are you there? Look here, we've got to do something about...'

John shrugged and smilingly handed her his coat and woolly hat, laying it on top of his friend's snow-coated Ulster. 'And how are you doing, Brenda? Back to normal?'

She almost broke out laughing. 'Normal? Round here?' Was he joking?

Already there were raised voices in the dining room. Whatever they were discussing, the two professors were doing it very loudly.

John lowered his own voice. 'Erm, does he know? Tyler? I mean, what have you and Evelyn told him? About our adventure in Daakholm?'

Brenda was about to answer him when Evelyn emerged from the dining room, patting her hair and noticing John with a beaming smile. 'Hello, stranger!'

He blushed. 'Good morning, Evelyn. I was just asking Brenda whether you have told your husband anything about...'

'Him!' she snorted. Quite a vulgar snort. 'I haven't told him anything. He doesn't even really care. He wouldn't understand, I don't suppose, even if I told him where we ended up.'

Now the voices in the dining room were even louder and more forceful. Someone bashed their fist on the table, making the breakfast crockery clatter. 'Brenda, you'd better go and clear everything up,' sighed Evelyn wearily. 'Otherwise they'll smash things. Can you believe it? They're arguing about the Gipsy fair! I mean, how ridiculous. Shouting about an innocuous, funny thing like that.'

*

So Brenda beetled about her duties, clearing away breakfast, as the two Professors talked loudly to one another, and Evelyn and John conferred in the sitting room, leaving her out of things. Brenda was feeling quite miffed as she loaded up the hostess trolley.

'You saw it with your own eyes!' Cleavis was bellowing. 'My... assistant vanished. He disappeared where he sat. Taking the armchair with him...'

'I saw nothing of the sort,' Tyler shouted back. He glared at his colleague. 'Your assistant - as you style him - simply left the room while no one was looking. While everyone was focused upon listening to my reading.'

'No, no,' Cleavis snapped. 'I *saw* him vanish into thin air. Others among the Smudeglings witnessed it too. John literally faded out of existence. Also, I have his word about it, too. He has told me exactly what happened during his time away.'

'Time away?' Tyler sneered. 'Poppycock!'

The shorter professor was exasperated. 'And... he was *there* with your wife. He's told me all about it!'

'What?' shouted Tyler. 'With Evelyn's mother? In Scotland?'

This knocked Henry Cleavis sideways. '*Scotland?*'

Tyler shot Brenda a glance and she realised that she was standing there with her mouth open, a fully-laden hostess trolley before her. 'That is where my wife claims you and she went to, is it not, Brenda?'

Brenda couldn't say Evelyn had lied to him. She had to back her up. 'Er, yes sir. We went to visit the mistress's mother.'

Tyler looked at Cleavis with a triumphant look of, '*See?*'

'Rubbish!' cried Cleavis. 'That's not what John says! He says the three of you spent some time together in another world, another dimension, another place entirely, tangential to this one.'

Tyler let out a curious, huffing noise and waved his arms at Brenda, 'Get back to your duties, my dear.'

And so she was forced to leave them to it.

By the time she trundled the trolley into the kitchen, put the hot water kettle on the hob, and returned to the sitting room, Evelyn and John were as deeply in conference as the two Professors. They were a bit more harmonious, though.

'Brenda, dear, bring us tea would you? And biscuits? We have much to discuss.'

In the kitchen Brenda waited for the water to boil, and the tea to brew, reflecting that she would much rather be in Daakholm again. There, she had been no one's servant. She was just as equal as everyone else, and they even wanted to hear her opinions about things.

While the tealeaves mashed together in the big brown pot she nipped outside to take in the frosty morning air, sitting on the bench by the back door. Last night she had been someone as well, she thought. Even here in the everyday world. Meeting the freak show folk. They clearly thought she was something. She was someone special. She wasn't just the lumbering chief cook and bottle washer.

Just then she noticed she was being studied by a robin, who had come to land on the other end of the bench. He was standing in the thick crust of snow and his head was on one side. Quizzical-looking. Brenda was about to say something to him, amazed by his braveness in standing so near, when she noticed there was something attached to one of his thin legs. A fluttering piece of paper, tied with a knotted strand of wool. Bit like a label affixed to a parcel. On it there was some writing, the scratchy sort of writing that Professor Tyler did with his messy, splotchy nibs. But why would he be labeling the birds? It didn't make any sense. Brenda narrowed her eyes and leaned closer, trying to read the tiny words.

The robin took fright and jumped into the air. He circled her head and fluttered down the garden path. Before she knew it, she was on her feet. For some reason she was following it through the snowy garden, down the covered path, between the stark fruit trees. The robin landed on the green bark of the apple tree and caught his breath. Now Brenda knew she needed to read that scrap of paper. It was important. It was surely a clue to something. It would impart some important information that she would be able to take indoors and tell the others, and they would all be amazed...

Of he went again, in a little rush of scruffy feathers. He might be about to take to the skies at any moment, and shake her off. But he was going in little leaps and bounds, checking that she was still coming after him. Playing a game with her. But Brenda was determined. Now he was on the tall garden wall. Directly above the gateway that she and Evelyn had used last night on their circus jaunt. It was clear he wanted Brenda to leave the garden.

He took flight again and she unlatched the gate and shouldered it open. The frost had welded shut it overnight. Then she was in the alley, which had been smoothed completely by fresh snow.

She couldn't see any sign of her little friend and his strange note.

But two clowns with horrid black and white faces were standing there in full regalia. Snarling at her.

One made a grab for her.

She cried out in shock. The other was behind her, taking hold of her arms.

'Wait! What are you doing? Who are you? Get off!'

She was shouting any old rubbish. Just to draw attention. Just to bring others running.

The clowns were eerily silent. The air filled with plumes of hot breath from the three of them as they struggled together. One of them had produced – out of nowhere, like a magic trick – a sack and a rope and they were trying to get it over her head. This made her panic terribly and she resisted them with every fibre of her strength.

This made both clowns start to giggle. They stifled their noise, but they couldn't suppress their mirth. But they couldn't be doing this, could they? Clowns couldn't just take housemaids hostage. They couldn't kidnap her in broad daylight, in a public alleyway, in the middle of the morning. That kind of thing just couldn't go on…

She roared in protest. She lashed out with her clumsy fists. She got in a few good punches and made them reel and stagger about. They exaggerated their reactions, mocking her. She wasn't really hurting them. She wasn't in any danger of escaping from them, she realised. They were wiry and vicious. One produced a small handkerchief square soaked in something that smelled truly horrible as he brought it up to her face and covered her nose and mouth with it, and she passed out into deep blackness, asleep in an instant and falling face forward into the snow…

*

She slept a very strange sleep.

There were thick, fuggy fumes that wouldn't disperse. A fog that rose up from a river, somewhere nearby, cloying at her. A darkness that never lifted and a headache that plagued her for what seemed like years. Her whole body ached. She remembered these sensations. She used to feel like this all the time. But when was that? What kind of person was she then?

She just didn't know. Images, faces, ideas went flitting horribly quickly past her mind's eye. Her very confused mind's eye. Part of her felt like simply giving up and wailing and letting out all the tears of despair and everything she had keen hidden deep inside for all these years. *Just take me. Do what you will with me. I'm fed up with running away...*

But she also know she couldn't do that.

She opened her eyes and she was lying on the floor in a candle-lit room. There was a smell of exotic incense curdling in the air. It was masking something nasty. An animal smell.

It was a very fine, Arabian carpet she lying on. Musty and intricately-patterned. She wished she could mutter the correct magic spell and order it to carry her away.

But she couldn't. And it was just then that she realized that a rather large gentleman was sitting in a chair and staring down at her. He was buffing up a shiny top hat with the frilly cuffs of his evening shirt.

Brenda stirred miserably and attempted to sit up.

How like his own father he looked. That's what the Gold Leaf Princess had said, hadn't she? This was Dr Diodati's son, all grown up. Looking very much a chip off the nasty old block.

His grin was lascivious. He was very pleased with himself.

'You are quite a prize,' he said, in a tremulous, excited voice.

'Am I?' She tried to stand up. She was wriggling helplessly on the ground on her belly, like the serpent in the garden of Eden. She couldn't get up. She was tied and bound up like a bomb disguised as a parcel and she couldn't unwrap herself at all.

'I grew up hearing all kinds of amazing things about you. The star of Doctor Diodati's Freak Show. You broke his heart, you know. My father's. When you ran away. He did everything for you. You and that other one.' Diodati Junior was sneering, his face blazing with hatred. 'And how did you repay him? By breaking out. Not even leaving a note. Absconding into the night.'

There was a pause. Yes, yes, she could remember this. Even lying here, belly to the floor, all tangled up in her cardigan, with rough old rope cutting into the flesh of her ankles and wrists, she knew what he was talking about.

The tents had been set up on the smooth green fields by the cliff tops. They were at the very edge of the coast. Tynemouth. Where the North Sea was wild and noisy and the whole place felt so violent and steeped in history and the big ships sailed into the harbour. And she told Joe... *if we could just slip away, one night when they least expect it, it's only a couple of miles to the docks and we could be away before any of them even suspected...* Yes! She could picture this now. Feel it. That freezing night, when the ice was in the harbour. When the Big Top was thronged and teeming and the freaks were doing their usual carnival parade. *We can be away, Joe. We needn't live like this. We don't have to live like this anymore...*

Diodati's son – the current ringmaster – was looking furious. 'You're not even listening to me!'

All at once Brenda didn't have any patience left. It drained out of her in one go. 'Actually, no, I'm not. I don't really need to, do I? You're only going to rant and rave and brag about how you've been so clever in finding me and dragging me back to your circus. Your tawdry, run-down circus. Which, by the way, you've let get into quite a state since I last saw it. Shabby monkeys and elephants, I thought. The lions look decrepit and the tigers haven't a full gobful of teeth between them. And those clowns are more disturbing than funny. Who in their right mind would laugh at that macabre lot?'

There came a stifled giggle from somewhere in the shadows and Brenda realised that the clowns were present, there with them, in Diodati's private room, listening to every word.

'I try my best,' growled the circus owner. 'For years I've given this show my very best. I've tried so hard. But what would you know? What are you? A housemaid! You've done nothing, accomplished nothing with the freedom you so rudely stole.'

'I wouldn't say that, exactly.' She lowered her eyes to the swirling, dusty carpet. She warned herself to say no more. She would not tell him anything else about her life since she had fled his father's carnival. He didn't deserve to know anything. And besides, what did she even know for sure?

'Anyhow,' he snapped. 'Pleasant as all this chatting is, you must know that I have kidnapped... or rather, invited you here... for a reason.'

'I assume you want to place me back in your power. I imagine you want to put me on show again. The old act. *The Discombobulated Lady.*'

'Oh?' He smiled ghoulishly, as if this prospect hadn't even occurred to him. 'Well, I shall have to consider that intriguing idea of yours. Are you still capable of doing the old act, eh? Would the crowds still be amazed?'

Brenda blushed with fury and struggled against her bonds. There was no worse fate for her, she believed, than to be forced into being the Discombobulated Lady again.

'Actually though, my dear,' he purred, in a seductive voice that reminded her horribly of his departed parent. 'There is something even more valuable that you can provide for me. And I think you know what it is, don't you?'

She ceased her hopeless struggles. 'W-what?'

And really, she hadn't a clue.

Then she thought: *No. Surely not.* Could he really mean *that?*

*

It had never come natural to Brenda, that much was true.

On the days she had to perform she would get very nervous. She would walk the streets beforehand for hours on end. Whichever town they had pitched up in that week, she would wander long lanes and ginnels, as if she was trying to get herself lost. As if, by disappearing into the provinces somewhere, she would never be called upon again to put on a show for Doctor Diodati.

Usually she would return in time. She found her way back to the ragged collection of caravans and trailers, where her friends and the animals were living this week. She knew she mustn't ever let them down.

When she walked the streets her stomach would churn. Her blood would stutter through her veins and her ears would sing with dizziness. When she walked she wore a heavy hood and cowl and her cloak trailed on the path behind her. She was a mystery woman in a purple cloak. She didn't like strangers to look at her. But they all knew she hailed from the circus anyway. Everyone who saw her knew at once she was from the show and wore the hood to cover up her freakishness.

Sometimes she would stop at a public house and take a quick nip of something strong to quell her nerves. The old men standing round her would shrink in her presence. She stood so tall. She looked for formidable. She could down a pint of murky bitter in three seconds flat.

But when she stepped onto the tiny, brilliantly lit stage that night she would be at her most glamorous. The other sideshow performers would gather in the wings to watch her do her thing. All they had to do was shuffle out under the lights and let everyone get a good gander at them. The bearded lady would occasionally sing a rather crude song. But mostly the freaks just stood there, turning round in circles so everyone could see what made them so special.

Brenda's turn was rather spectacular.

It was a kind of striptease. Exotic music would play (the Gold Leaf Princess had a penny whistle, and she was skilful with it) and Brenda would undulate her whole, large body in provocative style. She wore a kind of swimming costume, all of gold and black. Gloves that went up to her elbows. A hefty corset that went on with the help of everyone in the show, squeezing and pummeling her abundant flesh like they were in a tug of war. Brenda onstage looked like a Valkyrie, trussed up and shimmying very slowly on the spot. Every eye in the small tent would be fixed on her slightest movement.

It wasn't quite a striptease in the conventional sense. She was billed as The Discombobulated Woman and that meant something very particular and peculiar.

It was a trick. It had to be, for what she did each night on stage was plainly impossible. Everyone who saw it had to agree, but that didn't stop her doing it.

Quite carefully, and keeping up the rhythm of her sensuous dance, Brenda would gradually *pull herself to pieces*.

Off came her fingers, one at a time. She strewed them on the floor, where they crooked and wriggled and danced of their own accord.

Then she peeled her ears from the sides of her skull and they fluttered under the lights like two fleshy moths.

She unhooked her arms, one at a time, and they bobbed about at the edges of her cone of dusty lumination. Her palms waggled and went all come-hithery and made everyone shiver at the sight of them.

The music would go up in pitch, and get quite excitable when she yanked off her feet, then her legs broke off at the knees. Somehow she still managed to support herself and keep in time to the tune.

Off came her corset, springing open like a Jack-in-the-Box and everyone jumped in response.

Her breasts floated free like gravity was a thing of the past. They tumbled round and round, above the heads of the paying customers, looking just like flotstam and jetsam of starships in space, a hundred years before any such things were invented by Earthmen.

All around her drifted items of apparel. Lacey exiguities wafted about her smiling head. Her head came free of its neck and floated in the shaft of light, bobbing and spinning very slowly. Stockings wreathed and wriggled in lissom fashion, as did her long black gloves.

Her very eyeballs squirmed free of their sockets – in the very final moments of her act. As a final flourish they eased stickily past the clasp of her fake eyelashes and they swirled free of the darkness of her skull.

Then, the music reaching a climax, that darkness reached out to subsume the entire audience. Without fail they were all standing there, agog. Never having seen anything like this. They were each staring straight into the showgirl's skull as its dark interior grew impossibly large and impenetrable. Until it was all that anyone could see.

And then it snuffed out the limelight with a gasp – and Brenda's performance was over for another night.

When the houselights returned every scrap of her would be gone.

The punters goggled and stared. Had they really seen what they thought they had? Surely it was all done with fog and… and mirrors… but there had only been a little icy fog. They had seen everything very clearly, with their very own eyes. They had witnessed the impossible.

They would shuffle out. Dazed. Dazzled. Bedeviled.

Unable to understand where the woman had gone. Had she whittled herself down to her constituent parts and then, into even smaller portions? Had she turned herself into dust, and then blown away? Had she exploded into – though this thought would never have occurred to one of her audiences in the mid 1890s, of course – mere clusters of shining atoms?

The truth was, she had a very nimble stage assistant. He only needed a few seconds of darkness to scramble about that tiny stage. He had a large carpetbag and unerring feel, and lots of practice.

He groped around, knowing where each of Brenda's bits would be. All he needed was a good two minutes of darkness, while the audience were still stunned, to pop every fragment of his employer safely into his bag.

Then it was off to her trailer, to stitch her back together again. Which could be a long job and a fiddly one, requiring superhuman patience. Sometimes he was up half the night, putting her back into one piece with catgut and fish hooks and needles made of bone.

Victor, they called him. He was only twenty four, but very skilled at picking up the pieces.

*

Behind a little ragged curtain, lying on the bunk in his half of the caravan they shared, Brenda's best friend would listen to her describe that night's performance.

Naturally rather modest, Brenda changed during the years her atomizing lady act became popular. She was almost boastful, in fact. Her helper Victor would pitch in, adding bits that she missed out of her accounts, but mostly her voice carried out an interrupted monologue, swollen with pride, about how marvelous her show had been tonight, and how she had blown everyone's socks off.

Her best friend Joe lay propped up in his bunk, three straw pillows keeping him upright. He listened fondly and made all the right noises. But he knew Brenda was becoming too prideful. She was setting herself up for the inevitable fall.

Joe was a veteran of the freak show life. He had been with Doctor Diodati a number of years. And before that, as a much younger man, he had toured the continent – all of Germany, Switzerland, Italy and France. In freezing climes and muggy heat, he had been a part of a show. Traipsing around the sawdust ring with a burlap sack over his head and his feet in chains. Giving them the big reveal. Making them scream out with mingled joy and disgust at the shock of seeing him.

Once he had been the headline act at Doctor Diodati's. Now Brenda had that honour. At first there had been some tension between them, as she superceded him on the bill. But really, he was glad to shrink into obscurity. He was old and his knees hurt dreadfully. Everything hurt. His breathing was worse than it had ever been. When he got up to perform his ablutions – when Victor brought him a bucket and he stood in the shaded lee of his caravan and sluiced himself down – his breathing came ragged and harsh.

He managed to hide the worst of the discomfort and pain from his friends. But since Christmas it had been getting worse. He didn't think he could last much longer in this peripatetic life. But where would he go? He had no money, no retirement fund, no relatives. The doctor who had once shown him kindness? He was way down south. He'd never forgive Joe for running away, and Joe wouldn't blame him for that. How could Joe prefer being a part of a circus sideshow to living at the hospital, visited by the great and the good, prodded and poked and held up for display before learned, fascinated men?

But tonight wasn't the time to dwell on unhappy things. Here was Brenda, full of triumph. Glowing with it, in fact. Victor stitching away and lacing her up. Making her decent again. Joe encouraged her to chatter on and on, telling him about the local audience. What were they like, these people of the north? Different? The same? How did they react to the sideshow freaks? Joe was very fascinated by the differences between folk, in far-flung parts of the country. He loved to study the varieties of people. He wished that he could meet them, talk to them, find out about their lives. But there was little or no chance of his ever meeting and talking to any strangers without his monstrousness coming between them. He was quite used to anyone he talked to fixating on his misshapen skull and limbs. Their words would fail them.

Not so with Brenda, of course. This was one of the reasons he loved her. Right from the very first, when they met in London, all those years ago. She had looked past everything that was wrong with him. She'd seen straight into the real Joe inside.

He smiled, listening to her burble on. She laughed out loud as she described a new bit of stage business to do with her feet, and how she'd set them tap-dancing around the pedestal where she placed her head at the very climax of the act. How the audience had wailed in appalled dismay! How macabre! How *wonderful!* He heard her clapping her newly-reattached hands with glee.

She had such a dreadfully dark sense of humour. Sometimes he wondered where she got it from.

Even as he listened to her laugh his thoughts went back to the note on his lap. He'd crumpled it earlier, on first reading it. Quality vellum. Exquisite hand. Dark brown ink. The note was from Doctor Diodati himself. To the point, as usual. It voiced the very thing Joe had been fretting about. Since before Christmas. Back when he gave his last performance. His least ever spectacular performance. Shambling about, showing the people of Harrogate his twisted spine, his bloated skull. He had been in such excruciating pain, it was as much as he could do. He had been helped away from the stage area by Victor: sweating, feverish, exhausted.

Since then he was supposed to be regathering his strength. Recovering. It was February, though, and Joe knew that his days of performing were over.

And Doctor Diodati's note was telling him – in no uncertain terms – that either he got on that stage and twirled about and let the world get a good gander at him – or he was *out*. What was the point of having an Elephant Man on the bill, dragging him around the countryside, making sure he was watered and well-fed, if no one could ever get a bloody look at him? Surely Joe could see the ringmaster's point?

The thing was, Joe could indeed see his point. Times were tough. Everyone in the show must earn their keep. Everyone did more than one job, just in order to maintain the show on the road. What did Joe do but lie here on his bunk, doing his best to keep breathing; keeping his spirit tethered to the ground, keeping it from fleeing gladly away?

Tonight he would show Brenda the note. He'd have to. Once she was in one piece and dressed and ready to sit with him. When Victor brought their cocoa. Then he would tell her that his days were numbered. And she was his friend. She would know just what was best to do.

*

Victor was outraged when he heard their plan, several days later.

'It's impossible. You can't. Neither of you can do it. You'll be hopeless... You couldn't cope!'

Brenda was beginning to wish she had never told him. The dishevelled young man - dark, grimy, impossible to place by his accent, or guess how old he truly was. For some time she had assumed him to be a friend, and unequivocally on her side. Tonight as they walked along the cliff edge, gazing at the calm North Sea, scrambling around the pale stony lumps of the Roman remains, she realised she couldn't actually take Victor's support for granted.

She had told him that she and Joe were planning to run away. Together. At the earliest possible opportunity. She had assumed Victor would be glad to help. Now she looked at his keen, conniving face and she wondered whether his first loyalty wasn't to Doctor Diodati and his circus after all. Perhaps he had been placed to close to Brenda and Joseph in the first place so that he could keep an eye on them.

I've been a fool, she hissed, under her breath.

The wretched assistant pursued her with questions. Where would they go? What would they live off? How could she make sure that she could look after Joe? He was less and less mobile with each passing month. Surely she could see that? He was never going to get any better. Was she so blind?

'What do you mean?' she snapped.

Victor sighed. 'Joe is dying, Brenda. That's apparent to anyone. Surely you can tell? Can't you see that and hear that for yourself? Listen to the way he's breathing these days. The struggle that he has even to sit up. I've known him a long time. I've been helping him out longer than you've been around. He was never what you'd call the picture of health and vitality... But he's come right down in recent months. If he's talking about running away then he's just deluded. He's getting your hopes up, or you're encouraging him to get his hopes up... either way, it will never happen. For one thing, Diodati won't let it.'

Victor and Brenda returned to the encampment and, sitting with the others, enjoyed a hearty supper. Spicy stew, something like ghoulash. Brenda was glad of it, and the fact that there would be no show tonight. The coastal city's fathers had been quite clear about that. There would be no freak show on the Lord's Day.

Perched at the rough table beside her, the Gold Leaf Princess was pretending to eat. Brenda knew that the girl never really ate, that she never needed to. All that dainty nibbling was just for show. Did that mean she was lined with metal inside, too? Brenda sometimes wondered whether it meant that she wasn't actually human at all. The cool, beautiful girl turned with a jangling, chiming noise to look at her dinner companion and frowned.

'You'll never get away with it,' said the Gold Leaf Princess in her quietest voice.

Brenda's tired heart slipped inside her chest. Did everyone know her secret plan?

'I tried to get away once,' said the princess. 'I tried to flee. We were in Paris. This was a long time ago. A gentleman asked me. He said I shouldn't be on show like I was. I should be treasured by just one man. Him, he meant. We made preparations and plans. I was to be at the station. I remember its name. The Garr Doo Norr. It was a snowy, foggy night. And I was there. I managed to get there by myself, under my own steam. I was ready waiting, just before the ticket booth. Hardly anyone else was there that night. And I waited and waited.

'But my gentleman never came. Hours I stood waiting under the steel arches. Hearing trains shrieking and whistling and heading off down to the tracks to distant locations. Eventually someone came to see me. It was Diodati. Out of breath. Angry. Or rather, like someone who has been tremendously angry, but who is now exhausted with it. Who has come running through the night. He came up to me and said my gentleman would not be joining me. Diodati had seen him face to face earlier that very evening and... he had *dissuaded* him.

The Gold Leaf Princess was crying now, over her untouched bowl of food. No tears fell from her eyes. But her emotions were no less real for that, Brenda thought. She could hear them ringing and chiming through the girl's empty body.

'Doctor Diodati wants only the best for us. He knows how to look after us. He knows we wouldn't ever survive on our own out there, in the world by ourselves. Look at us...'

With that the girl gestured to the other carnival freaks bowed over their meals. Mingling with the clowns and the able-bodied, they no longer stood out as all that different in Brenda's eyes. She was used to the sight of them all. But they *were* different, she knew. Hairy or scaled, with too few limbs or too many, the wrong size or shape. Misfits all. Out in the world they would be conspicuous and vulnerable.

'Sometimes... I think that there must be other worlds besides this one,' sighed the biscuit tin princess. Her voice was like wind chimes in Brenda's ear. 'Worlds where different kinds of people live and no one thinks it's odd. Worlds where all the people aren't the obvious shape, or obvious in any way at all...'

There was only so much sitting around feeling wistful that Brenda could take. She was a practical woman of action, and always had been. The Gold Leaf princess was sweet, but she was hopeless, really. She was a doll. A demented, dented plaything who would never do anything to improve her own lot.

Brenda's mind was made up. And it would have to be that very night.

After supper she went to see Joe in their caravan. He was slurping his own bowl of thin soup. Victor sat with him, spooning it up and looking impatient.

Brenda told them: 'Soon, then. My mind's made up.'

*

Even though she disapproved and thought it was probably hopeless, the Princess agreed to help them in the end.

Word had gone round. All the sideshow freaks were pitching in. It would all happen immediately after the freaks' parade during the Big Top show on Monday night. Marvin the Man Mountain was going to take a nasty tumble, just as they were completing their circuit of the ring. He would fall disastrously, loudly, and take several others with him. Clowns would be trampled underfoot. Even the Nonesuch agreed to help, suggesting in her ethereal voice that, perhaps, the waterless tank she was wheeled around in might be tipped – gently - to the ground.

Brenda was touched by all their suggestions. No one really wanted her to leave. After this many years she was such a fixture. They even loved her. But they could see that she needed to get out.

When they came to say goodbye to Joe, they realised that this was the best thing for him, too. Being on the road all the time was killing him. He sat up in his bunk, his cloak drawn up around him, his great big velvet cap draped over his skull. They each in turn gazed into his tremendously wrinkled, wise yellow eyes and saw that he had to be away from here. Away from servitude and pleasing others…

Victor had it all planned. He had family that he belonged to, here in this smoky town, by the docks. Serried rows of little orange houses marched in stiff lines underneath the railway arches. Somewhere down there, in the salty smog of South Shields lived his Aunty Liz and her brood of kids. And they had one back room kept for best. Joe was welcome to come and use it, for as many days as he liked.

Victor's Aunt Liz had been to see the show and, she said, she would do anything to help. 'Eee, my heart went out to the poor ugly fella,' she said. Victor reported her words back verbatim. 'He can't have had an easy life of it, shuffling about like this with his hump and his wonky leg and that. And so anything I can dee to help, I'm more than happy to, wor Vic.'

Victor pointed out that his north country relations were much warmer-hearted than he was.

Somehow a hefty wheelchair was conjured up from an orderly who worked at the General. A rag and bone man's cart was scheduled to appear on the green by the cliffs during the performance on Monday night. Brenda and Joe would be hurried out and placed carefully atop the cart with all the other bric-a-brac and junk and covered with a snug tarpaulin for the short ride into the depths of the town. It would be perfectly straightforward, if not easy.

All that was needed now was some kind of distraction concerning the Ringmaster.

True, they could have waited till he was doing his patter in the ring. He spoke sometimes for more than five minutes at a time between acts. But when he wasn't onstage he was smoking cheroots outside the tent, whipping his staff into action as they came and went out of the tent, and listening hard to the roar of the applause and the laughter, frowning as if he was listening to important news from faraway.

Rather than playing guessing games with his schedule, the Princess took matters into her own hands.

'I will seduce him,' she announced, to the gathering of freaks who were making plans on Sunday night.

There was a sharp inhalation from everyone.

She was beautiful. She was untouchable, too. In those days she was much slimmer and more streamlined than in later days. She had the figure of a young girl. It was well known that many had come lusting after her and that she had repelled them all. She wasn't quite real. People didn't even know if she was made of flesh. She was more like an exquisite kind of wind-up doll.

Which, it turned out, is exactly what she was. Much older, too, than anyone knew. She hailed from the days of the Napoleonic wars and had been a gift sent to the Emperor himself by a foreign head of state. Even the Princess herself couldn't remember who, or what had become of the man who had first offered her as an exquisite token.

She had passed through any number of collectors' hands in all the vast spread of time since. Her life in recent years, as one of Doctor Diodati's freaks, was the least luxurious her existence had ever been. She never said as much, but everyone could tell she was used to better.

Everyone knew she was a good girl. No one had touched her, though many had tried. It was rumoured that her unique metal shell had one or two hidden features that allowed her to forcibly repel unwanted suitors.

Diodati had longed for her ever since clapping eyes on her, she knew. He'd do anything to get just a bit closer.

Tonight – that Monday – she had decided that his luck was going to be in at last.

She dropped him a note in her tidy handwriting. (She had raised type on each fingertip, and an inky pad. People loved this about her. In her little sideshow booth they would watch as she made message cards for them, the illiterate poor. These were treasured items: billets doux from the golden clockwork girl.)

Her hand-typed message told Doctor Diodati that at last his boat had come in. Here atop the cliffs of South Shields. She had seen the way he had been watching her. She was crumbling at last, like the cliffs themselves under those brutal waves. He must meet her tonight at seven forty five, while the show was underway, and the freaks were marching round to the accordionist's usual wheezing repertoire.

'Are you sure you can do this?'

The Gold Leaf Princess wouldn't go into details about it. 'Yes, of course, Brenda. Just you two get yourselves away. And never let the Carnival of Doctor Diodati catch up with you again.

'You will never, *ever* be able to escape twice.'

CHAPTER SIX

Henry Cleavis had to agree with his colleague, Reg Tyler.

'It's only a fair,' Evelyn protested. 'You are both being very snobbish and silly about it.'

Cleavis knew better. He knew more than she did. At least, he thought he did. 'No, no, you see, my dears. There is a glamour there. *Suffusing* the place.'

Evelyn was stacking their tea things on a tray, rather brusquely. 'What does that mean? A glamour?'

Her husband pursed his lips and handed her his plate of untouched Madeira cake. 'He means a magic spell, don't you, Henry?'

'I do. I'm afraid that's exactly what I mean. I went there this afternoon, for a little shufti around the grounds. And I didn't like what I saw at all.'

John was surprised by this. Why didn't he ask me to come along? he wondered. It was rare that John didn't get invited on one of Henry's investigations. 'What did you see?'

'A circus in decline. Poor folk eking out a living in shabby caravans. And I must say, I wasn't particularly happy with how the animals were being cared for either. They looked rather malnourished and mangy to my inexpert eye.'

Tyler was thoughtful. 'Then perhaps we can put a stop to them by appealing to the authorities. Have them shut down as a menace to public health? Or animal cruelty.'

'You'd have them shut down?' Evelyn gasped, carrying the heavy tray awkwardly. In the days since Brenda's disappearance she'd had to carry out any number of domestic tasks herself, and she was getting mightily sick of it.

'Put the kettle on again, would you, my dear?' Cleavis asked her. 'I think this may be a discussion requiring a second pot of tea.'

*

While the good woman was out of earshot (crossly spooning dry leaves into the giant brown pot) Cleavis told the other two his major discovery of the afternoon. 'Knowing that they are friends of a sort, I hardly liked to mention this in front of your lady wife, Reg. But I saw *that woman* on the Gipsy Green. Catriona Mackay. The Hexford Dean's Secretary.'

'Oh yes?'

'All dolled up and trolling about as if she hadn't a care in the world. Completely at home amongst the shambling circus and fairground folk. All duffled up in a very extravagant fur coat.'

'Anyone can go to the fair,' John pointed out. 'You were there yourself.'

'She was up to no good. I watched her. She was meeting with the owner. A swarthy, foreign-looking chap. Ridiculous moustache and beard. Top hat, the works. They looked thick as thieves to me.'

Tyler was still pursing his lips. 'These vagabonds. The city could well do without their type. Their influence isn't a good one. The students are going in great numbers to their horrible shows, every night. People were yawning in my lecture this morning. Would you credit it?'

John had to suppress a smile at this.

'They're up all night. Enjoying themselves on the Gipsy Green,' Tyler said sourly.

'Ordinarily I wouldn't mind,' Cleavis said. 'But for the magic I felt emanating from the place; plus, Catriona's meeting with Dr Diodati.'

'What did they say?' John asked urgently.

'I never got close enough to hear.'

'It's all supposition, then,' John sighed.

'But what about Brenda?' Tyler suddenly asked. 'Where's she gone, eh? Three days she's been away. Evelyn says she couldn't stop her the other night. She begged and pleaded with her. But the silly woman was intent on leaving the house and wandering over to the Green, to enjoy the coarse amusements of the sideshows and to mingle with the common rabble. We're both very worried about Brenda...'

*

Evelyn left their tea mashing in the pot too long and it became stewed. The reason was, she was on the phone to Catriona. Standing in the hallway she cradled the receiver and her eyes widened at what her friend was telling her. She whispered to her. Their voices crackled on the line, tinny, faraway, mingling together. It sounded as if Catriona's words were coming from a thousand miles and years away, even though Evelyn knew she was just the other side of town. She knew she had a phone and a line extension in her very own room. The handset was on her nightstand, right beside her bed in that room at the top of the leaf-shrouded house.

Oh, yes. Evelyn had visited that room by now.

'You know where she is?' hissed Evelyn. 'Then why didn't you tell me before?'

'We don't have time to quibble,' Catriona said patiently. 'Your servant is safe. But she has something we need. Something priceless and important.'

'Brenda does?' Evelyn couldn't see it somehow. What possessions did she have? A couple of worn old frocks. A number of battered old books. Anything worthwhile that belonged to her had been provided by the Tylers, or bought by the wages she had earned while living under their roof. At least, as far as Evelyn knew, this was the case.

'She has a trunk,' said Catriona. 'Brenda has a trunk.'

This was true. A very old-fashioned thing. Clunky, scratched and scarred. Covered in mostly-illegible, peeling stickers from some places Evelyn had never even heard of.

After a few weeks living in the Tylers' attic Brenda had asked permission to spend the day visiting London, in order to fetch this trunk containing her most important belongings, as she put it. Evelyn suddenly remembered the day well. Perhaps ten years ago? She and her husband had been mystified. But what could they do? Brenda was a charity case, but she was entitled to a day out like anyone else.

What could she own that was so precious? The Tylers were intrigued, it was true. Reg even went to meet her at the station that evening, to help carry the thing – something he regretted later – after helping her manhandle it all the way to 199 Steps Lane and then up their several winding staircases to the attic. His flare-up of lumbago had put paid to any further curiosity. The trunk had been installed in Brenda's room and a lace cloth had been placed over the top. It had done as a kind of dressing table for her ever since, albeit a low one. And Evelyn hadn't thought about it for a moment since.

But now her mysterious friend Catriona was telling her – in somewhat urgent, breathy tones – that there was something inside it. Something vital. Something that she and her friend, Doctor Diodati, very dearly wanted to possess. And Brenda had apparently told them that it was quite all right if they came to take it away...

*

Strange, the way Catriona's voice could send Evelyn into a kind of daze. She had noticed this before. It was rather like staring into space, the way she sometimes did, musing on nothing in particular. Then, all of a sudden Evelyn would jolt awake and find that fifteen, twenty minutes had gone by. Dolly Daydreams, Reg had used to call her. Back in the days when he let himself speak fondly to her.

Now she woke into clarity and she was at the top of her own house, stealing about like an intruder. Why was she up here? Wasn't she meant to be serving the men with more tea? Ah yes. She recalled what Catriona had said. She was on a mission for Catriona. Something simple and harmless, and Brenda wouldn't mind. The missing housemaid had given her permission. Evelyn slipped into the housemaid's tidy, spartan room and glanced around.

Still, something at the back of her mind was telling her there was something odd about this. Why was Catriona passing on messages from Brenda? Why hadn't Brenda simply come home? Had the great lummox gone and joined the circus, maybe?

Very carefully Evelyn found herself crouching beside Brenda's makeshift table. She removed the cracked mirror, the claw-footed candlesticks (horrid things), and several pots and jars of thick, sticky make-up and other medical-looking unguents. Yes, the maid's skin was quite bad, wasn't it? She had to slaver herself in all kinds of stuff. She had some awful scars, Evelyn had noticed, over the years, but didn't like to pry into how Brenda had come about such injuries.

Off came the lacy cloth with a little puff of attic dust and below lay revealed the scratched and pitted surface of the travelling trunk. It looked as if it had been floating through the outer reaches of the solar system, Evelyn thought fancifully. Scorched by comets and blasted by the heat of distant planets. Her luggage was mucky with cosmic dust.

What strange thoughts she was having today…

There were chains and a hefty lock. They were rusted and no problem to her. She did quick work with the hairpin she drew out of her golden chignon. She had learned to deal with such piffling obstacles many years ago, at boarding school.

The trunk opened with a really ghastly shriek.

The darkness within was almost palpable. It was as if she could reach in with both hands and scoop palmfuls of it out, like soot or blackberry jam. She would have to dig down and down to see what it was hiding…

'*Evelyn!*'

Her husband's barking cry brought her out of her comfortable spell. Yes – barking. He was just like a tall, skinny terrier. Yapping at her, yapping at her constantly all the years they had been leashed together in marriage. She twisted round awkwardly in her crouching position and saw him framed in the doorway. That Cleavis and the lovely John were standing behind him. All of them were staring at her.

'Evelyn, what are you doing?' cried John, stepping towards her across the thin carpet. Nothing in this room has any colour, Evelyn realised all of a sudden. The carpet and the patterned

212

wallpaper. All had been faded into dull neutrality by the sunlight through the attic skylight and the passing of time.

'I-I didn't think I was doing anything wrong, John...' she stammered, getting up off the floor. The trunk still yawned open before her. It contained everything Brenda had wanted to preserve. Everything that Brenda thought of as precious. And she, Evelyn, had been about to search through it. Was that really so bad?

'I was doing a favour...' Evelyn said. Her voice sounded muddled even to herself, as if she was feeling less and less sure about her mission. 'There is something Brenda needs. I need to find it for her and take it to her...' Yes, yes. That was right. This was all for Brenda's sake. This would help her.

'For God's sake woman,' shouted Tyler, advancing on her. 'What are you yammering about? Have you heard from Brenda, then? Has she been in touch with you?'

'On the t-telephone... a few minutes ago...'

'Steady on, Reg,' Cleavis said, bustling into the room. 'She's clearly upset.'

'*I'm* upset!' roared Tyler. 'There's been nothing *but* upset in this house for weeks! Women disappearing and coming back! Then disappearing off the face of the Earth again! Clowns and carnival freaks roaming the streets! Well, I've had about enough, Evelyn Tyler! Do you hear me?'

John was standing there next to her, speaking gently. She relaxed in his proximity. The tallness and strength of him were reassuring to her, just as they were in the other place, Daakholm, when they visited there in recent weeks. 'Evelyn, you talked with Brenda?'

She shook her head. 'No, no. It was Catriona. My good friend, Catriona. But she knows where Brenda is. And she says she is safe. She knows where she wants to be. But there is something vital that she needs... from the trunk. The trunk that contains all her worldly goods. Everything she has preserved down the years. Her special things.'

John turned, expecting to see Henry Cleavis scowling at the mention of the Catriona person again. But instead he saw that his friend was rummaging around busily inside the dark trunk. He didn't care that this was someone's holy of holies.

Out came strange gee-gaws and souvenirs. Objects and fetishes and items the purpose of which John could only guess at. They were scattered on the bare wooden floorboards as Cleavis searched. Everything was wrapped in dirty rags, it seemed, like relics from the tombs of the Pharaohs. There were puffs of ancient dust and some curious odours as the others gathered around Cleavis, who was grunting with fascination as he uncovered each secret specimen. He held up a withered, preserved primate's paw. The tiniest book anyone had ever seen. A silvery bottle with a tiny lid that made the strangest wailing noise when you held it to your ear. A fresh red apple, impossible preserved. Something that looked very like a ray gun from a Saturday morning space serial. A corn dolly. Voodoo dolls. A hangman's noose. A single baby's bootee.

And right at the bottom of the trunk – wrapped in a faded burlap sack – a human skull. When Henry Cleavis held the thing up for them all to look at, each of them drew in a sharp breath and held it for a few moments as if in horrified tribute. Whoever the skull had belonged to was the victim of cruel and extravagant deformities. The rictus smile and the hollow pits of the eyes still managed to look stricken under the weight of that monstrously misshapen dome.

'This is what Catriona Mackay phoned you up about, isn't it?' Cleavis asked Evelyn. 'This is what she asked you to find.'

Evelyn nodded, dazedly, still staring at the horrible thing. 'She said, look in the trunk. Brenda keeps a skull at the bottom of the trunk, and has done for years. She keeps the skull of the Elephant Man alongside the most precious of her things...'

*

The name 'Elephant Man' meant nothing to Reginald Tyler. He had never before heard the professional name of the Whitchapel freak and the star of the travelling sideshows. All he knew was that he wasn't prepared to give house space to such a hideous thing. He looked upon it with superstitious dread.

'This has been under my roof for ten years?' he said, in a choked voice. He pictured himself helping Brenda with her trunk. Damaging his back in the process and all the while thinking he was doing her a good turn. What kind of woman was she, that she kept things like this in her room? And those other queer relics from her trunk. It all had a whiff of the arcane about it. Something unholy.

Reginald wrested the skull out of his wife's unprotesting grasp. It even felt strange. Rough and pitted in places like cracked concrete, in others, smooth and polished like a beautiful shell. 'If they want this thing, they can have it,' he said decisively. 'I won't have it in my house a moment longer.'

Cleavis jumped up and intercepted him before he headed for the door. 'Wait! Reg, please. Don't be rash about this.'

'Rash?' spluttered the Professor. 'What are you talking about?'

'I only mean that, if Catriona Mackay wants this skull in her possession, then there's more to this. There's danger here. Something untoward.'

But Tyler wouldn't pause to listen to a single further word. His patience had fled. Evelyn, Henry and John hurried down the stairs after him, but he wasn't to be deterred. In the hallway he set the skull on the telephone table and pulled on his heaviest cloak. Through the transom window it was clear that evening was falling rapidly and snow was swirling down. 'Do we have a large bag or something?' he snapped at Evelyn. 'I can't very well go traipsing about holding a deformed skull aloft.'

There was no bag big enough. It certainly wouldn't fit in his briefcase, or Brenda's customary shopping bag. Evelyn found a tartan shopping bag on wheels under the stairs, which their housemaid used on days when she had a larger grocery list than usual. The outsized skull fitted inside quite snugly.

'Please, Reg, think again,' said Cleavis. 'Don't just deliver this into their hands…'

Tyler fixed him with a steely glare. 'You know, I thought that you might have been some help. I foolishly believed that you might have been a kind of ally for me in the midst of the strange things that go on in this town.'

'And so I am, Reg,' said Henry Cleavis darkly, choosing his words carefully as his mind ticked over.

'You're as bad as the bloody women!' Tyler shouted and, with that, he turned on his heel and hurried out through the porch into the evening, pulling the tartan shopping bag behind him.

Evelyn hovered anxiously as flurries of snow came into the hallway. 'Do you think that they'll return Evelyn to us? After he gives them the skull?'

John smiled at her. 'Let's hope so.' Right at that moment, though, he was more concerned with his friend, who was stomping up and down the hall and muttering crossly to himself.

'Did you hear that, John? I'm supposed to be his ally. I'm only here because of my history in dealing with untoward and uncanny events...'

John said, 'But you knew that already, didn't you?'

Cleavis stopped and sighed heavily. 'It would be nice to be wanted – just for once – for my intellect.'

Evelyn Tyler looked from one to the other. 'What are you two talking about? Stop quibbling! We must go after him. We can't let Reg go there alone...'

Cleavis stirred into action. 'You're quite right. We'd best stir our stumps...'

They took only a couple of minutes to wrap up against the advancing night, but by the time they'd crept into Steps Lane it was blowing a gale and the snow was so thick they couldn't see more than two yards ahead of themselves. Reg Tyler and his wheeled trolley were nowhere in sight.

'I've never seen snow like this,' Evelyn gasped, struggling with the stylish snood she'd brought back from Daakholm.

'It isn't natural weather,' shouted Cleavis, looking worried. 'These are rather freakish conditions in more ways than one.'

*

There was no show that evening. There was no need to send the message around the town that the weather was too poor. Everyone could see that for themselves. Snow was gathering on the tarpaulin of the tents and along the unlit beams and cranes of the fairground rides. All the bulbs were off and the Gipsy Green was quieter than it had been for several days. Only the groans and yowls of complaint from the animal trucks could be heard. All the fair folk, clowns and freaks gathered in their own caravans and sat about their stoves, listening to the wind rise in pitch outside.

Brenda sat on a rumpled bunk bed with a mug of Bovril clutched in both hands. She looked at the faces crowding about her in the cramped confines of the caravan belonging to the Gold Leaf Princess. She blinked slowly, taking them all in.

'You were all there. I saw you in my dream,' she said.

'Not dreaming,' said the Nonesuch, who was perched on a small cabinet, sounding piqued as usual. 'They were memories coming back to you. Everything you'd lost or blocked.'

'We weren't all there, of course,' smiled the vampire fox. 'Some of us are too young to remember you. But we've heard all the stories.'

'My friends,' Brenda smiled. 'You helped me... and Joe. You helped us get away. We ran away. You helped us just when we needed you.'

The Princess stooped over the kettle, making drinks for everyone. She looked stockier than Brenda remembered. It was as if the years had seen her adding more layers of metal tissue to her body and limbs and her face. 'And we warned you too,' she said gently. 'We warned you never to get captured again. We said you should get away and never come back.'

Brenda nodded. 'But here I am. I'd forgotten the dangers.'

'You must tell us everything,' said the Nonesuch. 'What has your life been like in the everyday world? You've had more than thirty years amongst ordinary souls... there must be so much you have to tell us...'

Brenda shrugged. Where could she even start? 'To be honest, it's only the last ten years or so that I remember with any clarity, though I do remember living in London, in the house of a very grand lady... some time before the war...' Her voice dwindled away as she heard someone approaching the caravan and thrusting open the door. The chilling wind blew into the cosy room and everyone turned sharply to see who was coming in.

Doctor Diodati stood staring at them all in contempt. He tossed his head arrogantly. His son – his callow duplicate, Tony – was standing beside him, looking uncertain in his shabby greatcoat. Diodati nodded roughly at Brenda. 'She's coming with me.'

*

'Helloooo…?'

Reg Tyler wandered directly into the middle of the encampment. He preferred never to shilly-shally around and so, even with a curious task like the one he had this evening, he marched straight into the heart of things. He struggled through the snowstorm to the hulking, silent mass of the Big Top and poked his head through the flaps.

'Helloooo?'

He sounded querulous. Annoyed. Exhausted, too. The journey through the snow had tired him out more than he'd expected. He'd had to battle almost every inch of the way, dragging the wheeled shopping bag behind him.

The skull inside felt like a dead weight. He almost fancied that it was gaining mass. Deliberately, somehow. As if weighting itself down with dread. Stubbornly resisting being taken from Tyler's home.

It made him shudder to think of this wretched relic being in his house for all this time. He wasn't sure why. There were worse things in his home. Things even Evelyn didn't know about. Smaller skeletons. Stuffed creatures. Things preserved in soupy unguents in jars at the back of his cupboards. Things that had, over the years, caught his fancy.

But for some reason he didn't want this... this hideous elephant's head thing in his home. It gave him a bad feeling.

In fact, he felt rather like Mirabilia and Foulsum as they made their way through the perilous journey that took up the final third of his book. Beset by Gyregoyles amid the loftiest peaks of Valcea, hadn't they been carrying a portion of a long-dead skeleton? Hadn't their quest been all to do with returning the skull to its acolytes in the far northern province of Queng?

A noise. The crack of a knee. Or knuckles.

Someone was in the tent with him, he was sure of it.

Great inky pools of shadow stretched across the ring. The tiers of seats were empty and subtly haunting. As he crossed the sawdusty performance space it was like he could feel a thousand pairs of eyes scrutinizing his every move. But Tyler was quite accustomed to eyes watching him from ranks of flip-down seats like this. When he lectured, however, he was the esteemed expert. He was the great professor and he was used to a respectful hush and automatic respect. This quiet sounded somehow mocking. The invisible audience members were watching him like they would watch a clown, waiting for him to slip or do something ridiculous.

Oh, stop it, man, he cursed himself. That ludicrous imagination of yours. Always playing tricks. It's like a curse on you. You can't help making things up... even when you really don't want to...

He crossed the wide ring, shuffling leadenly through the sawdust, which was pale in the fitful light. It felt rather like moving through porridge oats.

That noise again. Yes, definitely footsteps. And breathing. He could hear someone quite close by...

He came to a halt in the middle of the Big Top and addressed his unseen host. 'Very well. Here I am. I understand I have something that you require.'

There came no reply.

Tyler coughed, quite nervously. 'Well, I have brought it. But I insist on a cessation of all... strange and hostile actions. I insist on the return of my housekeeper. A-and no more funny business with the clowns, or people dressed up as toad men and whatnot. D'you hear?'

By the end of this speech his voice sounded shrill and defiant. I sound so old, he thought. Really, who would take heed of me?

A giggle. Somewhere deep in the shadows.

He shaded his eyes. There was a light there. Torchlight, waving about.

'H-hellooo?'

Another giggle. Probably at the sight of him. Clutching the worn handle of the tartan shopping bag.

'Please,' said Reg. 'Just bring Brenda to me. I'll leave you the skull...'

Why was he so scared? What were these people? Just circus folk, surely? Just a common rabble...

His thoughts were drowned out then. Even inside his own head. There came a vast upswell of cacophonous noise. Audience noise. Enthusiastic applause. And laughter. Long, loud, rollicking laughter. Loud as a waterfalls, crashing over him, almost knocking him flat onto the ground.

Reg whirled about in horror. Everywhere he could look, everywhere about him. The audience noise was coming from everywhere at once. The seating banks were suddenly filled. Hundreds, perhaps a thousand pale faces. Mouths open wide with dark laughter.

Thunderous applause. Hideous, cheap music played on an accordion.

And Reg standing helpless in front of them all.

Suddenly he was the star of the show.

*

'What have you done to him?' Brenda hissed.

Diodati father and son stood either side of her and the three of them were watching Tyler's performance from the shadows.

The Ring Master scowled at her. 'Do you want me to promise not to hurt a single hair on your beloved professor's head?'

Brenda watched, straining against her bonds, as Tyler whipped his head about, crying out in rage and terror, turning circles in the centre of the ring. 'What is he seeing?' she demanded. 'What are you doing to him?'

'The big cats are in the rings. The lions and tigers are having a paw at him. Oh, don't worry, Brenda. He can't come to any harm...'

The son, Tony, looked less certain. 'Father, this is unnecessary. And, you know, when we let him go, he's bound to go straight to the police. He could make our lives here very difficult...'

Diodati snarled at his son. The contempt was plain on his face. 'What's wrong with you? Aren't you enjoying this?'

Now the old man was on his knees, panting hoarsely. From this vantage point it was clear that his clothes were soaked through and that his breath was coming raggedly. His face was white with exhaustion and fear.

'Diodati,' Brenda said, in her most furious tones. 'Let him go at once. He has done what you asked. He has brought you the skull of Joe Merrick.'

The circus owner sighed. 'I suppose he has.' Absently, he clicked his fingers and all at once all the tension went out of the air. Just ten yards away from them Professor Tyler flopped face-down onto the sawdust, unconscious.

'Let me go to him,' Brenda begged. 'Let me check that he's all right...'

Diodati waved her away. Then he nodded at his son. 'You go, too. Bring me the skull.'

*

The falling snow revived Reg somewhat as they dragged him out of the tent and into one of the caravans. He muttered and stirred, struggling in their arms. He tried to resist them, but Brenda whispered into his ear: 'Please, Professor – it's only me. I will see that you come to no harm.'

And she vowed that she would. He and his wife didn't deserve any of this bother. This was all Brenda's fault. If the Tylers were involved it was because they had been kind enough, ten years ago, to take her in with no references and no knowledge about her at all.

The grandson of Doctor Diodati was silent as he helped manhandle the prisoner into the caravan. Brenda shot him a murderous glance. 'How can you help your father do this?'

He didn't answer.

'What is he planning anyway?' said Brenda. 'He's got Joe's skull now. Can't he just let us go?'

Joe's skull, she thought miserably, and recalled the horrible, gnawing feeling in her gut just moments before, when she watched Tyler produce the thing out of her shopping bag. That gnarled, almost inhuman-looking object. She herself hadn't looked at it in years. But she had known where it was. She'd known it was safe. Seeing Joe's skull held aloft in the circus tent was like some terrible violation. And she had broken her promise to him. She had promised that the circus would never claim him back.

'What's to stop me stoving your head in?' she snapped gruffly at Tony Diodati. 'I'm stronger than you. I'm stronger than most men.'

'You won't, though,' he said, a little nervously, as he slammed the caravan door behind them.

Brenda slumped onto a flimsy bench, propping the semi-conscious professor beside her. 'What makes you so sure? I could carry this one. I'm strong. We could go right now.'

Tony produced a stubby revolver from under his scruffy jacket. He brandished it half-heartedly, as if he hated having to resort to such tactics.

Brenda bit her lip and swore under her breath. 'What if I said my unnatural hide was impervious to bullets?'

'I know it isn't,' said the young man. Nevertheless, he looked very nervous. A white mouse was peeking out of his top breast pocket. Its pink eyes looked at the charged scene with alarm.

'Have you heard all about me?' Brenda asked. 'From your father? He was about your age when I last met him, when your Grandfather was still in charge.'

'He's told me plenty,' said the boy. 'You ruined the show. Nothing was the same after you... and Merrick... ran away.'

'Is that a fact?' She took the smallest, slightest pleasure in this. After she and Joe absconded she never once wondered about the fortunes of Diodati's show. But her friends were there. The other freaks. The ones who had helped her escape. What if they had all starved and perished? Hadn't she cared? Had she really never thought about their fates?

'There was no big draw,' said the young man. 'People were coming to see your act. They were lured by the legendary Elephant Man. Even when he couldn't do much, they still wanted to see him in the stinking flesh. But the rest of them... they weren't such a draw.'

The Gold Leaf Princess and the Nonesuch. They were still in the show. Brenda had seen them. But everyone else she had met in the past couple of days was relatively new and unfamiliar to her. The Princess and the Nonesuch didn't need feeding, of course. They didn't need much of anything to carry on and they were genuinely miraculous beings. But what of the others? I've scarcely given them a thought, Brenda realised, with dismay. Did they all starve? Were they turfed out by Grandfather Diodati?

All of a sudden she was aware that Professor Tyler was awake. His skinny, bent frame was like a broken deck chair on the bench beside her. 'E-Evelyn...?'

Brenda curled one of her hefty arms about him, supporting his weight. She realised that there wasn't much to him. How touched Evelyn would be, she thought, to know that her old man thought of her name first. But Evelyn wouldn't hear that. Nor would she believe it if Brenda told her...

'Sssh, Professor. It's me.'

'Brenda?' He looked up, all confused. Then his face drained of colour as the memory of recent events returned to him. 'The seats were all full and they were... looking down at me and laughing...'

She patted him and glared at Tony Diodati. 'All a nasty illusion. I think.'

'An illusion?' he said hotly. 'I'm not one to be taken in by illusion..!' He struggled to sit up in his damp clothes. He'll be getting pleurisy, she thought, if we don't get him somewhere warmer than this shabby caravan...

'I must go to help my father,' said Tony suddenly.

'Just you wait there..!' Brenda tried to get to her feet, but it was too late. He was outside, locking and bolting the door behind him.

Brenda swore extensively and colourfully.

'B-Brenda?' frowned Tyler. 'Is it truly you? You seem... different.'

She tossed her head. 'Probably I do.' She made an effort to control her anger. 'Are you feeling all right?'

'I don't know.' A dozen thoughts seem to flit across his face all at once. 'Look here, what's going on? Those circus chaps... and that hideous skull! What on earth were you doing harbouring it in our attic, eh? And why do these... vagabonds want it so badly?'

Brenda sat back down heavily. Maybe she could smash down the door. But in a moment. First she needed to gather her strength... 'It isn't a hideous skull, Professor. It belongs... well, it belonged to my best friend in all the world.'

'A circus freak?' Tyler demanded. He was returning to his usual, querulous, beaky-nosed self.

She laughed bitterly. 'We were both circus freaks in those days.'

He stared at her. 'I hardly know you at all. You... you are using complete sentences, for one thing.'

This really made her guffaw. 'Professor Reginald Tyler! I love you, you daft old clot!'

'I beg your pardon?'

'Amidst everything that's going on – all the violence and weirdness – the first thing that strikes you as untoward is that your housemaid is speaking the King's English for once?'

He frowned deeply. 'You must admit, it's rather unusual.'

'I've been keeping a low profile,' she said confidingly. 'The less anyone knows about me, the better. Especially those I am close to. Or care about.'

'Care about?' he said, as if she had said something peculiar. 'Anyhow, what's all this about an Elephant Chap? That skull appeared to belong to some poor unfortunate who had suffered from terrible deformities...'

Brenda sighed. 'They say his mother was in the circus. A beautiful trapeze artist. When she was heavily pregnant she was trampled by an escaped elephant in the circus ring, during a performance. And there was a curse upon Joe from that day on...'

'Poppycock,' muttered Tyler.

'I'm inclined to agree,' Brenda nodded. 'Anyhow, I met Joe in... I suppose it must have been the late 1880s, when he was put on display St Thomas' hospital in London and I was...'

Brenda was just warming to her theme when there came an urgent clattering at the door. Someone was rattling the locks and bolts.

'He's come back!' Tyler cried.

'I don't think so,' Brenda said, hopping up and listening hard. 'That's not a key they're using. It's an axe!'

All at once the thin door shivered into splinters and it was obvious that Brenda was correct in her surmise. Except it wasn't exactly an axe that their rescuer was using to liberate them. In the shredded doorway stood the gleaming figure of the Gold Leaf Princess, with her blade-like arms held up before her like deadly weapons.

'Bugger me!' Brenda cried out. 'You could never do that before!'

'I've learned a thing or two since then,' smiled the Princess. 'Come on. You've both got to hurry up. They're planning something completely dreadful.'

Tyler was on his feet. 'Good gracious! What manner of being are you?'

The Princess looked him up and down. 'I might say much the same about you. But I trust you're a friend of Brenda's?'

Tyler stammered. 'I – I... suppose so. She's my servant.'

The Princess looked as shocked as her rigid face would allow. 'That can't be true. She ran away from the show. She can't be another man's servant.'

Brenda wedged herself between the two of them. 'I'll explain it all later, Princess. Perhaps, in the mean time, we ought to get away from here? What did you mean by 'something dreadful'?'

The Princess's voice sounded more hollow than ever when she told them: 'Diodati has a new ally. A witch. He has found a witch here in this town and she is going to help him perform the most awful of rites. And it needs lots of blood apparently.' She looked at them both with her brilliant glass eyes gleaming. 'Blood from the two of you. Oh, and Ferdinand as well.'

Professor Tyler didn't get a chance to voice his reaction to her revelations, let alone enquire who Ferdinand might be. The very next thing he knew, he and his housekeeper were being bundled into the tumultuously snowy night and they were surrounded by a whole gaggle of people, whose identities he couldn't quite discern. They surrounded the escapees like a phalanx of bodyguards, shuffling determinedly through the terrible weather. He could only make out the fact that there was a wild variety of heights and sizes of persons, and they were all wrapped up in what seemed to him to be rags.

Brenda had grabbed his arm and was dragging him along and, for perhaps the first time in his life, Tyler felt actually old.

The Gold Leaf Princess marched ahead, unperturbed by the blasting wind. She was like a shining beacon, showing them the way. And yet the Gipsy Green seemed like an endless expanse now. It was as if they would never find their way back to civilisation, as if the storm had disordered their senses and had them walking round in circles.

Reg found himself hoping that Evelyn and the others hadn't foolishly followed him into the night. What would he do if they too – especially his wife – wandered into this freakish nightmare? He prayed that she was at home, bored and cursing his name. At least nothing terrible would become of her…

All at once the Princess came to a dead stop, holding up one of her slender arms as a warning. The raggle-taggle mob following stumbled to a halt beside her and, for the first time, Reg got a good look at his rescuers. A woman with ice crystals hanging from her beard was partially supporting him, and a child-like being with a gnarled old man's face was holding his hand.

'What is it, Princess?' Brenda frowned.

She was answered by a ferocious cry, which cut through the noise of the storm. There was a flash of liquid gold, and then another. Furious, ravenous noises came from all around them and the truth quickly became apparent.

'They've let the cats out,' said a voice behind Reg. 'They're circling us...'

Now the night all around them was rank with the smell of the cages.

The Princess turned to look at them all. 'I never thought he'd do this,' she said, aghast. She looked guilty, as if she knew she had led them all to their doom.

'He can't let the cats eat us!' shouted the Bearded Lady. 'We're his show! We're his livelihood!'

'They're rounding us up,' said Brenda. 'They'll take us back to him.'

Ahead of them materialised the largest of the cats. The oldest and most deadly of all belonging to Diodati's show. Beside him was a woman in pale sable furs. She looked untouched by the storms around her. Even her hair was neat, clipped close to her head. She gazed solemnly at the runaway freak show, and everyone quailed under her stern green eyes.

'Who is that?' hissed Reg.

'I think I know,' Brenda said. 'That's your wife's best friend, Professor.'

He squinted blearily. 'Is it?'

Catriona was looking very pleased with herself. 'What a ghastly night it is. I can't possibly let an old man like you come to any harm.'

He lurched forward, shouting at her: 'Call off your beasts, you witch woman! What the devil do you think you're playing at?'

She laughed at him, looking delighted by his spirit. 'I don't think so, Professor Tyler. We need you, you see. And your friend there.'

Brenda stood protectively at the Professor's side. 'What could you want with us?'

'I'm sorry,' said the Princess in a hollow voice. 'I tried my best. I thought I could help you.'

'That's all right,' said Brenda. 'All you could do was your best. You weren't to know that Doctor Diodati had the infernal help of this... this person.'

'I did know, though,' said the Princess dully. 'Everything has been much worse since she has been involved with the show.'

Catriona was still shouting at Reg: 'You could have avoided all of this nastiness, Professor. All you had to do was accede to my request. I wasn't asking for much. I was very polite. But you wouldn't let me. You wouldn't have the likes of me in your foolish Fellowship.'

The big cats snarled greedily. All that could be seen of them was the odd flash of emerald eyes; a gleam of fang and claw. But it was clear that they were squeezing the circle around the runaways...

'Come back to the circus tent with me,' said Catriona. 'We have a lovely surprise prepared.'

'W-will we be punished?' asked one of the sideshow freaks, sounding very scared.

'Not very much,' said Catriona, producing an evil-looking bullwhip and cracking it expertly above her head. The big cats yowled as one, and shepherded the captives back towards the Big Top.

Behind them, Diodati's circus had come back to life. Defying the storm and the night, the tent was illuminated by pink and orange bulbs. From within came the very familiar hurdy-gurdy music pumped out by the elderly clockwork orchestra. Despite the gaiety, the captives trudged back to the tent with heavy hearts. There was no escape for them. There never would be.

Doctor Diodati and his son were waiting for them in the ring. The black and white clowns laughed at them with every step they took. They laughed soundlessly, pressing their dirty gloves to their painted mouths to stifle the noise.

The big cats padded meekly into the ring and went to sit, one by one, guarding the perimeter. Catriona led her runaways proudly, her face gleaming with triumph. She was white as alabaster, Reg was thinking. How could Evelyn ever have been friends with a creature like this? The malignancy came rolling off her in waves. She was thoroughly, hopelessly wicked.

Brenda grasped his arm. 'I-is that Ferdinand?' she asked.

'Hm? What?' said Tyler, suddenly aware of what she was pointing at. More of those hateful clowns were leading the largest elephant he had ever seen into the ring. The beast looked like it had given up hope.

'Welcome back to the show!' cried Diodati. 'Welcome to the part of the evening in which certain members of our cast are called upon to perform… the ultimate sacrifice!'

*

It was Henry's fortitude and mostly unerring instincts that got them through the storms that night.

None of them was wrapped up warm enough against that piercing frosty wind. Cleavis, John and Evelyn clung together as they made their way through the howling back streets of Darkholmes. The two men tried to shelter Tyler's wife but there was no escaping it for any of them. Plastered with frost and numbed to their core they struggled bravely on, relying on Cleavis's sense of direction to take them to the Gipsy Green which, incredibly, he managed to do.

'There's nothing natural about this weather tonight,' he muttered, as they paused in the lee of a garden wall. 'Someone is trying to keep us away.'

Evelyn looked shocked and close to despair. Her husband had been taken from her: he was lost in this wilderness. All of a sudden she felt very sorry for her years of harping and nagging. If he could have heard what she was thinking, a small, rueful part of her mind decided, he might even be gratified. She didn't want to lose him. Certainly not to whatever unnatural thing was turning Darkholmes into Antarctica.

At last they could see the circus lights, glimmering faintly on the dark horizon. Eddies of sound reached them through the roaring storm. Snatches of hideous, distorted music, and the bellowing roars of starving beasts.

The three took hold of each other and set off across the green, ploughing through the deeply-settling snow…

What will we do when we get there? Evelyn was wondering desperately. What can we do? If there are forces here that can act magically upon the weather like this, what are we going to be able to do against them? Nevertheless, her numbed feet kept moving forward, and her pale hands kept hold of John and Henry's. Thank goodness for them. Thank god these two were her friends…!

*

The candy-striped pink and orange of the Big Top was lurid, almost obscene, against the obliterating whiteness of the snow. It glared at them like a lighthouse and, as Henry led John and Evelyn closer to it, the ululations of the circus beasts became louder and the rise and fall of the cacophonous music came at them in waves. All three were feeling nauseous by the time they reached the buckling canvas walls. It was clear that something within really didn't want them to come any closer.

Cleavis was muttering to himself about the magical charm that was being evoked even as it sought to repel them. 'Perhaps the inverse of what the Circus Master uses to draw his crowds here, hm? The same kind of atavistic pull... but directed the other way around, hm? That's why everyone has been acting so... mesmerized and came here even when they wouldn't normally choose to..?'

With the still-rational part of her mind Evelyn caught the gist of his words before they went swirling off into the wind and she knew he was right. Yes, mesmerized... it was just how she had felt when she had come here with Brenda... what? Only a few nights ago. The night that Brenda had disappeared, leaving Evelyn wandering alone through the packed and heaving pleasure grounds. She had passed faces she knew – neighbours, familiar local people – and no one greeted her. All had been intent and distracted as they jostled through the fair.

There was something unnatural about all of this.

She noticed John and Henry exchanging glances as they stepped up to the rippling canvas walls. There was no opening. Where was the entrance? Buffeting waves of noise made the huge tent thrum with energy, but there was no sign of the entrance nor clue to what was actually going on inside.

John stepped forward, producing from a hidden pocket a sharp blade. Like a boy scout, Evelyn thought, endlessly prepared for any eventuality. She watched as he stepped bravely forward and plunged the blade into the canvas. Like living flesh it appeared to flinch and shrink back at the blade's touch, but John wouldn't be deterred. He lunged forward with all his might and in a few seconds had used his penknife like a dagger, drawing a great slash in the side of the Big Top.

The music was impossibly loud. It blared as if it was going to crush the three of them and grind them into the frozen earth. Evelyn was sure at first that her eardrums had popped. She couldn't even hear herself screaming...

The next thing she knew, the three of them were stepping through the aperture John had cut. And clutching onto the ragged sides. She wished she hadn't screamed at the noise. It was a bit of a giveaway for someone wanting to sneak their way indoors. But the noise emanating from the circus ring was so fierce her shrieks had made no difference whatsoever.

She saw John mouth words at Henry and wasn't sure if he was shouting aloud or not: 'Are we too late?'

Henry Cleavis shook his head grimly and led the way down the dark canyon between the banks of seating. He and his friends were completely covered in snow. Evelyn felt like laughing wildly. We look like snowmen... creeping in from the night outside...

'Oh my...!'

Her hearing was coming back. She heard John's words before she could catch up and see what it was he had exclaimed at.

They stood at the very edge of the bright central ring. From here they could see the circus' full complement of performers arrayed, all in their most garish attire. Clowns, freaks, acrobats. All were frozen and staring at some central tableau. All of them were staring aghast at the spectacle before them.

Evelyn and the others followed their gaze and saw the figure of Dr Diodati in all of his gold and scarlet regalia presiding over a kind of ritualistic or religious ceremony. On a sacrificial altar – a rather small, precarious one – was laid the gargantuan figure of a sleeping elephant. Its wattled throat was exposed to the silver, deadly blade of a high priestess in gorgeous ermine robes. She held the dagger aloft and was intoning some ghastly verses in a shrill voice.

On the sawdust at her feet were two bound and gagged figures. Evelyn recognized Brenda at once and then almost screamed again when she saw that the other was her husband Reg, looking half dead as he lay on the circus floor.

A strange golden cage was suspended between the participants in this ritual. It contained a skull. A hideous, yellowing, slightly familiar skull. The eye sockets seemed to be flashing with infernal life.

The priestess reached the end of her chanting with a final, triumphant screech.

And all the music suddenly stopped. There was silence all at once.

'Ah my dears,' said Catriona Mackay. 'You made it just in time. Do step forward, would you? I'm sure you'll be interested to see.'

*

Evelyn tried to make sense of it all.

'You can't be here, doing this, Catriona…'

Her friend looked amused. 'Why's that?'

Evelyn wanted to say, because it isn't like you. But what did she know really, about her friend? Only what her mother had told her. And, oddly enough, mother hadn't mentioned strange, sinister ceremonies held in circus tents.

'What have I been saying all along?' said Cleavis glumly. 'Hm? The woman is wicked, through and through.'

Catriona laughed at him. 'What gives you the right to say that? You still don't know what I'm endeavouring to do.'

'It can't be anything very... um, nice,' said Cleavis. John stared at him. He looked rather less steadfast in the face of danger than usual. Could it be that this Mackay woman actually frightened him?

Across the way, the ringmaster cracked his whip. 'Enough of this talk! On with the ceremony! I'm keen to see if it will work!'

'Of course it will work, my pet,' sighed Catriona. 'Just let me slit these throats...' Toying with her sacrificial blade in a listless fashion, she spoke down to Professor Tyler, who made various, furious ummph noises through his dirty gag. 'I'm sorry that everything has become quite so bloodthirsty and *obvious*, Professor Tyler. But needs must.'

Was Brenda actually snarling? Catriona and the others looked at her, and she was thrashing energetically against her bonds and making the most disturbing racket.

'It's all very unfortunate from your point of view,' Catriona sighed. 'You're in the wrong place at the wrong time. At least, when it comes to the matter of your survival. However, from the point of view of my plans and my ambitions, you're very much in the right place and quite conveniently located in time.'

'What are you talking about, woman?' thundered Cleavis, recollecting his ire. 'Put down that weapon at once!'

The witch-woman flashed him a look. 'What a pity you haven't been resident in Darkholmes longer, Professor Cleavis. But your blood is of no use to me or this experiment. You haven't lived at the Nexus Point long enough.'

'Drivel!' cried Cleavis, bustling forward, and finding himself held firmly by clowns. 'You're talking absolute rot! Put down that knife at once before you do someone a mischief…'

Evelyn was weeping and struggling against those who held her. 'Don't you dare do anything to hurt my Reg…'

'Your Reg?' scoffed Catriona. 'Really, what do you care about him? Remember all the things you told me, Evelyn? How much you hate and resent him. And yes, how you fear him. How he's ruined your life by locking you up here in this town that you despise…'

'No..!' wept Evelyn. 'I never meant a word of it. I swear, Reg…! That woman put words in my mouth! She had me so that I didn't know where I was…'

Various angry umpff noises emanated from the floor and, at this point, John's attention was drawn by something that none of the others had noticed. They were too busy arguing amongst themselves to see that a woman seemingly made out of metal had positioned herself close to the supine elephant upon the makeshift altar. Unseen by the others, she seemed to be using the flat of her golden hands as blades and was sawing away at the thick tarred ropes that held the creature still…

'Catriona, you can't do anything to my Reg,' Evelyn gabbled. 'I don't know what I'd do without him… I'm not anything without him, whatever I may have said to you before, when I was unhappy and mad…'

'And what about Brenda?' smiled Catriona, waggling her deadly blade. 'Would you be lost without your servant, too?'

Evelyn nodded firmly, and covered her face with her hands. She couldn't take any more of this.

'Catriona, come on!' thundered Doctor Diodati, storming up to where she stood in the limelight. 'We haven't time for any more of this. Prove to me your magic works. Show me everything you promised.'

'I shall,' she told him solemnly. 'It is as I promised. Everything. This is the meeting place for tremendous magical forces. All it takes is the shedding of blood from particular, special beings... and the right invocation...'

'And you will restore Merrick to life?' said the Ringmaster eagerly. 'You will restore my fortunes?'

'Hm?' she glared at him. 'Oh yes. Amongst other things. Yes. This should do the trick...' She advanced on Tyler.

'Noooo!' Evelyn howled.

At this precise moment Ferdinand the elephant realized that the ropes that had been holding him so cruelly upside down were no longer tight about his throat and limbs. He was free to sit up. He blinked his eyes and lashed his trunk about and righted himself. All at once he was aware of the crowd gathered about him, and something queer and murderous stirring in the air. He saw the metal girl backing away from him, looking pleased with herself, and he realized that it was she who had liberated him.

He trumpeted his delight at this turnabout in his fortunes.

'What?' roared the circus master, Diodati. The bane of Ferdinand's life. For some many years he had trotted around at his bidding, lowered himself onto his knees, and allowed this bullying show-off ride around on his back. But no more. 'Wait! We must secure him again... he's... he's got a crazed look in his eye... he's going to... he's going to charge!'

In the very centre of the circus ring under the Big Top at Diodati's long-running show, in the midst of the most violent snowstorm Darkholmes had known for a very long time, Ferdinand the elephant went beserk. He went beserk in a very fastidious fashion, wreaking havoc in a quite localized area. In short, he hurried thunderously towards the screeching Diodati, howling out his lust for revenge down the length of his trunk as he went those few deadly yards. Then he raised up one massive, ancient foot and knocked Diodati to the ground. He took great gleeful pleasure in trampling his oppressor into the earth. This took several moments and there was nothing any of the others could do but watch in appalled horror.

Halfway through the killing of the ringmaster anyone might have turned to see Catriona backing away from the scene of would-be sacrifice. Given the sudden death of her colleague she had decided to give up early on the evening's plan. She slipped backwards, through the crowd of astonished circus folk. Obviously she regretted not fulfilling her ambition of using the shed blood of her captives in order to open up a *hole* in the dimensions. But then, you couldn't have everything. Not all at once. Catriona refused to look upon the climactic events of this evening as any kind of defeat. She was eternally an optimist and, besides, she had further plans to hatch.

So off she went, out the back of the circus tent, across the wind-blown fairground, muttering under her frosty breath the spell that would stop the weather blowing her about so violently.

And meanwhile Ferdinand the elephant, having satisfied himself that Doctor Diodati would never be able to enslave any creature ever again, headed off into the night, free at last.

The humans and circus folk all watched him go, smashing his way out of the tent and making the whole flimsy edifice sway alarmingly. Anything not to look at the remains of Diodati, over which the son and heir was crouching and weeping copiously by now.

*

Several students and locals were witness to the elephant pounding through the streets as the storm blew itself out and the last of the snow came tumbling down in a jumbo flurry. Others snuggled under their duvets, blocking out the noise of the howling wind, convinced that they were only imagining the hullaballoo of an escaped behemoth.

Only one or two saw Ferdinand heading for the river.

And no one at all but ourselves were witness to the rather elegant way he slipped into the dark, sluggish, partly frozen waters of the river, swimming with hefty strokes down into the wintry deeps.

*

It was very late that night when they assembled in the Tylers' parlour. Professor Tyler insisted that he would not go to bed yet. He was a ghastly colour and his wife fretted over him, but he would not be dissuaded. They must talk – the five of them – before dawn came.

Evelyn put a tartan rug over his knee and made Brenda bring brandy for him. Then she told the housemaid to brew a huge pot of tea. Half-dead herself, Brenda lumbered heavily between the rooms, doing as she was told.

Henry and John warmed themselves by the fire. Brenda brought them rough blankets and towels and they sat steaming in their thermal underwear, gradually thawing out.

Evelyn was Queen Bee, wearing a silk Chinese robe and bossing everyone about. They all let her, realizing that she needed to boss them in order to feel sane and in control.

All of them were mulling over the strangeness of the night's adventures.

Brenda stood hunched over the kettle, shedding a tear or two.

'What's the matter?' asked John gently.

'I left his skull there. In all the brou-haha. All that time looking after his last earthly remains for so long... I actually left his head behind in all the kerfuffle of getting away...'

Awkwardly John tried to hug her. She was so large though, even his long, muscular arms couldn't quite manage to go round her. She seemed gratified, however, that he had tried. She finished making the tea.

'Professor Tyler can't deny it all now,' Brenda said, stirring each mug carefully. 'Now he has to admit it. He knows that peculiar things are happening. His writing is making it happen. He has to admit it, doesn't he?'

John stared at her. 'His writing is making it happen?'

'Yes. Making *holes*,' she said. 'That's what's going on. *Holes*.'

'Henry, too?' he asked. 'Do you believe that his writing is having the same effect?'

'I do,' Brenda nodded. 'Help me with these teas. Bring that tin of shortbread, would you?'

In the parlour they discovered Tyler looking distraught. John was startled to see tears running down his face. Evelyn knelt at his feet, looking worried and Cleavis was trying to buck him up.

'Look here, old fellow. Nobody was hurt, were they? We all got away safely...'

But his words pricked at Brenda's rough hide. We're all okay, she thought. But what about the Princess and the Nonesuch? And all the other sideshow performers? What would happen to them after the night's events?

And Doctor Diodati was hurt, of course. Hurt beyond repair. Her mind shied away from the thought of his flattened remains.

'S-should we phone the police, do you think?' Evelyn asked, darting a look at Brenda and then at the carriage clock on the mantelpiece. Somehow it had reached five thirty-five in the morning without anyone noticing. Outside the dark world was smeary with mist and snow. John peered through the heavy parlour curtains and blinked.

'I'll phone them,' he announced. 'I'll say we witnessed... an accident. The accidental killing of the ringmaster. Thank goodness the animal ran away, otherwise they would have it destroyed.'

Funny, he thought, heading for the hallway phone. There's an elephant rampaging about somewhere in the night-shrouded streets and none of us has given it a second thought...

They all took their mugs from Brenda and Cleavis laced them with brandy. 'What a night,' he kept saying, a bit too jovially.

He turned and was surprised to see Tyler's sharp eyes on him, still pink and brimming with tears. The old man's twiggy fingers clutched at the tartan blanket as he told Henry: 'This is why I inveigled it.'

'I'm sorry?' Cleavis frowned. 'Inveigled what?'

'Your new post. Your job. Your being here. I knew... I knew you could help. You had form.' Tyler started to laugh. It was throaty and wheezing and alarmed his wife. 'You'd dealt with demons before. You knew how to rout these monsters out. I had a feeling I would need your help here in Darkholmes.'

Henry nodded. He already knew as much.

Brenda spoke up. 'You've made it worse, Professor Tyler.'

Everyone was startled to hear her interrupt like this. They all stared at her.

'Henry Cleavis has worlds inside him as well. He has monsters and demons inside him, too.'

'I beg your pardon?' asked Cleavis, looking dismayed.

Brenda sat down heavily on a threadbare chair. 'We were all drawn here to live in this town. No matter how much we think we made choices of our own. Ten years ago I walked out on a life I had in London... I was following vibrations in the ether... and they brought me here.' She looked at them each in turn. 'I think we all did. We are all here for a reason, you see.'

Everyone's attention was on Brenda. Evelyn tried to shush her. 'You're tired, dear...'

'No, I must say what I think,' the housemaid said. 'I must tell you what is true. Now, I'm not magic myself. I can't do magic. I can't control magic. But I am old. I'm older than you'd ever believe and I've seen some amazing things. Things like you'd never believe.'

'I think... I'd believe it,' said Cleavis. Right at that moment he would believe Brenda capable of anything.

'Well,' she went on. 'Believe this. Darkholmes is right in the middle of a cosmic disaster. As we've been told by the goblin men and by Mr Tweet and his birds, there are *holes* opening up between the many dimensions.'

'Mr Tweet? What *birds*?' asked Tyler stiffly.

'Sssh,' said his wife.

Brenda went on, as if in a trance. 'The curtains are fraying apart. The breeze is stiffening. Catriona Mackay has told us that.'

'That witch,' growled Cleavis.

'Don't,' said Evelyn, with a sob. 'I still can't quite believe what she was trying to do...'

'We are here as a... a team,' Brenda said, cutting through their interruptions. 'The five of us have been assembled here. Moved like pieces on a chessboard by forces unseen. It has taken these forces many years to put us in the correct positions, but here we are. We are here in order to protect the world we know and also, the worlds beyond...'

Tyler was boggling at her. 'Yes...' he sighed. 'Yes, I see...'

'This is our role here,' said Brenda. 'And we must all recognize this and bond together in our work. Our secret work. As a team of equal members.'

By now John had returned from making his phone call in the hallway. He stood in the doorway, hanging on Brenda's every word, just as the others were doing.

'Monsters will seek us out,' Brenda was saying. 'They will come from every corner of the omniverse, wanting to exploit this strange state of affairs; this very sensitive town. They will come here from our own world and from many others and we must stand in their way. You, Professors Tyler and Cleavis, you Evelyn, you John and me, also. We all must work together.'

John coughed and came fully into the room. 'Erm, sorry to interrupt. But I've talked to the police. They're sending a man out to Gipsy Green, to see what can be done. I think when it's light I'll head over there myself.'

'Good,' Cleavis nodded, still staring at Brenda. 'Did they say anything about the elephant?'

'No one's reported seeing an elephant,' said John. 'It's vanished into the night.'

'Good,' said Henry. 'Well! Did you catch everything Brenda's been telling us?'

John nodded, and turned to look at her. She was opening a large tin. 'Shortbread, anyone?'

CHAPTER SEVEN

'I left you behind, Joe. I did it again...'

Brenda tossed and turned in her attic room in the early hours. She dreamed that Joe Merrick came to see her and he stood there wordlessly, looking disappointed in her.

'I'm sorry, Joe. It was all I could do to get away alive... They were going to cut my throat and bleed me dry. They would have sacrificed me to bring you back to life... Though I'm not sure that would even have worked. But the magic here – it's so strange at this Nexus Point, between the dimensions... who knows? Perhaps my sacrifice would have been worth it. You could have lived again! You might have walked again!'

She wept silently in her sleep, for her friend who she hadn't seen in so long; whose skull she had preserved so carefully in her travelling trunk for so many years, along with the rest of her macabre bric-a-brac.

But even as she slept her memory was doing strange things. It had always been so unreliable. She could remember running away with Joe and hiding in a series of bolt-holes, and living off charity... always trying to get further away and elude notice.

'I won't let them have you, Joe. I won't let them take you and put you on display again...'

To Brenda, the doctors and the ringmasters were all the same.

'Brenda?'

The Gold Leaf Princess came to see her, her innards chiming like the workings of the clock. 'You abandoned us again. You ran away and left us all over again...'

Brenda cried out and sobbed more loudly, but even her cries couldn't wake the other, exhausted inhabitants of 199 Steps Lane.

Evelyn had her own dreams to contend with. She was back among the animal faces of Daakholm. She went back to Woodbegood's Hotel, where she was happily pulling open the wardrobe, expecting to find all the new dresses she had had to leave behind. But when the doors flew open they revealed nothing but a flock of dark, furious birds with razor-sharp beaks. They billowed out of the wardrobe and swarmed about her, filling the small room so that she couldn't even catch her breath...

Beside her in their marital bed Reg was even deeper inside his dreams. He was in Hyspero. Taking tea in the market square where, had he but known it, his own wife had been sitting with her friends not so long ago. He dreamed that he was sipping iced tea and looking at the busy square, keeping a keen eye out for the tattooed guards of the Empress. On the tiled table before him were three children's books, seemingly left there. The name on their covers was the same in each case: his new friend, Henry Cleavis. Tatty, trivial books for children, Tyler thought crossly.

He paid a drab-looking otter his tab and a decent tip, and was about to move off through the market place. 'The circus has gone,' the otter told him, sotto voce.

'I beg your pardon?'

'You'll find that it's done a moonlight flit. Somehow, Diodati's show has whistled away in the night. Every vehicle. Every clown and big cat. Each and every one of the freaks. They've left a big burned patch in the middle of the snowy green. You'll have no more trouble from them.'

'That's a relief,' frowned Tyler. 'But... ah, how do you know this?'

The otter shrugged, clearing the table onto his tray. Picking up the books. 'Want these? No? Oh, it was a little message brought by carrier pigeon. Before you even sat down here. But it had your name on it. You're Professor Tyler, aren't you?'

'Indeed,' said Reg, gruffly. He wasn't at all happy about people – let along messenger pigeons - knowing all about his movements.

Then Evelyn was shaking him awake. Her fingers were very cool on his arms. 'Reg? Reg! Can you hear that? In the attic? I think Brenda's taking a funny turn...'

There was the most ghastly row coming from the servant's quarters.

*

Tyler was surprised to see his wife nipping up and down the stairs, taking milky drinks to Brenda and telling her to stay in bed.

'You ought to stay in bed too, Reg,' she told him, bringing him an execrable cup of tea, and slopping it in the saucer, and over the books on his nightstand. 'Sleep all day. Get your strength back. You and Brenda both had quite an ordeal...'

Tyler nodded and reached for his glasses. As he moved he remembered what the otter had told him in his dream. Diodati's circus was gone. He knew that it must be true. Reg was quite used to believing the communications in his dreams implicitly though, of course, no one knew this. If they knew it, they'd think him mad.

Ah, but this was the time that things were coming out into the open, wasn't it? That was what the others believed, anyhow.

He thought about Brenda's long, peculiar speech last night. Talking about Nexus Points, *Holes* and other dimensions. Things had come to a pretty pass when even domestic servants seemed to know as much about the workings of the worlds as he did.

He needed to make some notes. He needed to write things down before they faded from his mind. He felt around on his nightstand for his papers and pens…

*

Evelyn was pleased with her own efficiency that morning. While the world was still and silent outside she set about reclaiming her house and kitchen and tending to her two patients upstairs. Perhaps she could even make some porridge or somesuch.

When the phone rang she was passing through the hall on her way back upstairs and she was startled to hear the complacent tones of Catriona at the other end.

'My dear, I hope you're all right,' her friend said.

'What?' Evelyn could hardly believe Catriona had dared to phone. 'What are you doing? After what you did last night? After…'

'Yes, I know. And I am sorry, Evelyn dear. But things became rather complicated. Sometimes, you see, we find ourselves having to do certain things and act in ways that go against one's nature. Some difficult nights we have to make strange choices… and last night, for me, was one of those nights.'

'You're telling me!' said Evelyn hotly.

'Now, now, Evelyn,' said Catriona. Evelyn could imagine the way she was smiling. Sitting up in that very smart armchair Evelyn had coveted, in the corner of her tiny room. The one with the peacock print fabric. 'You mustn't sound bitter and nasty. You must endeavour to be cheery and inspiring. Never, never sound bitter and ill-natured. It's very unbecoming.'

Evelyn closed her eyes and counted slowly in her head to five. What was she supposed to say to this woman? This woman who was meant to be her friend. Evelyn could picture her, clear as anything, tottering around with a silver knife and shouting about ritual sacrifice. Reg lying trussed up like a spatchcock at her feet. What were you meant to say in these situations?

'I have a piece of news for you,' Catriona said.

'What?' Evelyn felt dozy. She felt like she couldn't muster the wherewithal to say anything to her so-called friend. She didn't know where to start. But this didn't seem to matter to Catriona Mackay anyway. She didn't seem to expect any kind of statement from Evelyn. She was breezing along quite contentedly. 'W-what news do you have?' asked Evelyn, feeling very stupid.

'I have contacted your mother,' Catriona said. She sounded delighted with herself. Evelyn could imagine the way she was smiling into the receiver. She even thought she could feel her hot peppermint breath in her ear.

'My mother..?'

'Yes, my old friend. Your mother. And she's very alarmed to hear about things that have been happening here in Darkholmes, my dear. I'm sure you'll be cockahoop to learn that she's on the train now. She's coming to grace us all with a visit.'

*

Hers was the last train to arrive in Darkholmes before Christmas.

The weather in the north was very bad that year. The tall hills and the wide fields that she saw from the window of her carriage were coated in thick drifts of snow and, as the day wore on, more and more came falling.

Dorothea alighted and changed trains at Inverness, Perth, Edinburgh, Newcastle... moving south and tacking along the coastline as the journey went on. It wasn't very often that she ventured into England; it wasn't very often that she saw her daughter Evelyn, but this time she found she was looking forward to it. Mother and daughter were good friends, as it happened. The tensions and uncomfortablenesses of the past were all mostly forgotten. Evelyn lived a good, useful and respectable life as a don's wife, and Dorothea was able to relax. She had succeeded in seeing her daughter settled.

At seventy, Dorothea was an impressive, imperious, handsome woman. She sat in a bubble of her own righteous composure, surveying the wintry world outside as it thundered by, and thoroughly enjoying the sensation of being rocked steadily towards her destination. Others passengers came and went, nodding politely and respecting her quiet as she read her book, or knitted bootees or reread her daughter's peculiar recent letters. Planning ahead as usual, she had brought plenty of things to divert her and to dissuade any fellow travellers from engaging her in unwanted conversation. Crosswords, oranges, mint humbugs, smoked salmon sandwiches wrapped in wax paper, several murder mysteries.

That still didn't stop the vicar from talking to her. When he clambered into her carriage as they idled smokily in the cavernous interior of Newcastle station, she knew at first sight that he would be trouble. The nervy, garrulous sort, keen to curry favour with well-to-do ladies of her type. And, sure enough, before they had even set off, he was gabbling away. All about being a college chaplain at a university and what a tricky job it was. How the students and the faculty were all godless heathens. How none of them really deserved to live in the hallowed, reclusive surroundings of Hexford at the top of Darkholmes. How it was an enchanted place, and one where he had lived for many years, and where he would be content to finish his days…

Dorothea, sighing, glanced at him narrowly over the top of her murder magazine. 'Oh really?' she said, not really listening.

'Of course, this Michaelmas term has been a very challenging one,' worried the Reverend Mr Small. 'And not at all indicative of what life is like… what with various peculiar events and so on. The poor porter. And our Dean acting so strangely…'

'Oh?' Her ears pricked up only slightly at his tone. She still wasn't properly paying attention to him, but the wretched vicar took this as his cue to divulge further.

'I've actually been rather disturbed by several things this term. Nothing tangible, as such… not much, anyway. It's more like a kind of feeling… yes, an atmosphere that has been generated in the place. Well, as I've said on numerous occasions, there have been new people in our college this autumn. New presences. And perhaps, if there is a change in the ambience, then it is they we ought to be looking to for explanations, hm?'

'Possibly,' nodded Dorothea, groaning inside. She had the sudden impulse to seize hold of the babbling fool and to shove his bald head out of the window. She'd wait until she saw the hellish dark mouth of a tunnel appear, and threaten him with decapitation. Give the old idiot something real to be scared about.

Now he was counting names off on his fingers. 'Well, there's the new porter, of course, who is so brusque compared with Mr Mack. And Professor Cleavis, of course, and his young... erm... companion, as it were. Plus the year's intake of students, of course. But those fellows all blur into one, I'm afraid. When you've worked in a place as long as I have... they seem a pretty harmless, mundane bunch. Same old faces each year... Oh, and there's the Dean's secretary, of course. She's new, as well.'

Abruptly he stopped talking, as if he had thought of something rather nasty, or had hit upon a topic he wasn't allowed to discuss. His words had skidded to a halt so suddenly that Dorothea lowered her murder magazine. She was intrigued despite herself. 'Go on, Reverend..?'

He was pale and, even though the small compartment wasn't overly hot, there were drops of moisture on his face. To Dorothea's disgust he looked rather clammy. 'Tell me, my dear, have you ever been in the presence of a person you would actually describe as evil?'

She drew back sharply, startled by his words, just as the train ducked into a tunnel, dousing them both in deep shadow. The whistle screamed.

It was almost a full minute before they emerged again into the light, on the other side of a high range of hills. On the forested plain beyond, the snow was even deeper, the sky even stormier. The vicar was looking embarrassed. 'Please forgive the ramblings of an old man. I am exhausted. I thought a few days away at the coast would do me good. Wall's End. My sister Minnie has a guesthouse and gives me a good rate. But it is no good... I still feel oppressed and... and I actually find myself dreading my return to college. After twenty-eight years as Chaplain...! This is absurd, is it not?'

Evelyn wasn't sure what to say to him for the best. To her eyes he seemed to be having a kind of breakdown, or an episode of some sort involving his nerves. She wasn't one for kindly platitudes. 'I suggest you try to calm down. We'll be there soon. There's simply no use working yourself up into a frenzy.' And she handed him a boiled sweet and her murder magazine.

Then she dismissed him from her mind, and returned to reading her daughter's recent letters, which she had bundled up and put into her handbag at the last minute before leaving this morning. They were so odd and fantastical, she felt she must read them again before arriving, but had put off the moment. She wondered whether Evelyn might be having her very own nerve-storm herself? Or whether she had taken up the writing of outlandish novelettes. Either way, Dorothea wished that she could have written more mundane and everyday letters home.

I'm too old for mystery, thought Dorothea Fisk, as the snow came whirling out of the darkening skies and the vicar avoided catching her eye once more, fearful of annoying her. And then she thought: No, I'm not. She rather liked the idea of sweeping into town on the last train before Christmas, bearing some modest gifts, a new nightie, and her monogrammed luggage. She liked the idea of there being a juicy mystery awaiting her at her destination: she simply couldn't help it.

*

She struggled to get her bearings as the city came into view. Suddenly, a glimpse of the cathedral and the castle towers, high above the snowy trees of the island, and then swift passage over a tall viaduct, then they were pulling into the small station. Was it this side of the river, or the other that her daughter lived? Dorothea remembered that she had found this place rather confusing, the last time she had visited. It was the way the place had been organized, with everything looping back on itself in a most annoying fashion.

As the train settled in for its brief rest and smoke billowed round the platforms she caught a glimpse of her daughter looking worried. All bundled up against the snow, Evelyn seemed pale and distracted. Her face was looking rather pinched, with some old headscarf wrapped around it.

Dorothea manhandled her own luggage swiftly from the rack above, brusquely letting the vicar know that she wouldn't be requiring any help from him. She bade him a curt farewell and hurried to open the door.

'Mother,' Evelyn said, with a catch in her voice. She hugged her mother as she stood there, still clutching her bags and cases. A most unusual welcome from Evelyn. Rather warm. As if she was relieved to see her, in fact.

'Evelyn, my dear,' Dorothea said, studying her face carefully. 'What the devil has been happening here?'

'Can we talk about it later?' Evelyn's face creased, and she started taking hold of her mother's bags. 'Let me help you.'

The vicar eased past them, through the small crowd, tiptoeing past the shoveled banks of snow on the slippery platform. He tipped his wide-brimmed hat at Dorothea, who could only muster a grimace back. 'Dreadful man,' she murmured to her daughter.

'You'll be glad you got here in one piece!' Evelyn said, with fake brightness, leading the way down the steps to the stone tunnel and the exit. Ah yes, Dorothea remembered the way now. Such a convoluted little town. 'There have been all sorts of ructions on the railways today. Lines closing. Journeys cancelled. And look – the sky here is simply full of snow. We're getting ready for another big fall. Yours is the last train that's stopping here until Christmas...'

Evelyn was gabbling and Dorothea let the words go rushing by, drowned in the noise of the train whooshing and shunting its way onwards, out of Darkholmes.

'We'll catch a taxi,' Evelyn said, as they emerged into the street, where the shop windows were glowing with festive lights and Dorothea felt her heart open up a little at the sight. Charming. It really was a very charming little town, and she was glad to be spending the holiday here with her one and only daughter.

'Let's get a cup of tea somewhere first, could we?' Dorothea asked. 'I've been gasping since Edinburgh and our buffet car was closed for some reason.'

Evelyn led them directly to the nearest tearooms, one she didn't know well. It was a little rough around the edges, with plastic tablecloths and sauce bottles on the table. It really wasn't their kind of place at all, and she apologized to her mother, who waved her hands graciously.

When they were seated, Dorothea scrutinized her daughter's face and asked: 'He's not gone off the deep end, has he?'

Evelyn looked blank. 'Who?'

'Why, him, of course. Your husband!'

'Deep end?'

'Yes, exactly. Much I say I like him, and I'm very respectful of his job and position and everything, I do think he's rather highly-strung and slightly peculiar. And I'm your mother, so I need to know if he's mistreating you in any way, or if he's the one making you unhappy...'

Evelyn's eyes widened. 'But I'm not unhappy, mother!'

'Your letters tell another story, dear.'

The waitress brought them cups of tea in cheap china, and chipped plates with flaky pastries. She was a young woman wearing a woebegone expression, about as cheery as the few sorry swags of tinsel that failed to brighten the place up. 'I wish we could have found a nicer café,' Evelyn said. 'It's not a very nice welcome for you.'

'Never mind that,' Dorothea snapped. 'I need to know, before I set foot in your house, what my attitude to your husband ought to be. Need I be on my guard?'

'No, no, Reg is fine,' Evelyn said. Then she paused for thought. 'Well, actually, he's not. There are all sorts of things going on here at the moment and he's been under a certain amount of strain...'

Mother rolled her eyes in a way that Evelyn knew all too well. She sipped her tea and put the cup down quickly. 'Haven't we all.'

Evelyn said, 'We've all experienced some rather odd goings-on in recent weeks, Mother.'

'Yes, I've read your cryptic letters. Some of what you said I couldn't make head nor tail of. At once point I thought you had left your husband, but it seems not.'

Evelyn felt embarrassed now, when she thought of her mother scanning through the many pages of cramped handwriting. Evelyn hadn't told her everything that had been going on. In fact, she had kept it quite oblique, and didn't really allude to the supernatural aspect of things directly. As a result, her mother didn't know what to make of her queer accounts of events at all. 'Well, we can't talk it all out here, in this place,' Dorothea sighed. 'I suggest we finish our nasty tea and catch a taxi.'

It was suddenly twilight in the street outside and the air was becoming frostier. Evelyn took the bulk of her mother's parcels and kept a keen eye out for a black cab.

'It isn't as busy as it was when I was here last,' Dorothea pointed out. 'There was barely room on the pavement, last time, with all those young people thundering about the place...'

'That was in term time,' Evelyn laughed. 'Almost all of the students have gone home. Darkholmes is quite different in the holidays.'

Dorothea pursed her lips and steadied herself in the slippery, tea-coloured slush that covered the pavement. 'It's more than that, I think. It's different to when I was last here... It feels quite changed, somehow.'

Her daughter gave her a worried look, aware of her mother's sensitivities in that direction. A cab pulled up then, and Evelyn was relieved. She didn't want her mother feeling wet and cold and having to walk another step. It was time to get her home and warmed up. Brenda would have a proper afternoon tea prepared. They could sit by the fire and Mother could admire the Christmas tree and other decorations Evelyn and Brenda had spent the morning putting up. Evelyn was determined to make Christmas more than reassuringly normal. Despite everything, she wanted it to go with a swing.

Monsters and strange dimensions and *holes* in the omniverse notwithstanding.

As she told the driver where to take them, and installed herself next to Mother in the backseat she knew that Dorothea already had the measure of her. There was no fooling her with a falsely cheery front.

*

It seemed to take Reg a huge effort, but he came downstairs to welcome his mother in law. His eyes were bleary and his thoughts were elsewhere, thought Evelyn critically as she watched him put his bony arms around her mother. But at least he was there. He had left his work for an hour or so to take tea in the parlour.

'Evelyn *said* that we would be having a very large old bird for Christmas this year,' he said, in a jocular tone that didn't come naturally to him.

'I beg your pardon?' Dorothea's eyes flashed. 'Evelyn, dear, help me with all my things would you? I don't know where to put anything. Your hallway is so cluttered...'

At once Evelyn started to see her house through her mother's careful, watchful eyes. She surged forward to relieve her of her various cases and bags and was already feeling hopeless. Our house is messy, cluttered. We've let it get out of hand and Brenda can't cope. Worse: our house looks eccentric. Reg's bike was propped up against the staircase. There were stacks of books piled everywhere, pausing mid-journey between upstairs and down. Letters were spilling off the telephone table and there was a drift of them on the wooden floor.

Dorothea took everything in as Evelyn relieved her of her coat and hat. 'I always forget how charming your home is,' she told the Tylers, and Evelyn flushed.

'Happy Christmas, Mother dear,' Reg said and the two women shot him a glass, suspecting sarcasm. Dorothea was always particularly irked when he called her 'Mother.' She was only four years his senior.

Once they were sitting stiffly in the parlour Brenda came lumbering in with her favourite hostess trolley. 'Oh, I see you still have your... help,' said Dorothea.

Brenda didn't say anything. It was best to keep her head down on occasions like this.

'You haven't decorated your tree,' Dorothea said, holding up her china cup and saucer and waiting for Brenda to pour.

'We thought we'd wait till you were here, and you could help...'

'I'm allergic to pine needles, I'm afraid.'

'Ha!' Tyler laughed. 'You live in a forest! You're surrounded by acres of firs!'

Dorothea glared at him. Brenda poured her tea. It was a perfect orange, just how she liked it. 'Thank you... erm...'

'Brenda, ma'am.'

'Ah yes. You're the girl my soft-hearted daughter took in off the streets, aren't you?'

Brenda nodded gruffly and hurried away as Evelyn protested: 'It wasn't quite like that, mother...'

'Hmf,' Dorothea said, and took a large swig of tea.

The next hour dragged by rather awkwardly, with an artificially cheery Reg making conversational gambits and Dorothea shooting them down, one after the next like a sniper in a gun turret. At last she said, 'Are you still writing, then? Hm? Your interminable novel?'

Evelyn said, 'Oh, Reg never stops, mother. You would never believe how busy he is these days.'

'I'm sure I wouldn't,' said Dorothea stiffly. 'I'm surprised that your academic duties leave you any time at all for messing about with writing.'

Reg grumbled into his own cup and managed to rein in his reply. 'Some things we simply have to do,' he said. 'No matter how busy we are. We must give up our time to the things that matter.'

'Indeed,' Dorothea said. 'Such as one's spouse. It's very important for couples to spend time together, I find. Not too much. But some, at least. It doesn't do for one to feel neglected. Does it?'

Evelyn was mortified. Less than an hour in the house and her mother was interfering already.

'You must excuse me,' Reg said, a few minutes later, rising stiffly (he was still aching and exhausted after his night in Diodati's Big Top.) 'I have much to do in my study.'

'See you at dinner time,' Evelyn said quietly.

'Yes, quite possibly,' he said vaguely, patting her on the shoulder.

Both women remained quiet until they heard him going up the stairs.

'He doesn't look very well, Evelyn,' Dorothea drained her tea, smacking her lips in a way her daughter had always found unpleasant. 'Is his will up to date?'

*

Later, while she was unpacking her bags in the best room that 199 Steps Lane had to offer, Dorothea happened to peer out of her window. She glanced critically at the walled garden that seemed to her, even though it was covered in snow, to have been left by the Tylers to go to rack and ruin. There was nothing Dorothea could stand less than people who couldn't be bothered to keep their garden spruce. She stood there in a kind of tired trance, watching the birds flitting between the bare branches of the chestnut trees. Strangely, several of them appeared to be sporting ragged little tags on their legs, like messenger pigeons.

She noticed a burly figure going up the smothered garden path, across a tussocky lawn. It was Brenda, that mouth-breathing maid. She seemed to be making for a broken down shed at the far corner of the garden. It was almost hidden by a shapeless laurel hedge, but it was clearly the maid's intended destination. There was something so furtive about Brenda's movements that Dorothea felt compelled to keep watching as the big woman fiddled with locks and chains on the shed's door. She opened the door only a crack and slipped in, keeping a watchful eye behind her.

Up to no good in the woodshed at the bottom of the garden. Dorothea could have guessed as much.

There was a knock at her door. 'Mother? Are you all right?'

'Don't fuss, Evelyn,' she snapped, as her daughter's worried face appeared. 'You never used to be so jumpy. What on earth's happened to you?'

Evelyn sat on the stool in front of the dressing table. She had arranged things so nicely for her mother in this best room the house had to offer. Dorothea saw that now. Reasonably expensive face cream in a fancy bottle. An elaborate powder puff in a cerise jar. Scent in a bottle with a squeezy bulb. Everything was arranged very carefully, as if Evelyn had spent time imagining how her mother might like it. Dorothea sighed, caught unawares by the memory of Evelyn as a girl, messing about with the things on mother's dressing table. Playing at dressing up under Dorothea's watchful eye.

'I'm not sure what's happened to me, mother,' Evelyn said. Her shoulders slumped, which was most unbecoming. Dorothea longed to tell her to buck up and sit straight. 'But...

something has been happening to all of us here. Something strange... and I think, wonderful...'

*

'Helloooo..?'

Brenda shouldered her way into the tiny, dim space of the shed, where it was even mustier and more cobwebby than she remembered.

'We're here,' said a small, tinny voice.

The brown paper bag in Brenda's hands was soggy with cold blood. The liver inside squished unpleasantly. 'I brought this...' she said, holding it out. She felt long, delicate fingers take it out of her grasp. Then she heard someone chewing hungrily, messily at what she'd slipped from the Tylers' refrigerator. She shuddered at the noises.

'I'm sorry,' Brenda said. 'This was all I could think of. I couldn't take you into the house...'

There was a clockwork chiming noise as the Gold Leaf Princess nodded. 'We understand.'

By now Brenda's eyes had adjusted to the scratchy light coming through the frosty shed window. Amongst the garden tools and bric-a-brac were huddled fugitives from the vanished carnival. The metal Princess, looking worried but calm. The foxy-faced Charles in his heavy cloak, lapping busily at the liver, wholly absorbed in his bloody meal. And propped up on one of the cluttered shelves, on top of a heap of yellowed story papers, was the Nonesuch in her shabby box. She seemed to be in a furious sulk with everyone.

Brenda was embarrassed. When they needed her, all she could offer was this dreadful outhouse. And this after the Princess had saved Tyler's life, plus everyone else's. 'I should have taken you into the house,' Brenda said. 'But they've got a visitor today. Evelyn's mother has come down from Scotland, and I'm not sure how she would react to seeing you... She's a very shrewd kind of person, and I think she would know at once you were there, if I tried to smuggle you inside...'

'It's all right, Brenda,' said the Princess, with a smile so gentle and sincere she made Brenda feel even worse. 'None of us three feel the cold. I am mostly tin, as you know, the Nonesuch has had no feeling in her body for many years and Charles, is of course, undead.'

Brenda nodded. 'I know. But I do feel bad. One day... oh, one day I shall have a place of my own. I'll save up, or something, and I'll buy a big tall house with lots of rooms. I'll have them all done out so beautifully and extravagantly. And do you know what? I'll invite everyone I know to come and stay. It'll be a kind of sanctuary for them who need it... Perhaps... by the seaside... That's what I'd love...'

With a fastidious smacking noise, Charles was finishing off his liver and sucking the ends of each of his fingers. 'That's all very well, Brenda dear, and I'm sure one day you'll do that. But in the mean time, what are we to do, hm? We have been liberated. We've never known freedom like this before. The circus has gone without us and we find ourselves with our whole shabby lives ahead of us. But what do you propose we do with them?'

Brenda bit her lip. 'What would you like to do?'

The Nonesuch was still squeezing her eyes and her wizened mouth tight shut and pretending she couldn't hear anything. She was trying to block the whole world out, Brenda realized. She was scared. All three of them were. She remembered that she too, had been so bewildered and scared, all those years ago, when she had first run away. She'd had Joe then, though. Joe and Victor had helped her to acclimatize to life in the world again. She just wished she could remember what had happened next... It was no good though. Her memories had stopped leaking back into her skull. It was as if snow had fallen inside her head, as well as everywhere else.

She was struck by a sudden inspiration. 'I know who can help you. He'll surely know what to do!'

The Nonsesuch's eyes open a little way at her words. The Princess' face shone with hope, and Charles bared his tiny, deadly teeth.

Brenda locked them all inside the shed again and hurried back across the garden, hoping that she could use the phone in the hall without anyone hearing. Evelyn would be changing for dinner, perhaps. Her mother would be unpacking and napping, if her previous visits were anything to go by. Tyler himself wouldn't hear anything from his study. Brenda wasn't supposed to ring out on the phone by herself. But who did she know to phone anyway? She knew how to use it, though. She had watched Evelyn carefully. And she knew the number she wanted was pinned to the board by the telephone table...

*

'I wish we'd never had it installed,' Cleavis said grumpily, picking up his papers. The phone's shrill ring had made him jump with a yelp, scattering everything off the tray he rested on while he was writing.

John suppressed a smile. 'The college insisted,' he shrugged. 'Mod cons, Henry. That's what it is. The modern world encroaching on your seclusion.'

'That noise is driving me crackers! Pick it up!'

Smiling, John picked up the phone and was pleased to hear Brenda's voice coming down the ear-piece. 'You'll have to speak up...' he told her.

'Who is it?' frowned Henry Cleavis, clutching handfuls of pages. 'Hm?'

John's eyes were widening as he listened to Brenda burble urgently and quietly in his ear. 'Yes... yes, of course. I understand. We'll... of course we'll do everything we can. We'll come at once.'

Henry rolled his eyes. 'What? I'm not going anywhere. Have you seen it outside? I'm settled in for the night. Nothing can budge me.'

John put the telephone down and stared at his friend. 'Brenda needs our help.'

'What with?' said Cleavis. 'Something dire? Something dangerous?'

'I don't know,' said John. 'She wants our help. For friends of hers. They've escaped from the Carnival. She's got them hiding in the shed.'

'It's not the *elephant*, is it?' Henry's eyes widened. 'We haven't got the space for a runaway elephant...'

John couldn't help smiling at him. 'Come on. Let's get togged up. We've got work to do.'

*

Brenda had to hurry that night. She had dinner to see to, and didn't even have time to fret about Evelyn's mother's presence. Dorothea would just have to like it or lump it.

'Whatever's this?' she heard the old lady say hotly, as soon as her back was turned.

'Chinese,' said Professor Tyler mildly. 'Chow Mein, I think.'

Evelyn explained: 'Brenda lived in Limehouse for a while, she once told us. She picked up a liking for Eastern cuisine.'

There was a pause and Brenda could imagine the Scotch woman's disgusted expression. 'Did she indeed. And what am I mean to eat it with?'

Bessie couldn't exactly recall her Limehouse days, but she knew it was true. Chinese cooking came so easily to her. Her hands moved between chopping board and wok almost of their own accord...

Plus, it was quick. And this evening she needed all the time she could get. While the Tylers were preoccupied with their exotic banquet, Brenda was busy herself with a spot of smuggling.

At precisely eight pm she was in the dark garden, as snow fell again, waiting by the red gate in the wall. All was peaceful indoors. The curtains were pulled against the night. Professor Cleavis and John were only a few minutes late, knocking three times on the gate.

'Thank you for coming to the back,' she said. 'And I'm sorry for the subterfuge...'

'That's all right,' beamed Cleavis, his eyes shining above coils of woollen scarf. 'I don't mind subterfuge. Now, where are these friends of yours?'

John said, 'He's looking forward to meeting them. He said it was a shame the other night, that we didn't get a chance to talk to any of the... erm, members of the carnival show.'

They were led through the wintry garden by Brenda to its very furthest, darkest corner. 'They're worn out and a bit upset,' Brenda whispered. 'It's all new to them, this freedom lark.'

'I understand,' said Cleavis, still looking eager.

He wasn't disappointed, when Brenda unlatched the shed and the snowy moonlight shone down on the three fugitives. The Gold Leaf Princess looked like she was made of pure gold as she stood propped up in the far corner. Not a blemish or the slightest hint of a biscuit tin could be seen. The Nonesuch slept in the box in her arms and, crouched on the dusty floor with his deep cape pulled around him, Charles the fox was snoozing. His eyes opened a luminous crack when he realized they had company.

'My friends,' Brenda explained breathlessly. 'These two men are my new friends in this town. Professor Cleavis...'

'Please,' said Cleavis. 'Henry. We're Henry and John.'

The Princess smiled at them both in turn, her insides jingling and chiming as she moved towards them. She held up the Nonesuch and got her to wake and greet their rescuers.

John saw that Henry was staring at all three of them as if he was enchanted. Even that fox with the vicious-looking teeth. John felt the hairs on his arms and the nape of his neck bristle and stand on end as the fox drew closer and the rancid scent of his breath became apparent. But Cleavis didn't seem at all wary of him as he said, 'Good evening,' in a deep and velvety voice.

'Well, then, goodness,' said Henry. 'We'd best be off. Good idea not to involve the Tylers, Brenda. We don't want to over-complicate matters.'

Brenda explained about Evelyn's mother staying, and how she wasn't the easiest of people to accommodate. Explaining the strange visitors would have proven quite impossible.

The small party exited the shed, keeping as quiet as they could. John winced at the mechanical noises that the Princess couldn't help making as they moved towards the door in the wall. She bit her lower lip with effort, trying to keep her body as quiet as she could. The fox tried to mask her gleaming body with his dark cloak, but when the clouds rolled away from the moon she was a brilliant presence, filling the garden with light.

Brenda just prayed no one was looking out the French windows at that moment.

They made it out of the garden, and into the alleyway. Cleavis wished that they had a car or a vehicle of some kind. It seemed like a long journey across town... But there was no way around it. The snow was falling heavily now and surely the streets would be fairly empty this time of night. He put on his bravest face for his colleagues: 'Come along, then! Next stop – Hexford College.'

And on the way he would set about thinking up a plan for getting them unseen up to his and John's apartment...

*

Brenda bade them farewell at the end of the alley, with promises to come to Hexford the following day. It was a prospect she quite relished, having only glimpsed the place previously. She loved the idea of seeing where Henry and John lived.

Good. Job done. She glowed with pride.

Then it was back to the house, to clear away the dishes.

When she bustled into the dining room she was surprised to find that Dorothea had eaten more than the Tylers put together.

'Brenda, that was delicious! What did you say it was called again?'

'Just Chow Mein,' she said, reverting easily to her monosyllabic persona.

'I would say that's one of the best meals I've had in ages,' Dorothea sighed. 'Those delicious little prawns! How clever you are, my dear.' She eyed Brenda carefully.

'That's all right,' Brenda said, looking down at the table as she loaded up the used plates. 'Ice cream for afters.'

'Oh, I couldn't manage another thing,' Dorothea said. 'But please, you young people, do go ahead.' Then she dabbed her lips with a damask napkin and laced her fingers together before her. 'Before I forget. Dinner. Tomorrow night. I have been in touch with my old, old friend. Naturally, I would like to see her as soon as possible. Many years have past since I last saw her. I took the liberty, Evelyn, dear, of inviting her here, to dinner, tomorrow evening. I promised her a kind of early Christmas feast. It's the twenty-first, isn't it? The shortest night. Anyway, Catriona has said she would be delighted to come here.'

Reg had been sitting rigid throughout this speech, staring open-mouthed at his mother in law.

'Is that all right with you, Brenda dear?' Dorothea said. 'It's you who will be doing all the work, of course, and I don't want to impose upon anyone. But I gather Catriona has become something of a good friend of yours, too, Evelyn and...'

Suddenly Professor Tyler was on his feet. 'NO!' he roared, flinging his soy-stained napkin down like a gauntlet. 'I will not have that heathen witch in my house again!'

Dorothea jerked back in her chair, as if she had been slapped. 'Reginald!'

His face contorted with anger, Reg said in a low, nasty voice: 'That woman gets in here over my dear body.'

Evelyn put out a steadying hand, 'Reg, mother doesn't understand about…'

He shook her off. 'I'm going upstairs to work.' And then he was off, without sparing the women another glance.

Dorothea waited until he had stomped off down the hall and up the stairs and his study door had clattered shut behind him. Silence fell on the house and then she glanced at her daughter. 'Goodness, but he's touchy these days.'

Evelyn's smile was sickly.

'I wish you would tell me what's going on,' her mother said. 'Because something is, isn't it? Something peculiar.'

*

All of Darkholmes was frozen.

The railway lines, the roads, all the countryside that surrounding the Medieval town: every stitch of it was solid with ice.

Next morning, the inhabitants woke late to find that they had to dig themselves out of the snow. Even the lofty towers of Hexford were affected. The porter called for volunteers to help him shift the great sliding drifts that had sealed the doors and gates of the old college shut.

From their cosy eerie John and Henry looked down on the town and both felt perplexed at how peaceful it looked; both knowing that such a spell of weather could be disastrous.

That morning, though, they had other duties to take their mind off conditions outside. The three sideshow freaks in their sitting room were a worthy distraction.

'We don't take much feeding, or looking after,' smiled the fox-faced young man, sitting the armchair where he had slept the remainder of last night. 'In fact, of the three of us, only I require food of any kind. Though what I need is quite... specialized.'

'Yes, quite.' Henry clapped his hands briskly and rubbed them together. 'It's quite parky in here this morning, isn't it? Erm... good morning ladies and gentleman.' He surveyed the rag-tag runaways in his sitting room quite solemnly and it was clear that he was still wondering what to do about them.

'We aren't your problem,' chimed the Princess, smiling at him. 'What you've done for us so far, leading us through town last night – that was plenty. We don't want to be a burden to you.'

'Nonsense!' said Cleavis. 'You're no such thing, are they, John?'

John smiled, as reassuringly as he could.

'The thing is,' Cleavis went on. 'You may in fact be holed up in here with us for several days... The weather, you see...'

They understood. They knew all about waiting, and sitting still, and hoping the right moment would come along.

The Nonesuch stirred in her battered cabinet. Her simian arms twitched and her wrinkled eyes opened in her shaggy head. 'Where are we now?' she asked, her voice harsh and crackling, as if it was being broadcast from miles away. The others explained to her how the Professor had been so kind, and now they were in his rooms.

'Professor, eh?' the homunculus cackled. Then her expression went distant and her glass eyes blazed. 'Hexford College is in danger. The walls have been breached. There's been a death here... a killing...'

'What's that?' asked Cleavis, trying to sound jocular. 'She's got the second sight, has she?'

'I'm afraid so,' said the Gold Leaf Princess. 'The Nonesuch doesn't quite see all, but what she does see is generally true.' She looked worriedly at them all. 'I've never known her to be wrong, especially when she goes into one of her strange turns.'

*

It was John, who went down to the porter's lodge to help with freeing the gates to the college of snow, who returned with the news. He was ashen-faced and covered in snow. 'You'd best sit down,' he told Henry.

'Damned if I will! What's up?'

'The whole place is in a state of panic. Everyone's locking themselves into their rooms. The... the Nonesuch was quite right. There has been a... killing in the night.'

'What?' Cleavis took a step closer to him.

'His rooms were broken into. Much as ours were. There was one witness, an undergraduate. He described a creature very like the one who was here that time...'

'A Gyregoyle?'

'They've been sighted above the college. Several of them, turning in circles like vultures above us...' John shuddered, clearly recalling his deadly struggle in the arms of one of those beasts.

'But who have they killed?' Cleavis burst out.

John told him: 'The Dean. They found him first thing this morning. At his desk in his pyjamas, as if he was working very late. Not a very pretty sight, apparently.'

For a moment Henry Cleavis looked as shocked as John did, then his face darkened with resolve. 'This is a terrible thing.'

'The doors were smashed open. The window was shattered.'

'And no one heard this in the night?'

John shook his head. He became aware that the three escapees were staring at himself and his friend. They looked worried and eager to know what was going on.

'Can we… can we be of help?' said Charles, hesitantly.

'I'm afraid not, my friends,' said Cleavis, with a watery smile. 'Something very ghastly has happened.' Then, all at once he thought of something terrible. What if people in college became aware of the strange beings he was harbouring in his rooms? Scared, furious, paranoid about the murder of the Dean, how would they react to the presence of such unusual people seeking sanctuary here? All at once Cleavis knew that his friends were not as safe as he'd previously assumed.

'There's something else,' John said, touching Henry's arm. 'I'm not sure if it's relevant or not.'

'Everything is relevant,' snapped the professor.

'It's to do with who found the Dean's corpse. Who was first on the scene.'

'And?' said Cleavis, although with dawning dread, he already knew what John was going to say.

'It was Catriona Mackay,' John said. 'And after raising the alarm, and having the body removed and discovering that the college and just about the whole town was frozen solid with ice, she took over the Dean's duties herself. She has placed herself in charge of the whole college.'

*

Across town, where the snowdrifts were just as heavy, and the coming and going were perhaps even more complicated and arduous, the Tyler household had awoken stiffly and gradually. And, in the case of Reginald Tyler, with fury uppermost in his heart. His first act upon waking was to sit up and glare at his wife across the arctic wasteland of their white candlewick bedspread and to tell her, once again, in no uncertain terms that Catriona Mackay would not be entering their home that evening, come hell or high water.

Evelyn was still befuddled by sleep. 'Of course not. Mother doesn't understand. You know what she's like. I'm sure if you'll explain your... your objections, then she'll understand...'

'Catriona Mackay took me prisoner and tried to slit my throat!' Reg said harshly. 'Just a couple of nights ago. I don't care if she was under some kind of supernatural influence or not. Whatever you say, Evelyn, I believe that we are all responsible for our own actions, and that woman was intent on doing me harm. And poor Brenda, too. She is a sorceress!'

At this moment they were interrupted by the phone ringing down in the hall. It was five to eight in the morning. 'Who the devil rings at this hour?' coughed Tyler.

Brenda answered it and came to their room moments later, to deliver the awful news about the Dean.

'Good God,' said Tyler, untangling his threadbare dressing gown and dragging it on. 'You're absolutely sure you didn't jumble up the message, Brenda?'

She shook her head. 'Apparently he was torn to pieces.'

Evelyn looked as if she might be sick. 'Oh, that poor, dear old man...' She had only met him a handful of times, at her own cocktail parties at the beginnings and ends of terms, but he had always seemed harmless enough to her. The idea of his meeting with a violent end was shocking to say the least.

'Who did you talk to?' asked Tyler sharply.

'The acting Dean,' said Brenda. 'That's what she called herself. Ms Catriona Mackay. Who, incidentally, said she'd be delighted to come to Steps Lane for dinner this evening. It will be a soothing diversion. That's what she said. A soothing diversion from the business of murder.'

*

After a swift breakfast Reg set off on his bicycle into the snow.

'How extraordinary,' said Dorothea, lathering butter and marmalade on her toast. 'Your husband seems intent on doing himself a mischief, Evelyn dear.'

Evelyn didn't say anything. She wouldn't rise to her mother's bait. She was too busy fretting about Reg. He had been intent on trundling his way into town, to Hexford College, foolhardy as it seemed. 'Just stay here with us,' she had told him. 'Get on with your book... stay here where it's warm and safe...'

He had laughed harshly in her face. 'What book, eh? There are seventeen chapters missing, aren't there?'

Evelyn recoiled at the bitterness in his voice as he pulled his balaclava on. Then, having secured his bicycle clips, he was wheeling his rickety bike down their drive. Evelyn was thinking: he'll never forgive me. What was I thinking, handing that most precious manuscript over to Mr Tweet? She mustn't have been in her right mind.

Brenda prepared dinner early, stuffing a chicken and chopping her vegetables. She set them out ready to go into the oven, and then she pulled on her coat. Evelyn caught her in the hall. 'You're not going out as well?' The wind had picked up, late in the morning, and already the sky was dingy with oncoming snow. Brenda nodded and answered gruffly, not to be put off.

'Please, Brenda, stay here...' Evelyn was feeling herself getting hysterical. She was furious with her own feebleness.

'I can't stay,' said Brenda. 'Look, I'll be back to make dinner. Got things to do. In town.'

All she could think about were her three fugitives and fellow freaks. Thanks to her they had sought sanctuary in that college, where a murderer had struck in the night. As she trudged down Steps Lane a terrible thought came to her. What if it had been one of her escapees? She knew the Gold Leaf Princess, and she knew the Nonesuch. Neither were capable – temperamentally or physically in each case respectively – of killing anyone. But what did she really know about Charles the vampire fox? Was he really, for example, a vampire? Had Brenda unwittingly – and with all the best intentions – unleashed a monster upon the venerable college? All of this churned through her mind as she ploughed through the ever-thickening snow, making her way down into the town.

Lights burned in windows. Chimneys smoked. She saw hardly another living soul. Not even students larking about and enjoying the snow. Everyone, it seemed, had gone to ground, as if they knew these weren't natural conditions. As if they knew that something disturbing underlay it all.

*

Cleavis rapped smartly on the Dean's office door. As he did he cast a sour glance at the secretary's desk that lay emptied and unoccupied outside. She has got what she wanted, he thought, just as the call came from beyond the door: a cheerful, 'Come in, Professor.'

He shouldered his way in and stamped across the room, where the lissom Ms Mackay was sitting in the dean's chair. She was sporting a ludicrous outfit in Lincoln green, with a dashing little hat, complete with feather. What on earth did she think she was doing? Playing dressing up games when the Dean had been murdered?

Had it been here, in this very room? She had been very swift in getting in all cleared up, if it had. No, of course. It had been the Dean's own chambers. That's where it had happened.

Still, the Mackay woman had wasted no time in making this place her own. All the Dean's books and papers had been boxed up and the shelves stood empty. She had set out books of her own, plus some nasty little gee-gaws. They looked like they had everything to do with necromancy and black magic, Cleavis decided. Especially the golden basilisk ornament that stood on her desk before her.

He barged up to her desk and got straight to the point: 'You cannot take the Dean's place.'

Catriona smirked at him. 'Professor Cleavis. How I've longed for a tete-a-tete with you. I gather you're not altogether pleased with my presence here in Hexford? Wait, let me order some tea…' She tinged a little bell and then devoted her whole attention to him. 'I'm a great admirer of yours, Professor Cleavis. I must tell you this. And it grieves and hurts me terribly when you bad-mouth me everywhere.' She made a pantomime of frowning and weeping and then smiled at him brilliantly.

'I know who and what you are,' he growled, jutting out his chin.

'Do you, I wonder?' There was a light knock, and then one of the students – a blond, rather beautiful boy – came gliding in bearing a tray of hot tea things. Her servant. Her bowed when she told him they could manage, and he vanished silently out of the office.

Cleavis flung himself down on a chair. 'You've got everything arranged the way you want it, haven't you?'

'Don't be absurd,' she snapped, some of her steel showing through at last. 'Do you really think I'd wish the Dean dead? He was such a lovely man. Such a gentle soul. He was so very good for me, welcoming me to this college. No, his death was caused by a creature, Professor Cleavis. A creature with very sharp teeth. A drinker of blood and a nightstalker. Let's not be coy, Professor Cleavis. We know all kinds of creatures are patrolling the halls and back lanes of Darkholmes these days. Their numbers will increase. And it's all because of the Smudgelings.'

'Balderdash,' gasped Cleavis. 'Absolute rot. You know nothing.'

'Your combined mental willpower and imaginations. Such fierce energy. The walls between dimensions are so very thin here in Darkholmes. Your feats of invention prove... corrosive.'

'I've hardly been here any time at all,' he protested.

'Tyler and his fellows have been rubbing away for years. The addition of your good self to their number is disastrous. You and your Other Place. Your other dimensions. Your creatures from beyond.' She laughed heartily and poured out tea that looked violet and smelled like wild flowers.

He harrumphed. He wasn't about to be drawn into speculations with a malign creature like this, and he certainly wasn't about to sip her strange concoctions. 'Now look here, dear. What is it you want?'

She laughed again. 'Most doddering, middle aged professors I've come across so far in this place have fallen over themselves, just like the Dean did, to comply with my bidding.

They couldn't resist me, Cleavis. Old Sneagle, for instance. I've got that one wrapped round my finger.'

'So?'

'You're not very easy prey for feminine wiles and charm. I wonder why that can be?'

He glared at her steadfastly. 'Just tell me what you want.'

'As I said, Professor. There's no need to be coy. You and I are higher, enlightened beings, aren't we? There's no need for either of us to be tied down by the societal codes and taboos of the day, nor even the foibles and weaknesses of the flesh. But know this, 'dear'. I know everything about you. All your secrets. Everything you'd rather not have the world at large know about you. I know it all.'

Cleavis flinched inwardly, but he maintained his composure with a huge effort of will. What did it matter, what this witch knew? What could she know anyway? And who the hell was she to threaten him like this? 'I believe this meeting is at an end,' he said stiffly, and rose to his feet.

'Please, Professor,' she said, a note of... was it panic? in her voice. She stood and came round the desk after him, and he saw that she was clutching a book to her skinny chest. A flat, square, velvet-bound volume. 'This is all I want. Such a small thing. A modest thing. You'll think it absurd. But it means such a lot to me. I... I have written stories. My own stories. Something like... a little like those that you and Professor Tyler write. I have made a clean copy here. Look, would you take this? And read them. That is all I want... an acknowledgement from one such as you that they are... at least readable. I just want to think of you reading them... and seeing a little of my world...'

He looked at her, incredulous. 'That's what all of this is about? All of your shenanigans? Your enchantments?'

'I practise no enchantments,' she said. 'Nothing like that. Honestly. All I've ever tried to do is to get closer to Professor Tyler and yourself. That's all it's been about. I want to know whether my tales ring true.'

He stared into her eyes for a long moment. She looked back without blinking or altering her expression. She seemed sincere enough.

Reluctantly he took the purple velvet book from her grasp. Its cover felt odd. Like something alive. It made his fingers tingle as he turned and walked away, out of the poor late Dean's office.

*

It was in one of the narrowest, curving streets that Brenda was attacked. In one of the upward-sloping ginnels through which only the narrowest chink of light could fall. She was hurrying on her way up to Hexford College and then, without warning, without the slightest noise, she was set upon.

There were two of them. Burly, fantastic beings with scaled hides and elegant wings. They were like stone devils come down from the tallest towers of the cathedral. Their limbs were frozen but their rank breath was hot on her face as they seized hold of her.

She shrieked for all she was worth, and lashed out with both pan-shovel fists. They hopped and capered around her, scratching at her with their horrible claws. Teasing her, toying with her, clearly thinking she was easy meat. Just a foolish housemaid gadding about in the night, where no other citizens dared to venture. A ratty old coat pulled over her apron and a woolly hat that one of the creatures seized and slung through the air. Brenda pushed both hands down on her wig. There was no way she was letting them remove that.

'W-what do you creatures want with me?'

They laughed at her. Their eyes were like molten lava, glimmering with mineral hatred. She felt that they had no intelligence of their own, no volition or agency. They were just toys, wound up and set free in the world to cause chaos. She had seen such beings before, of course.

'You have to let me go unharmed,' she said in her bravest voice. 'I have... a mission. I have things I must do...'

The gargoyles advanced on her. There was nowhere to run in the frosty alley. Her feet slipped on the cobbles when she tried. Her knees hit the stone with a terrific crack and she cried out in pain. Where *was* everyone? Why did no one poke their heads out and see what was going on here?

Next thing she knew, the two monsters were taking a firm grip on her and... all at once she felt lighter. She felt very strange indeed. Her head started spinning and the air became very much colder. She was held between the stout bodies of both creatures and she was suspended between them as they rose effortlessly out of the alley and into the skies above the twisting rooftops of Hexford Hill...

*

The door crashed open and Professor Cleavis hurried into his rooms, furiously.

'Well! She's confirmed everything!' he brandished a hefty purple book at them all. 'Everything I knew was going on!'

283

'What?' John stood up. He'd been deep in conversation with the carnival people and Henry's entrance had made them all jump. 'Henry, calm down...'

'Calm down, he says!' The Professor stomped up and down the room, where the new carpet had already been flattened by all of his recent thinking. 'She told me that everything that I feared is true, John. She is in control here and she'll do what she will. No one is safe.'

The Nonesuch made a harsh, despairing noise at this and Cleavis turned to look at her. Beside the withered mermaid-creature the Gold Leaf Princess looked extremely worried. The late afternoon light burnished her skin beautifully, but also showed up those patches where the biscuit tin lettering could be seen. 'Where's the fox?' Cleavis said.

'Oh,' John said. 'He... er... he had to go.'

'Go?' Cleavis thundered. 'We're harbouring him here! We're helping him escape! What's he doing going off by himself?'

The Princess looked apologetic. 'He was having pangs. Hunger pangs. Sometimes, especially in stressful situations, Charles must go off and hunt...'

'Hunt!' The colour drained from Cleavis's face. 'Are you saying that I've brought a vampire into the college and he's gone hunting?' He flashed John a look. 'How could you let him go?'

'I couldn't stop him,' murmured John. 'I turned my back when I was in the kitchen, getting my cake out of the oven. He was off out the window, shinning down the ivy...'

'It's all right!' the Princess jangled, standing up. 'He wouldn't hurt a person. Honestly. When he hunts he takes only rabbits or mice. The students are safe...'

Cleavis flung himself down in his chair. 'Pah. Safe, relatively speaking. There are still hideous creatures out there. There's still that terrible witch woman in control of everything...'

John could see that Henry was getting over-excited. What was required was a plan. Something practical they could fix on. 'I've had an idea, Henry. About where we can take our friends. Somewhere they might be safe.'

'Oh yes?' said Henry.

'What's that you've got?' The Princess interrupted, pointing at the book Henry was clasping to his chest. All at once he realized that the thing was warm in his hands and becoming warmer. The bare flesh of his fingers touched the pages inside and he cried out in alarm. They were hot. The pages were glowing silver and they were hot to touch.

He tried to look at the writing on the pages where the volume had fallen open, but the script was in a language that even he – with his massive experience of tongues ancient and dead – didn't recognize. It was as if the tiny, circular letters were moving. They were spiraling like tiny vortices on the page, burrowing into the shimmering heat haze...

*

After twilight, when the town was stiller and quieter than it had been all that day, Catriona Mackay dressed for dinner. She put her hair up into an elegant knot, and donned a black evening gown she had been saving for just this occasion. The very night that she would at last enter the Tyler stronghold.

She painted her face. She called her basilisk down from her desk and bade him grow to full size. She waited for him to cool and he bowed his head in her presence, careful not to stare into the eyes of his revered mistress. He must not turn her, of all people, into stone.

Then Catriona climbed onto his back and he set off, quite nimbly, down the plush corridor that led from the Dean's office to the pale stone stairs, down the turret and into the grounds of Hexford College. The porter in his small, cosy room, toasting muffins on his open fire, was the only soul to observe their passing. He sat there amazed. The Dean's secretary was astride a gleaming creature out of myth, and they were battering down the frozen gates and melting the drifts of snow that had sealed the old college shut. But he didn't believe any of it. Not a scrap of it. The porter concentrated on his muffins and his racing paper and tried not to believe anything he had seen in recent days. Gargoyles come to life and vampire foxes went capering in the quads. Students sleeping all day long and the days being frozen before Christmas could come. The porter had decided not to think too hard about any of it.

Bounding away from the college, bounding down the empty lanes, past the glimmering shop windows and shuttered homes, Catriona rode her basilisk hard. She clasped his golden flanks and relished the knife-sharp brightness of the night.

CHAPTER EIGHT

Dorothea couldn't say anything very much for a while. It wasn't that she was shocked, exactly, or that she was welling up with emotion. Nothing like that. She wasn't that kind of woman. She simply kept quiet for the first hour of the evening's proceedings, following her old friend's arrival at the Tyler residence.

It was almost as if the formidable Dorothea had turned shy in the presence of her old friend.

Catriona was graciousness itself, of course, as was proper for a woman in her position. And hadn't she done well? Dorothea was startled to hear that Catriona had risen to become Dean of the college. The details weren't quite straight in Dorothea's head. Her daughter was so poor at explaining things. It sounded most impressive, anyhow.

Catriona looked chic and sophisticated, shucking her expensive coat in the hall. Evelyn fussed around her. 'How did you get here? How did you make it through the snow?' Evelyn was behaving like a fool, or a lackey, and Dorothea felt almost ashamed of her.

'Oh, I used my magic,' Catriona shrugged happily, and fixed her brilliant eyes on Dorothea. 'My dear old friend.'

They embraced and took a long look at each other. What had Evelyn been saying? That Catriona was a young woman still? That she seemed to be no older than Evelyn herself? That's what Dorothea's daughter had written in her letters. Utter nonsense, of course. Catriona was still a very beautiful woman, but she had aged, sure enough. The flesh was thin on those exquisite bones. There were finely wrought lines around her eyes and mouth. Her make-up was very carefully applied. No, this was a woman of Dorothea's own age and generation, but one who had spent a great deal of time and energy looking after herself properly.

Dorothea could almost despise her for indulging herself: for having the luxury to preserve herself thus.

They clasped each other's arms and stared into the other's eyes. 'How could we let so many years go by?' Catriona asked. 'Why did we fall out? Did we fall out? Is that what kept us apart?'

But still Dorothea couldn't find her voice.

Evelyn shooed them into the dining room. 'We've lost our cook again,' she said. 'I'm trying to manage in the kitchen, but...' She made light of it, but it was clear that she was harassed, and worried over Brenda.

Professor Tyler was waiting in the dining room, in his smartest suit, clutching a glass of whisky. He glared at Catriona as she held out her dainty white hand.

'I'm allowing you in my house for the sake of these silly women,' he growled.

'Are you?' she smiled challengingly. 'I'm surprised at you. Have you decided to keep me sweet? Or have you realized that I'm simply no threat at all to you?'

He scowled at her, and Catriona laughed.

Evelyn came back into the room to see that they had drinks, and she hovered nervously. She too couldn't see why Reg had given in so easily. All he'd had to do was put his foot down, and forbid Catriona from coming to his house tonight. For some reason he had given up all his protests. He was letting Dorothea have her old friend round to dinner, just as she wanted.

Was there perhaps something Reg wanted from Catriona? Evelyn wondered. Was her husband playing a clever game of some kind? Yes... surely he must be. She knew that furious look in his eye. He got it when he played board games too competitively, or when he related some complicated tale of academic politics.

Evelyn put it all out of her mind and concentrated on bringing Brenda's dinner to table, praying that she didn't make too much of a hash of it.

Worry about Brenda preyed on her mind the whole time. No way would she stay away out of choice. Clearly something had happened to her. Every now and then Evelyn would peer out the back door – letting billows of steam (and smoke, when she burned a pan) roll out into the dark garden. Now the snow was waist-high in places and she couldn't help picturing her maid struggling somewhere and freezing alone.

When she returned to the dining room with the hostess trolley, she found to her relief that her mother had at last recovered the use of her voice. She was haltingly describing her life in Scotland. It sounded lonesome and bleak, all of a sudden. Evelyn laid out the warmed plates and unstacked the silver vegetable platters and felt ashamed that her mother could make her life sound so sterile and empty.

'Is your life everything you hoped for?' Catriona said, in her purring voice. 'When you think back to when we were girls... do you have everything you dreamed about?'

'What? Why, of course not, Cat. Naturally not. Life doesn't work that way, does it?'

Catriona was drinking red wine out of an elaborate goblet from a set Evelyn had found in a cabinet. It was a set she had forgotten she owned. They looked too fussy and pretentious, really. In the candlelight she thought Catriona looked like a fairy tale queen sipping blood.

Reg broke in harshly, 'Catriona Mackay has everything she wants, don't you?'

She laughed. 'Do I? Not quite.'

'She only wants to belong, don't you?' Tyler went on. He hadn't touched a drop of his wine. When Evelyn pushed his dinner plate in front of him he looked at it as if it would poison him. 'She wanted acceptance. She wanted to belong.'

Dorothea stared at her elderly son-in-law. Why was he being so rude? It was embarrassing. Perhaps he had been drinking all afternoon in that study of his?

'It's true, in a way,' Catriona sighed, and turned to explain to Dorothea. 'I have petitioned Professor Tyler several times. For membership of his exclusive club. They are all writers you see, and tellers of stories.'

A sudden flare lit within Dorothea. It roasted her insides blue, just like the old boiler in her decrepit kitchen, which she had to coax into life each morning. Frozen, Scottish mornings in her empty house. Triumph each morning when the pilot light caught. And now that flare was within her. It was a brilliant idea, warming her. 'You tell such wonderful stories, Catriona. You always did.'

'Thank you, Dorothea.'

'Oh, but you did. You had us all… in your power. We were mesmerized by them. By you.' The old woman's face was glowing now, as she downed the rest of her wine and fixed her full attention on Reg. 'You must let her join your club, Reginald. I am sure you would love to hear Catriona's tales.'

'But he wouldn't,' Evelyn burst out. 'Dorothea's asked him. I've even asked him! He's steadfast. It's just for the men. Only the men can tell stories in his club.'

'What rubbish!' Dorothea laughed. 'No one could be better than Cat. I defy you to find a better storyteller.'

Catriona touched her old friend's hand. 'Bless you, my dear. I don't think you'll ever convince the Professor.'

'Professors, pah!' said Dorothea tipsily. 'Think they know everything.'

'I'll take these plates away, shall I?' fretted Evelyn.

By the time she returned to the living room, to find her elders in heated discussion, Evelyn was struck by something strange about the room. Something about the fire perhaps? The flames were licking higher, more brightly. Someone had put too much coal on. The room was becoming over-warm. No one was going to want jam roly-poly, that was for sure. Was there something amiss about the mantelpiece and its freight of nick-nacks?

No. It was the painting on the chimney breast. That desert scene with the mountains and the oasis. It had been there so many years that Evelyn had stopped looking at it. But tonight it was different. It was bigger. Somehow the painting had grown to fill the width of the whole wall. No one talking at the table had even noticed. Nor had they clocked that the light had changed on the painting, and the cool desert dawn had become blazing daylight, brightening the stark dunes. That heat, too, was pouring into the Tylers' dining room.

Evelyn teetered forward against the table, and the hostess trolley clattered with dirty dishes. Reg looked at her sharply. 'Are you all right, my dear?'

'But... can't you see?' she said, pointing at the distended frame, and the bloated picture and the ripples of heat haze above the dining table.

'Ah, yes,' said Reg. 'I rather hoped something like this would happen.'

*

Brenda never knew how long her flight lasted as she was borne through the skies above Hexford. Those grotesque Gargoyle things flew in a very eccentric path: long, swooping spirals through the clotted air. She was exhausted with shouting for help. She was limp as a dishrag in their stone-hard arms. It seemed that they were rising ever higher through the air, above the clouds – which shattered about them with a frosty roar like ice on a flowing river.

She thought they were carrying her as high as they could take her and then they'd cast her down to her death. She'd be impaled on the spires of Hexford College. But why? Why me? She wanted to cry out. What's so significant about me? Why was she part of everyone's schemes, and the target for their enmity? She was just a humble servant. Anonymous, useless, shambling along. Surely not even worth going to all this effort for...

One spire rose higher than all the others. A slender, pale, golden finger that pointed inexorably into the heavens. Curious thing. She'd never noticed it before. Surely the highest tower at the top of the hill was the Cathedral? And yet – when she dared twist her head round and look far below – there the Cathedtral was, swimming in the frigid mists. So what was this structure soaring past her, its pinnacle hidden in the darkness and obscurity above?

Brenda became aware that there were birds massing around her. They flew in loose, dark formation, like a tangled skein of fabric wafting and whirling about the spire. The creatures that carried her paid them no heed whatsoever, but as they passed through the dark flock Brenda was scratched by tiny claws, and felt their horrid, harsh wings brushing over her. Each of them – absurdly – had little tags of paper attached to their feet. She had seen this before, hadn't she? She had noticed those shreds of paper on the feet of wild birds before…

Then there was a dark hatch in the frozen stone of the spire. Her captors were swimming through the air towards it. Birds were passing in and out of the hole, about their business. Brenda took a deep breath as she was carried inside, where it smelled rank and ancient. She had a horrible feeling that, once inside that tower, she might never get out again. The whole edifice had such an ominous feeling about it.

And there, in a golden patch of light, standing on a little platform was an old man, staring at her as she was brought in to land beside him. He was a pale, skinny old thing, gurning with pleasure as the gargoyles dropped their prisoner beside him. Brenda saw that he was wearing a kind of cloak made out of many kinds of feathers. But the thing that struck her most strongly of all was that he was the spitting image of Professor Tyler. Even down to the tufty white eyebrows she sometimes longed to trim for him.

'Go, my friends! You may leave now, and be about your business!' he told the hulking brutes. 'Fetch the vampire fox for me, would you? He will flex his wings and try to outrun you, but you'll bring him here to me, won't you? We can't let him run around at liberty in the wrong world, can we?'

The gargoyles nodded their assent and soared off again, through the swirls of birds and out of the hatchway. When the old man turned to smile and address her directly, Brenda had some trouble following his worlds. The chattering, chirruping noise of the birds was so intense and furious within the tower. It was almost impossible to think straight, let alone cope with a whole new, perplexing situation.

'Welcome, Brenda,' he told her. 'Yes, I do know who you are. You needn't introduce yourself.'

She drew herself up indignantly. 'I didn't intend to! I think it's you who ought to be doing some explaining, don't you?'

The old man smiled wryly. Brenda already knew fine well who he was. Her friend and mistress Evelyn had already given her enough information about her trips to Vexing Tower for Brenda to realise. However stupid and slow Brenda often pretended to be, he knew how bright and fast she truly was.

'Welcome to Vexing Tower,' he said, spreading and rustling his feathery cloak and giving her an elaborate bow.

'A-am I back in Daakholm?' she asked. He didn't fail to notice the hope in her tone.

'Vexing Tower rises above *all* the worlds,' he said, looking very pleased with himself. 'Not just the one or two that you have visited…'

*

John offered to carry the Nonesuch, though he wasn't keen. To his surprise Henry was only too happy to take a spade with him on their expedition down into the snowy town, and to help the Princess dig their way through the drifts.

But the snow was freezing hard as the night advanced. It was like cutting through layers of permafrost. Both men were impressed by the seemingly indefatigable Princess, wielding her bladed arms and chopping and hacking away at the ice.

The Nonesuch kept up a stream of chatter, which issued out of the small wooden box and scratched away at John's nerves. 'Ah, the Princess has always been a marvel. She's a wonder. And she's always been very good to me, you know. I mean, what am I? Just a useless bit of tat. A faded scrap hoiked out of a house clearance sale. A nasty piece of Edwardian whimsy, that's all I am. I'm blighted with mould and cursed with sentience. But the Princess sees more than that, you see. She has a good heart under those layers of beaten gold and tin, and she perceives my heart, too, though it's a cold and whiskery, shriveled thing, somewhat akin to a dead mouse or an owl pellet.'

She burbled on in her whispery voice and John made noises every now and then to show that he was listening. Also within his arms he carried the velvet-covered book with which Henry had returned from his meeting with Catriona Mackay. What a curious thing for the witch-woman to give him. The repository of all her stories! Even if they couldn't make head nor tail of the swirling symbols covering all the silver pages, then surely she could? And they must be precious to her, the things she had written in this book? John couldn't make her out at all.

The steep, curving street that went down to the river from the market square was less clogged with snowdrifts. The crooked buildings with roofs that almost met had shielded the dark canyons from too much snow. This made the last third of their journey slightly easier, and John gave a great sigh of relief. What time was it? His watch had stopped. Of course they saw nobody else they could ask for the time. The town clock and the churches were silent and still. He hoped and prayed that *Chimera* would still be open...

His heart started thumping harder in his chest when he peered through the chilly mist ahead and saw that it was. The dusty windows were alive with a sulphurous glow. The old woman was in. She was there, apparently waiting for them, and so, he thought, his plan might work...

*

Evelyn Tyler didn't like what was happening to her house.

It was her home. Once upon a time she had been so proud of it. She remembered so very clearly the day Reg had told her that he had picked out the perfect place for them. In a secluded suburb in the north of the city of Darkholmes. At last they could move out of his rooms in Hexford College. Oh, his married quarters had been very nice. Luxurious, even. Evelyn hadn't had any housework to do. They'd send maids in to pick up and clean for her. But all the while all she wanted was her own palace. Obviously, that was what she was meant to long for, wasn't it?

Seventeen years ago. Seventeen winters past.

Reg had guided his youngish bride to Steps Hill and led her proudly up the gravel drive, through the dense foliage of the evergreens. And she had held her breath when they came in sight of number 199.

Everything was fixed up. He had talked to the bank. He had borrowed the necessary money. There was nothing for her to fret about, other than picking out new items of furniture, the pattern of carpets, curtains, which colours to paint the walls. So long as they were quite sober, Reg had counseled her. He didn't want anything too modern.

How proud she had been. A foolish little woman. She could look back at herself now and despair. He had offered her the whole world, and she'd accepted this drowsy, dowdy little house.

That night when Catriona was visiting, all these old feelings were revived within Evelyn. They came surging and bubbling up from her guts as she went back and forth to the scullery.

She didn't like what was happening tonight, even though she wasn't sure what it was. Catriona was talking now, in her low, sonorous voice. Evelyn could see that both her mother and her husband were captivated. Even her husband was bending his head closer and letting Catriona's words wash over him. When Evelyn came back in with the cheeseboard she felt very surprised. Why were they listening so intently? What could Catriona be saying?

It was obvious. She must be telling them one of her stories.

Evelyn felt envious. Just recently she had been Catriona's exclusive audience of one. She put the cheeseboard down with a clatter and the ripe brie spattered on the cloth. It was irrational, of course. She couldn't have Catriona all to herself. What was she even thinking of?

'Sssh,' Reg glanced at her. 'Sit down quietly here, my love.'

But something in her rebelled. All these old people. They were always telling her what to do. She had gone from her mother's house to Reg's house, all those years ago, and they had both dominated her and told her exactly what she should do. There was no let-up.

And just why were the walls in her dining room glowing?

They were pulsing with bright, lurid colours. Not just the chimney breast and the painting any more. The other walls had their own colours and their own strange scenes. They drank up her concentration. Their swirling, changing details snagged her attention. She stared at Catriona and met her challenging eyes. The drawn velvet curtains behind her started to drip and run away. They became a sheet of running water and beyond them, beyond the melting French windows, there was a jungle, all clammy and rank.

Evelyn backed away. 'What... what are you doing to my home?'

Catriona laughed at her. So did her mother. Dorothea snapped round and glared at Evelyn. 'Sit down girl, you'll ruin everything. Stop interrupting.'

'But the walls! My house! The walls are melting...'

Even Reg barked out laughing at this. Why, she was being absurd. As usual. She was saying all the wrong things. Silly girl. Getting it all wrong, as usual. She couldn't understand what was going on. And how could she understand anything at all? She had no real education. Not like her three elders. They were such distinguished people. They were sophisticated. They wouldn't set out the cheese on the board in a smiling face the way she had, with the red grapes arranged around the sticky wedges like hair...

Evelyn backed out of the room. She wouldn't stay with them. Something was going wrong and peculiar in her dining room. She didn't like whatever it was.

'Come back at once!' shouted Reg, and he sounded as annoyed as usual. Now he wasn't putting on airs and pretending to be a good husband. He was shouting like she was a dog, in front of her mother and her friend. He obviously didn't care what they thought.

She backed into the hallway and thought about going upstairs to lie down. Perhaps she had food poisoning? It would explain the way her head was pounding and her stomach was roiling around inside of her. She felt delirious and sick, but could food poisoning really come on that quickly? Yes, she thought it probably could – remembering a particular, grisly weekend away and an ill-advised seafood platter.

The hallway was glowing with its own colours, too. Each wall was different. Phantasmagorical – that was the word for it. Each stretch of wall shimmering and pulsing with bright new colours. Each hinted at different lands beyond.

When she tried to totter up the stairs they turned into chilly water, pouring towards her. Then they were a hill of rippling grass. The grass looked cool and inviting and fresh. She imagined being able to lie down in it and stare up at a wonderful, milk-blue sky.

Evelyn started to climb the stairs, feeling the long grasses and wildflowers twining and pulling at her ankles. She grasped the banister and climbed and climbed...

And met the basilisk coming down the stairs. He was grown to full size, about the size of a very large dog. For a confused moment she stopped and watched him approach. She wasn't quite sure where he had come from, and then she remembered. He was her gift, wasn't he? He came from *Chimera*. The shop she had been taken to by Catriona, when Catriona was still her special friend.

She was careful not to meet the basilisk's eye. He would turn her to stone in a flash, she remembered. He wouldn't be able to help himself.

'Climb on my back,' he told her. His voice was rather gruff. 'I'll take you away from here. Come along, Evelyn. We've got to catch up with the others...'

'I can't leave my house,' she gasped.

'You must,' he told her, urgently. 'You must catch them up. There's nothing more you can do here. Your mother and your husband are lost! You must find the others.'

'What others?' she asked, feeling scared and cross. But she knew very well who he meant.

She went to him and clambered awkwardly onto his back. And then – without another word – they set off down the stairs, through the molten front door and into the night.

*

Mr Tweet was showing Bessie his arrangement of speaking tubes. Each one was labeled with the names of different worlds. The curtained alcove where he kept this strange assemblage was rather confined and Bessie felt panic rising in her breast. There were dozens of worlds labeled here. And he could talk to them all?

'More than talk,' he beamed. 'Once upon a time I used to visit them all. I could go where I wanted. I was important in all of them!'

Then he went on to give an explanation of how all the worlds were like segments of a large and juicy orange. Could Brenda picture that? She nodded dumbly, furious inside about being patronized. He might be magical and all-powerful, but she hated anyone talking down to her.

'Like an orange, yes. Go on.'

'And so they all slot together, their thinnest edges in the centre around the central core of... well, pith.'

'And you're the central core?'

He shrugged and started pulling at various tubes. He was showing off to her. Why would he bother to do that? 'In many of these places I was the deity. I'd shout down this tube and my words would resound in the temples and holy places at the other end! What fun it all used to be!'

Brenda shook her head. 'You were playing with them. You were playing with the lives of folk in other worlds.'

He tutted at her. 'I hope I wasn't. I hope I was a wise and just god. And I wasn't always god. Some times I was just an advisor, or someone terribly humble. Some places I even went unseen, as just another face in the crowd, or a terribly dirty and obscure beggar. But still I wove my magic...'

Brenda had heard just about enough of his bragging by now. 'That's all very well and good, Mr Tweet. But why are you telling me all of this? I mean, who am I? I'm just nothing.'

He stared at her. He looked her up and down. Brenda might have imagined it but, for a moment she even thought he seemed nervous. Could he be wary of her? True, she was twice his size and, if he but knew, handy in a fistfight. She was surely stronger than this ancient old cove. But there was a curious cast to his eye when he looked at her. 'Some beings exist in more than one world simultaneously,' he said. 'Some special beings are archetypal. Eternal.'

'Oh, yes?' Now she was losing his drift. Just be polite, Brenda. Let him burble on until he decides to let you go.

'You are such a one as these,' he told her.

'I beg your pardon?'

'You are such a one.'

She still didn't get him. 'I'm sorry, I'm being very slow. It must be all the palaver of being dragged through the skies by gargoyles.'

'Gyregoyles,' he corrected her. 'They fly through the spiraling vortices of the centuries and the interstices between worlds.'

She waved her hands in front of her face. 'Stop saying nonsensical things to me! Please! Now, make yourself plain. What are you telling me?'

'You are a very important being, Brenda.' He coughed. 'Cosmically speaking.'

'You've got the wrong woman,' she said. Suddenly her claustrophobia was really getting to her. She shouldered forward, as if to barge past him. 'I don't know what you want with me, but I don't like it. I want you to send me back to my friends, right now.'

'But, your destiny, Brenda. You have a very particular destiny...'

She didn't like the sound of this one bit.

*

The white-whiskered bookseller glared balefully at her customers. 'I'm surprised to see anyone today. I was prepared for a quiet day. Catching up on my reading.' She had about twelve books open on the cash desk, and appeared to be reading them all at once.

'We need your help,' John said urgently.

She stared at him, frankly astonished. 'I'm not sure there's very much I can do.'

Henry Cleavis' patience had vanished. 'Now, look here. I suggest you listen to my friend here and try your best to comply with...'

Suddenly he was uncomfortably aware that the old woman was staring at him. It felt as if she was looking straight into his soul. He took a step backwards.

'Henry Cleavis,' she said.

'Yeee-ees,' he frowned at her, beetling his brows. 'What is it?'

'I'm very interested in you,' she said, abruptly.

'Are you, now?'

The old woman got up creakily from her desk and hurried out of her alcove, all the while studying Henry intently. 'Yes, I was hoping your boyfriend would bring you here to see me.'

'What?' asked Henry, turning pale. 'B...?'

She waved a clawed hand airily. 'Oh, don't worry about me, ducky. I'm not going to tell anyone about your funny proclivities, am I? Who'd believe anything I ever said?' Henry and John were darting worried looks at each other. 'No, no. What I'm far more interested in is how you can go about writing the books that you do: books that have such a strange and palpable effect on your world.'

'They don't usually,' he said. 'Just here. It's only ever happened here in Darkholmes.'

'I see,' said the crone. 'What's that?' Her hand darted out to clutch at the velvet-covered book they had brought with them. The book that Catriona had entrusted to Henry. For some mystifying reason she had wanted him to have it and now the bookshop owner's eyes were shining a goldish green with excitement. 'Is that what I think it is?'

Henry weighed the heavy tome in his hands. 'I've no idea. What I do know is that this belongs to a singularly wicked person and every single page of this book is completely unreadable.'

The old woman's fingers twitched spasmodically. She rubbed her palms on her filthy sweater like they were itching with scabs. She held both claws out beseechingly. 'Oh, not to me. I can read anything. This is important. I know it is. I can smell it... It has the distinctive flavour to it... I know that taste...'

Henry was at his most dour. 'What will you do with this book, if we hand it over to you?' John looked alarmed. He made as if to stop him, but Henry gave him a swift, reassuring glance. He knew what he was doing. Possibly.

'I must have the book,' said the old bookseller, wetting her lips. 'It belongs to... Cat Mackay, doesn't it? Cat Mackay. She was here... she was here in my shop, briefly, recently. I could hardly believe it. She was here looking at trinkets and jewels. She had no interest in the books at all. She hardly even noticed them. I wanted to talk to her... I longed to ask her about her stories...'

Henry was steadfast. 'What will you do with this book?'

'Why, nothing. It's only a book, isn't it? What can a book of stories do?' She gave her visitors a wintry smile. Her eyebrows went up creakily, as if noticing the Gold Leaf Princess standing beside John for the first time. Her eyes lingered on the beautiful, shining form of the Princess, and the box that contained the Nonesuch in her arms. 'One of you is missing.'

'It's our friend Charles,' said the Princess in her tinny voice. 'He... left us a little while ago. We don't know where he's gone.'

'Aha,' said the old woman said. 'The voracious fox. Finding his own way, just as he did in your stories, Henry Cleavis. Or will do, anyhow. So. Will you give me the book that belongs to Cat Mackay?'

'Certainly not!' replied Henry robustly.

John stepped forward, deciding to try another tack. 'If we do, what will you give us in return?'

She snickered to herself, pleased that one of these annoying visitors was seeing sense at last. 'Give me Cat Mackay's stories and I will let you go up to my attic, and you can allow these friends of yours to escape through my magic door.'

John grinned at his boyfriend, Henry, who found himself smiling back, almost shyly. 'The magic door, Henry. We're going through together at last...! Into the Other World.'

*

'Isn't that all any of us want?' asked Catriona Mackay. 'A magic door?'

'I picture one and it's green. The paint's flaking because of the elements. The door's at the bottom of the garden, in a crumbling wall of red brick. The stone of the bricks is frangible, like stale cake. It's a door in a wall like the one you've got here, Reg Tyler. Have you looked as far as the end of your nose? Have you been down the bottom of your garden recently? It's quite overgrown. Brenda doesn't have time in her packed and busy days to hack away the bushes and the vines...

'In less than ten years you'll have to make the garden neater. You'll have to dig your bomb shelter. You'll spend many, many nights at the bottom of your garden, shivering in the mouldy, worm-endy, dank, dripping bomb shelter that you'll dig out with your bare hands. But that's the future. One possible future.

'The magic door I'm thinking of could be the one in your garden wall, or the one into your ramshackle Anderson shelter, or it could even be the door into the cupboard under your stairs. It doesn't matter. The doors are where you want them to be. They could even be the walls. Any of the running, melting walls in your house. They're all you've ever wanted, aren't they? And I wonder why, Reg Tyler.

'Your life has been quite stable and sedate, up till now. Why, I could imagine your wife or your mother-in-law wanting or needing escape. I understand why they would like to take off, all at once, and fly elsewhere, or step through the molten walls into a new life. But you've always had it fairly cushy, haven't you, Professor? Cleavis, John, Brenda... all of them would be happy to escape beyond the bounds of their lives, but what about you? Why do you want to go elsewhere?

'Or perhaps you don't? Perhaps you're happy where you are. In your regular, rather easy, simplistic life. You like to keep it steady and bourgeois and almost dull, just so that you can give yourself up to the wildest adventures inside your head? And so you need everyone looking after for you – a wife and a servant and colleagues and a whole infrastructure around you. Supporting you and making sure that you have a calm life, a supported life. One that affords you hours of quiet for you to spend how you wish. And only then, in your safety and seclusion, you go into your most dangerous adventures and strangest dreams...'

The voice of Catriona Mackay was all he could hear. She was going on and on. Her voice was calm and wondering, as if she was thinking aloud to herself. She wasn't trying to taunt him but her words pulled and tugged at him nevertheless. He wished he could block them out.

He was outside, alone. On the thickly wooded hillside by the river. On Hexford Hill, quite alone. It was late and the moon had risen, the colour of lemon curd, over the ancient town. The snow had abated for once. The Professor had no idea how he had got here. Somehow Catriona's words were coming to him and he couldn't block them out.

What business of hers was it, the way he made up his stories? Why should she care anyway?

They were only stories. They were nothing. Why should they mean anything to her? Was she envious? But... but she made up her own, didn't she? In what way were his stories crowding out hers? In what way could his stories threaten hers? Stories existed in an invisible, infinite universe, didn't they? They didn't exist independently of the minds that created them or read them. To think otherwise was madness...

However he got here, standing knee-deep in the snow, he'd better get indoors. He'd die of exposure here...

But where was Evelyn and her mother? Where was Catriona? How long ago was it that he'd been sitting at his dining table and the walls had started to run away?

He didn't know. But the cold was battering at him now and his joints were paining him. If he climbed to the top of the woods he could seek shelter in Hexford College, perhaps. Get his breath. Get warm again. Try to work out what was going on.

He staggered and fell against a tree trunk, knocking his head. He saw stars for a second and steadied himself. Stupid old fool. What was he doing, running around in the cold night? He summoned up all his strength. It was perhaps a hundred yards to the top of the hill and the walls of the college. Perhaps there would be a door. He wouldn't have to walk all the way round to the front entrance. Perhaps he'd find a magic door in the wall.

The thought gave him strength and he pushed away from the wet, black iron of the tree trunk and went swimming through the crystallized air. Pushing, pushing hard against the drifted snow.

Then, when next he looked up, there was a figure standing slightly uphill from him. Standing quite still, quite calmly. Watching him. Studying him very carefully.

The man was wearing a long cloak. It hung straight down in the breathless night. The man's face was odd. Was it a mask? It had a long, pointed snout. Furred ears.

'Hello?' Reg said, and the sound of his own voice surprised him. It was harsh. He was parched. He picked up a handful of snow and melted it in his mouth and it stung him. His eyes watered and he tried not to sob. The figure still wasn't moving or saying anything to him. It was inhuman, in old-fashioned clothes. Boots and a cape and frilled shirt. Its eyes were green like angelica.

It was a fox. There was a rank whiff of fox on the air.

'Hello?' the Professor said again. 'Could you help me, please? I'm freezing here...'

It was a man-sized fox. It should be alarming, to see such a thing. But Reg had seen enough impossible things by now. Some assistance would be nice, even if it came from someone peculiar.

The fox sprang to life and came bounding across the crust of snow towards him...

'Thank goodness,' said Reg. 'Thank you...'

'You are old, aren't you? You're feeling your age...'

The fox was sniffing at him. Coming too close to him. Reg felt the stiff red bristles of his mane against his face.

'Yes, actually. I'm feeling wretched. You are..?'

'Charles,' said the fox. 'I'm here to help.'

'H-help me to the college... I have friends there.'

Charles surveyed the old man thoughtfully. 'No. I'll tell you what. Come with me, Reg Tyler. Come and be a fox in the woods.'

There was a beat of silence. Tyler stared at the grinning creature. The unnatural creature. There was something horrible about him, he could tell. All at once he wanted to get away.

'Now, don't be like that. Come along with me...'

His running was tentative at first. Aching old bones. Unused to vigour. His bicycle rides through the streets of Darkholmes were always at a sedate and measured pace. Reg wasn't used to belting about the place. He had never run like the fox did, hell for leather, skillfully darting through frosty thickets and dodging between the densely-packed boles of trees.

As the moments went by he become bolder. His heart began to sing. He took in a huge breath and felt his whole body exult with its newfound power. Everything was in accord. Everything worked. He flew across the brittle woodland floor just as fast as Charles was doing. But how was this happening to him? And when would it end?

They raced to the top of Hexford Hill, where the college walls rose sheer and tall. They were scabbed with ice and bearded with moss and Reg was no longer interested in getting inside. There was nothing in there for him any more. Just fusty old men and their boring old books and lives dedicated to nonsense. Nothing that he'd be interested in. All he cared for was the wild scent of Charles as he pounded a track through the forest floor for Reg to follow. Reg was following him round the perimeter of the wall and happy to be mindless at last...

Then, down the hill. Zig-zagging wildly through a slalom of mulch. They churned up the rotting carpet of dead things under layers of snow. They made a hideous muck of the gently sleeping woods. Under the jaundiced eye of the moon they came to a tumbling halt, yipping wildly, at the bottom of the hill by the slowly chugging river and howled in mirth together for the joy of it.

Then, without another moment's thought, Charles was racing towards the river.

'Wait!' cried Reg, panting after him. 'You'll freeze if you try to swim!'

But Charles jumped. Entirely trusting, Reg flew after him. Before they hit the bronze surface of the water they had changed again, into smooth, red-bellied trout, plunging down through the cold into the hairy green deeps.

*

Brenda seized the copper mechanism attached to the speaking tube closest to her, having noticed that it was labeled 'Darkholmes.'

'Your home,' said Mr Tweet. 'Yes, you may use it.' He smiled ruefully, knowing that the housemaid was trying to change the subject. She didn't want to hear anything further about the subject of her destiny. This amused the old man. Anyone else would have been keen, wouldn't they? Anyone else would have been avid to know the secrets he could tell. But Brenda was shifty and embarrassed. It was as if she already half-suspected the wild things he had to say about her, and she didn't want to hear anything more.

Yes, it was quite true. She was a remarkable person.

Brenda blew into the tube, and put it to her ear. She could recall using such devices, in the older days. When she worked in the big house. Even before the turn of the century. She remembered listening like this. Waiting for instructions from above stairs.

'I can hear voices..!' she said. 'Voices all the way from home!'

'You will hear the place your ear wishes to hear,' Mr Tweet said. 'The device interprets your desires...'

'Sssh,' she went, and squinched her eyes closed. 'I can hear... the women! Evelyn and her mother... and Catriona Mackay. They...they must be in the dining room still. They sound odd. I can't hear Professor Tyler...'

She listened hard. Mr Tweet smiled. 'Professor Tyler has been removed from his home. He's having adventures elsewhere tonight. He's having – as they say – his eyes opened at last. No way, once this night is through, will he be able to dismiss the possibility of magic in Darkholmes...'

Brenda waved her hand, begging him to be quiet. 'Oh! They're saying the Professor has vanished. He... he fell into a print that was on the wall. An etching of Hexford Hill and the woods under snow. I know the very picture. I dust its frame and glass every day. A beautiful piece... and now it has possession of the Professor...'

'Are the women scared and disturbed?' asked Mr Tweet, drawing closer.

'It's hard to tell. I can hear Catriona laughing. And Dorothea, Evelyn's mother, she sounds pretty upset. She sounds tired and scared. Evelyn is... Evelyn is pouring them brandy. They're debating what to do.'

Mr Tweet shrugged. 'The worlds have opened up for them. They have many choices. Catriona Mackay has her own way. Not as she imagined it would happen, but the walls have opened up and no one has been hurt. She's been lucky. We've all been lucky. And she's managed to use your friends to deliver her book of stories to Hyspero. Things have worked out well for the Witch Woman. I wonder what she'll do now. While Reg has left his house untended and the walls are glowing with colour...'

Brenda was staring at him. 'Are you saying that every one of those pictures in that house – the pictures I dust every day – they're magic doors into other worlds?'

'Only sometimes,' said Mr Tweet. 'There are many doors in Darkholmes. The fabric of the place is rubbing thin. Your

Professor Tyler is at the heart of it. His house is the very centre of the Nexus Point and now, while he runs around in the night, naked, joyful, turning into fish and fowl and wild beast, Catriona is in command...'

Brenda straightened up. Her face was set with determination. 'Then you must send me back there. Back to 199 Steps Lane. She mustn't be left in charge. I'll sort her out.'

Mr Tweet laughed softly. 'Are you sure, my dear?'

She nodded grimly. 'Can you send me?'

With a few harsh cries, and a swirl of his feathered cloak, Mr Tweet drew down from the hellish confines of Vexing Tower a great, dark flock of starlings and gulls. Their hideous racket blotted out his words and Brenda's thoughts. But she got the gist. They would carry her home. She simply had to let them, and not worry or be scared. They could fly her down from the tower, back to the north of the town, and into the world she belonged to.

'Godspeed, my love,' Mr Tweet's words barely came to her as she felt herself being carried away.

'Goodbye! Goodbye...!' she laughed, but her words were snatched away by the storm.

THE END